SUMMER AT GAGLOW

ALSO BY ESTHER FREUD

SUMMER AT GAGLOW

A Novel

ESTHER FREUD

ecco

An Imprint of HarperCollinsPublishers

HarperCollins books may be purchased for educational, business, or sales promotional use. For information, please email the Special Markets Department at SPsales@harpercollins.com.

Ecco® and HarperCollins® are trademarks of HarperCollins Publishers.

A hardcover edition of this book was published in 1999 by Ecco, an imprint of HarperCollins Publishers.

FIRST ECCO PAPERBACK EDITION PUBLISHED IN 1999

REISSUED BY ECCO IN 2021

Library of Congress Cataloging-in-Publication Data is available upon request.

ISBN 978-0-88-001672-8 (pbk.)

21 22 23 24 25   LSC   10 9 8

For Xandra and Alexandra

SUMMER AT GAGLOW

The Belgard girls did not admire their mother. They disapproved of her card-playing and the cigars she smoked when her husband was away from home. But their brother Emanuel they all adored. The following week he was to be twenty-one and the family were united for once in planning a party to span an entire weekend. The guests had been invited, the caterers informed and flowers were to be collected from the gardens and conservatories and arranged in monumental bouquets throughout the house. The party was to be held at Gaglow, and not at their Berlin apartment which, although large, was not large enough to hold the guests they expected to attend.

It was the summer of 1914 and it was also Eva's birthday. No one seemed to remember in the flurry of activity that, on the same day as her brother would be twenty-one, Eva was to be eleven. She held her head up high and defied them to remember. Marianna Belgard had arranged for new dresses to be made for each of her three daughters. Bina was to have a pale peach satin, ruched and tucked along the front, Martha a blue with a sash bow at the back, and Eva, really still a child, would wear white. Bina, at fifteen, considered herself excessively ladylike, with or without the new dress. She intended behaving at the party with incomparably perfect manners, and enjoyed the prospect of showing up her mother. 'She's so vulgar,' she protested, when after dinner Marianna continued to sit at table with the men, drinking beer and beating them at cards. Bina, Martha and Eva, their old nanny comfortably asleep, would often slip out of bed to spy on her through the thick drapes that led into the dining room. 'It's no way to behave,' Bina hissed, and the others nodded in vigorous agreement, adding solemnly, 'Poor Papa, poor, poor Papa.'

Eva sat in a large armchair, looking out through the french windows to where the grass was being clipped and mown, and thought with longing of the moment when Emanuel would come home. She thought how she would climb into his lap and tease him while he read. She would pull at the little hairs that grew singly on his chin and whisper the names of girls Mama had planned for him to marry. Eva shivered as she thought of the people her mother had invited to the party. Smart brash women with loud voices and thick necks. Emanuel would have nothing to do with them, she knew that, and, besides, he had made a promise to her. It was a promise secured on their shared birthday, the year that she'd turned seven, and she'd insisted that he swear to it, pricking his finger with a pin and blotting it against her thumb.

Emanuel's arrival was overshadowed by the talk of war that came with him from Hamburg. 'It's only rumour,' he consoled his mother. 'The consensus at my university is that there will not be a war,' and he repeated his theory to various groups of guests clustered around the piano in the drawing room or strolling on the upper lawn.

Emanuel also arrived with a birthday present for Eva. 'Did you think you were forgotten?' he teased, and she thanked him nonchalantly, gulping back relief. It was an inlaid Turkish box that shone in shades of rose and amber wood. Set in the centre was a pattern of mother-of-pearl uncurling like a flower. 'It has a key,' he told her, and when she twisted it, the box opened to reveal a lining of green felt and her name carved at the back between the hinges.

Eva had embroidered her brother five white handkerchiefs with his initials and a scattering of pink-eyed flowers in one corner. 'He'll never use them,' Bina teased, and Martha laughed that he would most likely hide them at the bottom of a drawer. Eva glared in triumph when Emanuel shook one out and tucked it into the top pocket of his waistcoat, the flowers bursting out against the cloth. He kept it there throughout the afternoon, transferring it to his evening suit when, with the guests, he retired to change for supper.

Of the three girls it was only Bina who was allowed to stay up for the night-time celebrations. Places had been laid for a hundred people at a long gallery of tables that spiralled round the dining room. Bina came up to the nursery where both Nanny and the governess, Fräulein Schulze, burst into praise over her dress and the way in which her hair had been arranged. Eva stared furiously into her green baize box and cursed that she was years too young. 'It's even worse luck for me,' Martha said, and it cheered Eva up a little to see that she was right.

Their mother came up to wish them both goodnight. 'You have been more than perfect today.' She smiled, glittering in the doorway of their double room, while Martha and Eva sat at twin dressing tables and stared sulkily back at her through the glass. 'Sleep well.' She blew them each a kiss and left them to rejoin the party.

'Did you see the earrings she had on?' Martha gasped, and Eva agreed that they were hideous. Great red rubies that dragged down the lobes of her ears. 'And such skinny arms.' She winced, continuing to give her hair the one hundred obligatory strokes insisted upon by Nanny.

'Well, at least we have Bina to report back.' Eva brushed vigorously. 'Not to mention,' she lowered her voice, 'our own dear Schu.'

'Now, now, children.' It was Nanny standing behind them with their nightdresses, freshly pressed and aired. 'I'm sure

3

Fräulein Schulze will be too busy enjoying herself to have time for such nonsense.'

'Oh, Omi, Omi Lise,' they both protested. They caught each other's eye and grinned. This was exactly what their governess had time for and what, above anything, she enjoyed. It was her wicked bedtime stories that had won them over at the very start, and the way she poked fun at strangers, livening up the walks they took even on the most dreary days, and filling her charges, each one, with a small, warm well of spite.

Eva lay in bed, listening to the distant strains of the music and running over in her mind the various eligible girls invited by her mother. Who would Emanuel be dancing with, she wondered, and she smiled at the off-hand way in which he had accepted their attentions.

'Martha?' she whispered. 'Martha, are you asleep?'

Martha answered drowsily that she was.

Eva let her lie in silence, and then, unable to contain her question, she hissed across the room, 'Martha, tell me something. Do you imagine, one day, that you'll get married?'

Martha turned grumpily under her quilt. 'What? Of course I will.' And she turned again, and burrowed her head down under the covers.

If Bina had been there, tucked into bed in the adjoining room, she would not have allowed her sisters to go to sleep but would have organized a spying party to outwit Nanny and slip down to the next landing where it might have been possible to see the people milling about in the tiled hall as they passed through from supper to dancing. They could have peered through the twist of the stairs, doubling back on themselves if anyone were to start ascending. 'Martha?' Eva called, feeling that they were possibly giving in too easily to their imposed curfew, but Martha lay rigid, insisting she had drifted off to sleep.

Eva forced herself out of bed. She felt honour bound to

attempt at least one glimpse of the proceedings. She knotted her long hair on the nape of her neck and, with slow fingers, inched the door until it was wide enough to slip through. Once safely out in the corridor she ran along the wooden floorboards, hanging for a second over the stairwell to check for adult hands circling the banisters and skipping down the first flight of stairs, keeping to the curve of the outside wall. At the next landing, she peered quickly over into the hall. A surge of talk and tinkling musicians floated up at her, and seeing nothing but the edges of dresses and the black elbows of men she craned further, holding on to the slippery wood and stretching her head and shoulders out into the scented air. At that moment a red-faced woman began to climb the stairs, looking short of breath in her tightened waistband. Eva flung herself back on to the landing and ran along a corridor, hiding in the deep doorway to a guest bedroom.

When it was safe to venture out again, she scaled the crook of the stairs, clasping the wooden railings with her knees and arching her back, imitating Bina on a dozen past occasions. She had to restrain herself from calling out and waving, and wondered that until now she had put up with so many second-hand reports. Eva hung there, waiting for someone to come into her view, and then she was rewarded by the sight of the two Samson girls exchanging flushed confidences at the foot of the stairs.

The Samson sisters were famous for their beauty, and their attendance at the party had been much discussed. Eva gazed down on their identical chestnut heads as they swayed towards each other in shared laughter. Her knees were starting to tremble with the effort of clinging, head down like a bat, when the girls, flushed and golden as French apples, were joined by her brother. Emanuel stood between them, his back against the carved post of the stairs, and lowering his voice, so that both sisters leant towards him, he began to tell them something. A story. A secret. Eva, her fingers whitening on the wood, strained impossibly for his whispery voice to rise above the music. And then as she watched, guessing at nothing, they all laughed, their three open mouths tilting upwards in the same split second to make crescents in their faces. They were still laughing, more softly and in interrupted chuckles, when Emanuel, a hand hovering around each sloping shoulder, led them away.

Eva, cold and furious, untangled her knees and slid down to the floor. She swung round, half expecting to see Nanny scowling in her stiff white nightdress, waiting crossly to escort her back to bed, but Nanny was sitting by the nursery fire, eating a plate of marzipan roses that had been sent up to her by Fräulein Schulze. Not caring now who saw her, Eva stamped up the last flight of stairs. She trailed along the low, polished corridor, and on reaching her own room, flung herself into bed. 'Martha?' she called, but Martha refused to be woken, and with the absent Schu-Schu's vengeful name on her lips, she cried herself to sleep.

Marianna Belgard had wanted all three of her daughters to be included in the night-time celebrations. She mentioned this to her husband in the hope of enlisting his support, but he made it clear that she would come in for too much criticism, and not least from their eldest girl. Wolf Belgard smiled when he said this, softening on Bina's name, and he caught his wife around the waist and kissed her. Marianna pulled angrily away. It was easy for him to make light of these hostilities. He was well loved by his children, and he either could or would not see how from an early age his daughters had turned their backs, poking fun and scheming up between themselves to undermine her. Marianna had tried several times to explain this to him, forcing back her tears as she spoke, but he refused to believe her, only laughed and teased and attempted to draw her back into the state of cheerfulness he relied on for himself. It was only Emanuel who understood, Emanuel who took her hand and pressed it when the girls refused to let themselves be kissed goodnight, when they ran away from her in the park, or called out for their governess in small plaintive voices when they were sick.

Marianna insisted that a place be set for Fräulein Schulze at Emanuel's birthday dinner. She still held out the hope of winning her round, and even offered up one of her own last season's dresses. But when Gabrielle Schulze entered the dining room, the dull red of the dress transformed by rosebuds stitched in satin and nestling voluptuously against the whiteness of her skin, Marianna found herself regretting it. The woman seemed to hold her head too high and Marianna noticed how, with cleverly exacting fingers, she had managed to disguise the necessary insertion of an extra panel across and under the wide sweep of her bust.

The party continued the following day with a lunch of cold meats, pickled vegetables and fruit, to be eaten in the garden. Eva woke early, her eyes swollen with tears trapped under her lids during the night. It made her skin look thick and out of focus. No one noticed. Bina was too busy telling anyone who'd listen about the dancing, and how admired she'd been by certain young men. Martha hung on every one of Bina's words. 'If you were so interested, why didn't you come and see for yourself?' Eva wanted to say, but she stopped herself, instead folding a piece of bitter bread around some cheese and chewing at the ends of it.

By mid-morning Marianna Belgard stood, in ivory taffeta, surveying her three daughters. Bina's bright face, she noticed, held a new ferocity, while Martha as ever was vague and shy. Eva had dark childish rings under her eyes. 'Are you quite well?' She put a hand under Eva's chin, and raised the girl's face to her own.

Eva scowled. Typical, she thought. Discovered by my enemy. And then, realizing how far she'd allowed herself to go in spite, she blushed up at her mother. The silly girl's in love. Marianna smiled, remembering herself as a child, and her heart lurched to think that they could not be friends.

It was only the overnight guests who had been invited to the picnic lunch. Tables had been set up, draped in white, on the flagstones behind the house that caught the early-morning sun. By lunchtime the stones had warmed and the sun had settled high above the house so that chairs could be arranged in or out of the shade. Eva knelt down and placed the back of one hand on a warm flag. Without intending it, and against all orders, she had come to love this house. She walked round to the front and looked down the straight drive to where the red roofs and the church spire of the village nestled in the valley. Apple orchards spread away to each side and the fields at the back were dotted with creamy, brown-faced cows. A carriage was hurtling, its black hood up, along the drive towards her. Four horses, harnessed in leather, trotted against the hill. Eva walked forward to see who it could be. She could make out Gruber, their own coachman, sitting high up on his box, holding the reins, and as the carriage swung into the drive it began to slow. A door flew open and Emanuel jumped down. 'Manu,' Eva called, picking up her skirt to race towards him, but from nowhere her mother had appeared, beaming and chastizing, and striding, with her arms outstretched, towards him.

Eva snorted and, just as they saw and waved to her, she took off to run round the side of the house and down to the stables where Gruber would be returning the horses to their stalls.

Eva watched her brother as he sat between the Samson girls, helping them to wine and sweet slices of frangipane, and sharing in the continuing joke of the night before.

'Which one do you think?' Bina nudged her.

'Which one what?' Eva scowled.

'Is he most likely to propose to?'

Eva put her elbows on the table and stared at the perfect smiling ovals of their faces, lit up and turned towards Emanuel.

Angelika and Julika. Julika and Angelika. 'Neither,' she said, and she felt a chill like a water spider run over her hand.

'You're useless.' Bina pinched her, snorting and moving to where Martha sat at the other end of the table. Eva watched her lips as she muttered, 'Utterly useless, what a waste,' into Martha's ear.

Eva leant forward to catch what her brother was saying. 'Oh, yes,' Angelika interrupted him, 'of course Paris is the only place there is.'

'For a honeymoon,' Julika added, and both sisters blushed a golden shade of pink.

'What rubbish people talk.' Eva swore under her breath. She stood up and ran into the house, stopping only to peer into the high hall mirror to inspect her scowl and the sticky lashes of her eyes.

The drawing room was filled with flowers and scattered with chairs and sofas, arranged in groups for the comfort of last night's guests. Eva stepped over the plum-coloured rugs, holding her nose against the cloying scent of lilies until she reached the grand piano. She let her hands fall heavily on the keys. They clashed and chimed, and her heart raced with the uneven notes. Omi Lise appeared in the door, her mouth puckered disapprovingly and a silk-fringed shawl draped over her arm. Eva caught her eye and ran.

She skipped past the high windows, catching at the curtains and not looking back until she reached a small door covered by a tapestry. She felt behind it and found the handle. The door opened and she slipped through into a long, vaulted passageway. This corridor was cold and lined with flowering pots of marguerites. Her feet echoed on the stone floor as she walked, more slowly now, straining her eyes into damp, half-empty rooms in which, not so many years before, the previous owner, Hans Dieter, had housed his collection of ivory-handled whips and guns. The sun fell onto white stone in harsh triangular patterns, and Eva trod as softly as she could to keep the echo to a minimum.

Through a last narrow door the corridor widened out into a circular hall. This was Eva's favourite room. It had a slanting pattern of black and white tiles over its octagonal floor and the curve of the walls made her want to spin. Through a side entrance off this hall Marianna Belgard had her own private study. It was where she talked things over with the gardeners and discussed the hiring of men and the upkeep of the stables, regretting regularly that her husband, against her good advice, had thought it safest to sell off all the land. There was a large, leather-topped desk in the centre of the room, on which lay a book of paper, ragged at the edges like raw silk, and so heavy it was hardly worth the effort it took to close it. Stone-edged windows looked out onto the flower garden, and each deep window-seat had a rug arranged on it, especially plumped and folded for Marianna's dogs. Marianna had a fleet of whippets, fawn and blue, who trotted daintily after her along the corridors, slipping occasionally and clipping the polish on the parquet floors. They stood, their eyes, like oil, popping out with sorrow when she stepped into her carriage, and when she returned to the house, even after an absence of a day, they greeted her with swirls and yelps and frantic, scampering circus twirls of joy.

Eva heard a noise. She stopped, still on tiptoe, her eyes on the circular ceiling, and looked across the hall into her mother's study. Marianna was standing, leaning with one hand on her desk and deep in conversation with the sturdy red-faced woman with whom Eva had nearly collided the night before as she hovered on the stairs. 'Frau Samson,' Eva muttered to herself, and she raised an eyebrow. You see, she thought, our mother has no qualms about marrying off poor Manu, even when she has the plain, hard evidence of how those girls are likely to turn out! And she hunched her shoulders in exasperation.

Eva kept an eye on her mother's profile, smiling and nodding to stout Frau Samson sitting in the window-seat, until they readied themselves to leave the room. Eva pressed herself into the curve of the wall and held her breath as her mother passed by, a whippet in tow, and walked with her companion back along the corridor, still talking lightly about troublesome cooks, suppressing a smile for the splintery patch of dog hair that had attached itself to the older woman's behind.

Eva escaped through the back door. She ran directly ahead, up the stretch of lawn to where the ice-house stood at the end of its own short drive. This tiny house was the one part of the estate Hans Dieter had taken the trouble to maintain, and the lawn that led to it was smooth and dense with years of careful tending. It had a roof like a dove-cote with rounded sloping tiles, and the pillars that supported it were freshly painted in a creamy white. Eva stepped into the cool shade of its interior and was startled by the sight of her governess standing with her eyes half closed against the door that led down to the cellar.

'Schu-Schu,' she said, laying a hand softly on her arm. Fräulein Schulze blinked and looked at her, and without a word picked up a long tin bucket. She felt with her hands for the hidden catch and swung the door open onto the freezing store of ice.

Eva lay down on the bench that curved into the wall and shouted down to where Fräulein Schulze rummaged underground. 'This isn't your job, collecting ice. Do you have gloves?'

Fräulein Schulze's laugh echoed up at her through the half-closed door. 'It's not a job. I wanted ice myself.' And she reappeared with a collection of shards lining the bottom of her bucket. Eva reached in and chose a flaking tentacle which she dripped over her forehead, her nose and into her mouth. 'I've asked Cook to prepare some redcurrant ice for you. I haven't forgotten it's your birthday too.' And before Eva had a chance to pull her down on to the bench and hug her, she strode off across the lawn and disappeared into the house.

Eva wandered back towards the terrace. She could see that the lunch party had reorganized itself into small groups clustering thickly round the table ends, while long sections of starched white linen, heavy with unfinished food, lay abandoned in between. The light legs of chairs knocked together, and girls' heads bent against the strengthening sun.

Eva saw her brother talking to a man in uniform. They were strolling away from the rest of the party, setting out across the lawn, the toes of their shoes kicking as if they were not entirely in agreement. Several of Emanuel's friends had arrived for the party in their National Service uniforms. Thick wool jackets the colour of dung with long, scalloped pockets across their chests. The soft hats on their heads were puckered at the front with buttons and, in some cases, a badge.

Eva took a handful of black chocolates from a bowl and followed the two men, trailing a little way behind, her eyes on the ground as if searching the lawn for stray spring flowers. Emanuel was talking in low, alarmed tones about the murder in Sarajevo of Franz Ferdinand. He put his arm on the thick cloth of his friend's jacket and wondered aloud if it would be an enforced conscription, were war to break out. 'But no one would need to be forced.' The other man shook him off, and Eva thought she saw her brother shiver in a long ripple down his back.

'Of course, of course,' he agreed quickly, 'I myself will sign up like a shot,' and they laughed, swapping stories of military adventures, tales of bravery and daring until Eva, distracted by a clump of golden celandines growing at the edge of the fountain, let them trail out of hearing.

CHAPTER 2

Sometimes while my father painted I stared up at the huge beast of my body, my gargantuan breasts, my widened thighs, and tried to find the charcoal outline of my former self. I hadn't known about the baby when I'd come for my first sitting, arriving smooth and pale and full of hope for how I was likely to turn out. I arranged myself in elegant profile, one arm limp across my stomach, my eyes fixed, half shut, on the corner of the room.

'When exactly are you due?' My father squinted as my painted body grew, masking the damask roses of the sofa, and at thirty weeks the canvas was sent away to be enlarged. Nine months had seemed such a never-ending stretch of time, and at first I'd put in extra hours, imagining the picture might be finished before I even started to show, but now with only six weeks left we had entered into a race. I moved my hand and laid it high under my ribs where the hard butt of the baby's head was pressing. 'Turn round,' I whispered, and I tried to catch the underwater fingers as they fluttered back and forth below the skin.

'Something rather extraordinary has happened.' My father had his back to me, scanning the canvas where the paint was piling up on my left breast.

'What extraordinary?' I asked, the high dome of my stomach tightening as I twisted round. He moved his eyes from one breast to the other and then peered back at his work.

'Well, some rather dubious-sounding man has written to

say that the descendants of Marianna Belgard, my maternal grandmother, are entitled to some property, now that the Wall's come down. There are some warehouses, apparently, and a theatre in East Berlin.'

'A theatre?' I struggled to sit up. 'Do you know what it's called? Where it is exactly?' And for a moment I imagined inheriting the Berliner Ensemble, pirouetting on the stage where Brecht had stood, employing myself, an out-of-work actress, single mother, and giving jobs to all my friends.

The baby hiccuped just below my navel.

My father didn't answer. I could see that he was waiting for me to settle down. I rubbed my hip and dropped back into position.

'There is a catch, of course.' He was widening (unnecessarily, I thought) a deep blue vein that ran in from my shoulder.

'Oh?'

'Yes, this man, Herr Gottfried something or other, insists he'll only tell us where the property is if we promise to give him sixty per cent of its value. It's a racket apparently, springing up all over East Germany.' And he stabbed his paintbrush hard against his leg. 'My feeling is,' he said at last, 'the whole thing's to be avoided.' I frowned in disappointment, already in my dreams having sold on the warehouse at enormous profit and, with my share, moved out of my tiny top-floor flat in Camden Town.

My father made a plate of salad for me, shaking olive oil on to *mâche* and cutting two thick slices of ham. 'Mustard?' he offered, but the baby was still hiccuping.

'You know what I *would* be interested in hearing about?' He reached over and whipped delicate leaves off my plate. 'Gaglow.'

'Gaglow?' I was eating too fast, hoarding the plate childishly against me, wishing he'd leave my food alone.

'It was my grandmother's estate. Very grand, somewhere in the country. Or it had been very grand.' A leaf curled over his lip. 'I used to go there in the holidays, although my mother

14

never stayed for long. And the awful aunt Bina refused to go at all.'

'Why? I mean, why awful, and why refuse to go?' I mopped up the oil with bread.

'Oh, you know, they disapproved of their mother. Thought she was vulgar.' He spiked some of my ham. 'Actually, I did ask once why they disliked her, and all they could come up with was that she drank beer. Beer, instead of wine. Although I do remember as a boy it was my mother's companion they disliked. A great big woman with huge feet like a man.'

And just as I was searching round for something more to eat, he clapped his hands and ordered us both back to work.

My father didn't usually talk about his family. He'd escaped from them early on, feuding and bristling to keep them out. But almost by chance he'd made a family of his own. Me and my two sisters. We had a mother each and separate lives, but looked unusually alike, with his high shoulders, and the same pale eyes. He never introduced us to his parents. I'd met a woman once who knew his mother, 'your grandmother,' she'd called her, and the blood caught up inside my chest. They'd talked over a garden hedge, somewhere in the country, by the sea, and I imagined them, hanging out their washing, pinning sheets, and not knowing how much I'd like to have been there.

I closed my eyes, breathing air into my hip. Why was it that even the most comfortable position became unbearable within the space of half an hour? Once I'd been under the misconception that the more difficult the pose the better the painting was likely to turn out, and I'd stiffened and twisted into strange contortions, priding myself on an ability to stall a blink. But now I lay stretched sideways, with a pillow below my ear, as close to sleep as I could get. I sighed, hoping for a response, and then to take my mind off numbness I asked what had happened to Marianna Belgard. 'At the end I mean.'

My father didn't answer, and I held my breath to hear the

worst. 'She came to live with us in London.' He was darkening the shadow of my jaw. 'And, now I think of it, it must have been very difficult for her.' He stopped and screwed up his eyes, gripping the sheaf of paintbrushes in one hand. 'You see, she didn't leave Germany until it was too late. She arrived with nothing, wasn't allowed to bring anything out, and so she lived in the small back room of my parents' house.' He had found the thing that worried him and was rubbing at it furiously with turps. 'She had to rely on my parents for everything, after once having been so grand, but I don't remember her complaining.'

'I suppose she was lucky to get out at all, so late?'

'Yes, she was lucky.' And we worked on, thinking of the endless others, until both my feet went to sleep and I had to beg him for a break.

CHAPTER 3

The day after Emanuel's party, Bina, Martha and Eva travelled back with the Samsons to spend a day and a night with them at what they called the Castle. It wasn't a castle but only a large square house with balconies below the first-floor windows and a row of small turrets above the eaves. There was no room in the brand new Samson motorcar for either their governess or Omi Lise to accompany them and, after much discussion, the decision was made that they should go alone. 'Gruber will drive over to fetch them tomorrow afternoon,' Marianna decided, and she waved after the receding vehicle, calling out how they must have a lovely time, unaware that her voice was drowned completely by the engine.

Marianna sighed deeply as she walked towards the house. Empty, she loved Gaglow more than at any other time. Today, with its rooms so recently vacated, the spaciousness that filled it was still warm. Each window hummed with talk and music, and the garden had a fleeting look as if a crowd of people had simply moved inside. As soon as the car was out of sight, her whippets, cowering in the porch, ran out to greet her. They spun round, stretching their front legs, growling and looking up at her with lovesick eyes. Marianna let them lead her through the garden. The eldest two, one blue, one fawn, had been brought over from England, a present to her from Wolf, and she'd never had the heart to part them from their litter. They trotted in a troupe, their tails jaunty as they swayed from side to side, and Marianna bent down to throw a stick for the pure pleasure of watching them fly. She followed them until they reached the parade Hans Dieter had so carefully preserved. The grass here was as short and warm as the blue coat of her favourite dog, cropped so close you could feel the earth humming underneath. She knelt to lay one hand against it, and saw the whippets standing, their noses raised, their ears arched in the direction of the ice-house.

Marianna straightened silently. She bit her lip and, without warning, loudly clapped her hands, laughing as all five animals sprang away, leaping and twisting, released by magic from a spell. They swarmed around her, smiling like a shoal of eels, and using both her hands she attempted to stroke them all at the same time, feeling their backs wriggling delightedly away. And then once again they froze, their noses twitching and their ears poised. Marianna listened with them. And then she heard a laugh. A woman's laugh, low and confidential. She shook herself and looked around. No one was there. 'Come on,' she called. 'Home,' and walked away down the gradual slope to the back door of the house. The dogs, their tails curving down in disappointment, trotted dutifully behind.

Marianna had an early supper with her husband and Emanuel. She smiled happily across at them, and asked how they thought the girls would be getting on that evening at the Castle. 'They'll be having a wonderful time,' Wolf laughed, 'and we shall be hearing about it for the rest of the summer. "Julika and Angelika, Angelika and Julika,"' he mimicked, and Marianna glanced over at Emanuel, catching his eye as he was about to raise a spoon of chilled soup to his mouth. He blushed, and a green stain smudged against his teeth.

'They're lovely girls, both of them.' Marianna turned a little sharply on her husband, and Wolf, missing her tone, agreed with a wink that lovely they most certainly were.

*

Eva sat on a low cane chair and listened to the conversation of the older girls. She had attempted to add to it, joining in with stories of her own, but found her interruptions frowned at and frozen out by Bina. When she persevered, looking to the Samson sisters for support, she simply met their patient, gentle stare, and with embarrassment she realized that the urgent, brilliant tales she was attempting were ones they'd probably heard before.

Frau Samson sat a little way away, her head bent over fine embroidery. She had placed herself carefully just far enough away to give the impression of not being able to overhear while still catching quite easily at each new strand of conversation. Eva felt inclined to join her. Today she liked the look of her large lumpy shoulders and the folds of her neck as she bent over her work. There was no sign in her of her daughters' delicacy and she wondered what had happened to the husband, and if he were the one from whom they'd inherited the tiny wrists and the heart-shaped apricot chins.

Angelika's voice lowered and she began to tell the others about a proposal of marriage she'd received while on holiday in St Moritz. He was a small, bald man of almost thirty who had failed to understand her when she said she couldn't marry him as she was still at school. 'I am quite prepared to wait,' he replied, and when she'd avoided him for the rest of that day, he proved that he was not in fact prepared to wait at all. In the middle of the night he'd begun hammering on the hotel door of an uncle who was travelling with them, and had demanded to know what was going on. The uncle was so annoyed at being woken that he told him quite plainly that nothing was going on or ever would be, and when they went down to breakfast the next morning Angelika found, to her relief, that he had changed hotels.

Bina and Martha laughed so hard that streaks of red appeared on their necks, and Eva had to close her eyes to force away the image of the little angry man hammering and hammering, in love. Julika burst in with a much more glamorous proposition from a mountain climber. He swore that to win her love would

19

be more marvellous than ascending the world's highest peak. Marriage to her, he insisted, could be the great adventure of his life. Eva found herself biting her lip for the end of this story, and it was with an uncomfortable sense of loss that she listened to Julika confide how it had been the sight of his frizzy red hair squirrelling out from under his hat that had decided her against him.

'A narrow escape.' Bina sighed, and Martha added tremblingly that she didn't know what she'd have done in a similar situation.

Eva closed her eyes and let the sun wash over her. She was waiting, as the others were, to hear what Bina might come up with. She was only a year younger than the Samsons and it was necessary that she offer up something against their dazzling display. The silence lasted fractionally too long and Martha began a dry, unconvincing cough. Eva opened her eyes, and saw her sister struggling. 'Binschen,' she smiled, 'it's not like you to be so shy,' and kicked her just above the ankle. Bina only glared at her, and to save the family name Eva added, 'So what about that doctor in Heligoland who had flowers specially brought over from the mainland?' The others turned to her, their faces brightening. 'Bina likes to keep him to herself,' she whispered, happy to have found a part to play at last. Bina looked modestly at her hands. 'Yes,' Eva took a breath, 'from one day to the next this young man would note down the colour of her dresses, and then order bouquets of flowers especially to match them. We don't know whether or not he ever got the opportunity of proposing.' Bina sat up a little straighter and the eyes of the others rested on her now mysterious face. 'But she certainly never gave him much encouragement.' And Eva added, rather too solemnly, 'Poor man.

'The day we left,' she continued quickly, 'the young doctor stood miserably on the pier and watched our boat pull out. He didn't wave or shout, and then suddenly from behind his back he produced a bunch of red and purple flowers, anemones, and waved them at us. I suppose he chose anemones because they were the most colourful flowers he could find and would be bound to match something Bina was wearing. Well, as we pulled away he began to throw them, petal by petal into the sea. Everyone on the ferry clapped and cheered and Bina . . .' she looked at her sister for inspiration '. . . Bina, who was dressed from head to toe in white, turned bright red, her ears went purple, and her black eyes glared, so that her whole face suddenly looked exactly –' Eva caught herself and stopped in time from running in the wrong direction. 'But the most terrible part of it was, Bina wouldn't even wave to the poor man. She took one look at him and ran inside to hide until he was completely out of sight.'

'Bina!' The Samson sisters exclaimed in one accusing breath. 'How cruel.' But their faces opened up with admiration.

Eva lay back comfortably in her chair. She screwed up one eye to glance sideways at her sister and was surprised to catch the dark fury of her scowl as she patted and smoothed the blush out of her cheeks.

'Manu,' Eva called, as soon as the Samson motorcar had set them down at Gaglow, and she ran through the house, along the downstairs corridor and out on to the back lawn to find him. Instead she found her mother, bent over a rose bush, surreptitiously plucking at the dead heads of the flowers. 'He hasn't gone away again?' she gasped, and Marianna, without looking up, said she needn't worry, they'd got him until the autumn.

'Emanuel,' Eva shouted, running down towards the orchard, but she could see between the rows of stunted trees that he wasn't there. The door to the walled garden was shut, and dragging her feet, she walked in a wide arc of the upper lawn, wading through a spray of wild raspberry and re-emerging on the sloping mound into which the ice-house had been built. The wall rose up out of the earth, only feet below the tiles, and as Eva scrambled round it, huffing and preparing to give up, she heard her brother's voice. He was talking softly, with a laugh between each word, and she could almost hear his slanting smile.

'I'm back, Manu, I'm back,' she announced, shrieking round a pillar, and her brother, as if she'd given him a fright, sprang out towards her.

'Manu?'

But there was her governess, leaning into the curved wall. 'Evschen, you're back already.' And she stretched out a hand. Her face was milky white and dense, as if she'd just woken from a sleep. 'We didn't hear you.' She laughed, and Emanuel dropped his shoulders and stepped towards them both.

'How was the Castle?' He put his arm around her, his face opening up especially for her, and Eva lolled blissfully between them, Schu-Schu and her brother, retelling every detail of each hour, until it was time to go into the house.

Emanuel had never been one of Fräulein Schulze's charges. She had come to them when Eva was still a baby and Emanuel, already quite grown up at eleven, was studying with a private tutor.

At first Marianna did not realize the effect the governess was having on her daughters. In the space of a few months, Bina, always wayward and given to fits of temper, became distant and cold, and the other two, ruled as they were by their elder sister, followed suit with their behaviour. It was only after returning home from a month-long visit to a spa town that Marianna clearly saw how they had changed towards her. Instead of rushing, their little arms outstretched and groping for the presents she had hidden in her cape, they lined up stiffly and curtsied, one by one. 'My darlings,' Marianna gasped, horrified at this cold reception. 'What manners!' But the children just looked glumly down, as if they longed for nothing more than to return to the private world of their nursery. She'd kept them with her for as long as she could bear it, and then when their formality showed no sign of easing she gave up miserably and sent them away. She imagined them prancing freely out of their regulation finery and throwing feather pillows at each other under the treacherous freckled eye of Fräulein Schulze.

Marianna became determined to find some ground on which to dismiss the governess. She watched her closely day after day, stinging with the sight of her children's growing adoration and unable to find the clue to her methods of seduction. She began to curse the bridge parties she had to arrange and the dresses that must be ordered and the three afternoons a week spent with a cloth over her shoulders while Herr Baum heated and rolled her hair. There were her piano lessons and her son's education and the health of her husband, which was not always good. All these things stopped her, month after month, from finding any cause for complaint, and she shrank from dismissing the girl without some specific reason. She had almost given up when an excuse was sent to her in the form of Eva. She was just rushing out to Wertheim's to buy stockings and new gloves when she noticed that the drawing-room door had been left open. Glancing in, she saw her youngest daughter standing with a marble in her hand. She was holding it up to the light, and as Marianna watched she popped it, like a sweet, into her mouth.

'Eva!' Marianna shrieked, seizing her by the shoulders, and Eva, who was relishing the smooth feel of glass rolling round her tongue, jumped so that the marble lodged hard into her throat. 'Spit it out!' Marianna ordered, pulling her round, and with her fingers she attempted to prise open her mouth. Eva choked and spluttered and began to turn a deep, dark red. 'Help, for God's sake!' Marianna shouted, panic rising, and before she'd had a chance to peel away her gloves, Fräulein Schulze was pushing her aside. She grabbed hold of the girl and with a quick twist of her arm flipped her upside down, thumping her sharply on the back so that the marble flew out and rolled away across the floor.

Marianna found that she was shaking. 'Whatever were you thinking of, leaving the child in here alone?' And when Fräulein

Schulze didn't answer, she seized her opportunity and ordered that she pack up her things and go. 'Evschen, my sweet child.' She went to wrap her daughter in her arms, but Eva struggled free, running towards her sisters who, white-faced and full of fury, were clutching at Schu-Schu's skirt.

'A marble?' Wolf raised an eyebrow. 'Is that so very dangerous? But Marianna refused to answer. She had spent most of that afternoon in tears, waiting for him to return, and now that the news had been passed on she presented a cold composure to her husband that he failed to understand.

'A month's wages, is that all?' he worried. 'She has been with us over a year.' And Marianna simply repeated that a seat was booked for Ulm in Fräulein Schulze's name and she would need to be at the station by eight o'clock the following morning.

Marianna Belgard stood with folded hands and stared down at the red-hot, raddled faces of her daughters. 'I shall manage,' she had said when, earlier that day, Wolf mentioned that he might just possibly be expected to have dinner out with grain merchants recently arrived in town.

'Come on now, my silly little loves,' she ventured, when the display of grief continued unabated. 'It cannot be the end of the world . . .' But her voice was sunk in wails and the endless maddening repetition of Schu-Schu's name. By late afternoon Marianna felt the strain of her own temper rising, and she had to stop herself from running to the kitchen for a basin of cold water. She imagined the gratifying sloosh of it as all three screaming mouths were startled into silence. But she gripped her hands, resisting, and sent out instead for Nanny from her evening off.

The following morning Bina still refused to eat, and Eva and Martha, having found small mementoes of their governess, a brooch and a bead-encrusted hairslide tucked under their pillows, howled with renewed strength. Marianna called the doctor out. 'A possible case of fever,' he diagnosed. 'Not always serious, but in this case we cannot be too careful.' And, with narrowed eyes, he prescribed a medicine to be administered at intervals throughout the day. Marianna, torn between respect and a reluctance to betray her children, wrote down his instructions and paid his bill.

'What if they really have become ill?' And having forgotten all about Eva, the marble and the suddenness of Fräulein Schulze's departure, she began to administer the bitter-tasting medicine, forcing it down and driving one more spoke into the claim against her. Nanny was no help: attached to her as the children were, in the course of the last year Fräulein had succeeded in undermining her authority. Where once Nanny might have silenced them with a stern look and the withdrawal of some treat, now they only laughed at her. 'I used to be your father's nurse,' she told them, 'many years ago, and he would never have given me such trouble.' And for a moment they were silent thinking over how their papa often stopped and pressed her chalky hand, laying it against his cheek, and calling her not Nanny but Omi Lise, as if she were a real-life grandmother.

After five more broken nights of wailing, it was Emanuel who suggested that Schu-Schu might be reinstated. He stood in the nursery and watched his sisters, red-eyed and unrelenting, while Eva, exhausted from the effort to maintain the vigil, sat palely in her cot.

Marianna refused her son's advice. Instead she drove with him to the zoological gardens, where they strolled along the gravel paths, breathing in the smell of the exotic plants and admiring the animals, the flock of pelicans and the great brown bear staring languidly out at them. 'How sad,' Emanuel said, his fingers clinging to the wire of the pen, his eyes fixed on the animal, whose paw scratched and scratched against the ground.

'Come away,' Marianna urged, the pink ends of his thumbs so vulnerable to one great swipe.

Emanuel took her arm. He was almost thirteen and growing taller by the month. He talked now and then about the day when he would begin work with his father, dealing grain on the exchange, and Marianna's pride in him occasionally rose up and overwhelmed her. It seized her by the throat and squeezed delicious tears from her eyes. She gripped his arm and led him in the direction of the sea lions.

There was a café in the centre of the park where they sat down and ordered ices. It was hardly the weather for it, and they smiled at each other over the cold silver of their spoons.

Marianna longed to ask his opinion of the governess Schulze and the strange power that she wielded, convinced he would have some wise words with which to comfort her. How much more eagerly she would accept his judgement than her husband's. Wolf, she knew, would be bound to tease her, turning her questions into an excuse to make light of the way she ran her house. As if the upbringing of her daughters could be compared in any way to a spring-clean. But she stopped herself from raising the subject, pushing away these thoughts and reminding herself that Emanuel must have his head free for Professor Essenheim, who came every morning to work with him on a whole variety of subjects.

Emanuel smiled mischievously across at her. 'Now what?' he asked, and she was sure he had guessed at what was really on her mind.

'Another ice?' she suggested, and they sat at their little table, chatting idly, and spooning up delicate mouthfuls of scented, frozen fruit, as they watched the people pass on their way to and from the zoo.

CHAPTER 4

For no obvious reason my father suggested we drop in to see his mother one afternoon after buying salmon from the fishmonger in St John's Wood. I was eighteen, in my first year at drama school, and as far as I knew my existence had never been disclosed.

'Will she know who I am?' I asked, as we drew up outside, and he took hold of my hand and said there were days when she didn't know who anybody was.

The house was flat-fronted and over-shadowed by a tree. It surprised me to find that my father had a key. 'Mutti?' he called, into the gloom of the front hall, and I followed him as he trod quietly through. There was a formal parlour, a pale rug over wooden boards, and a step down into the back room. And there she was. My grandmother. Eva. A person from another world. She looked at us and smiled. Her bright white hair was fastened in a bun and her eyes were pale and startling. 'Good afternoon.' My father kissed her hair, frowning down at a half-finished game of solitaire. I hovered in the corner. The room was panelled with dark wood, cabinets and shelves of varying lengths fitted tight into the walls on every side. There were drawers and small compartments and the flap of a hatch that led through into another room. I leant towards a photograph inside its frame, three young women in gauzy summer clothes, faded and beautiful with sun. 'Mutti, this is Sarah,' and my grandmother raised her eyes, opening them to let in white, and looked me over. I smiled and nodded but she moved her attention back to her game, and although I came and stood beside her, watching as she cheated marbles into holes, she didn't look at me again.

My grandmother had a live-in companion, Meg. My father called her from the bottom of the stairs and with a thud and a great hoot she came thundering down. 'Mr Linder! How lovely to see you!' She glanced sideways at her charge and whispered in a sing-song voice, 'She's a stubborn one, she is, stubborn and sly.' And then moving past us in a burst of whisky breath she put an arm around my grandmother's neck and kissed her roughly like a child.

'I'm Sarah,' I offered, as she fixed me with an inquisitive grin. 'Michael's daughter.'

Meg flushed and fumbled, wondering how she'd managed to forget. 'Sarah,' she said, 'Sarah!' as if it was just coming back to her, and she made me sit down and remind her what I did.

'I'm at drama school.'

She threw up her hands and told me she'd been married to an actor, well, two, in fact, and knew anyone and everyone there was to know in the business. 'I'll introduce you to the top producers,' she insisted, with a heavy hand, and I thanked her, moving towards my father who was shifting about uneasily by the door.

'Goodbye, Mutti,' he whispered as he slipped away, but she didn't look up from her game and my words to her were lost in a sudden and passionate embrace from Meg, insisting that we meet again very soon.

'We'll dine at Le Caprice,' she called, through the closed window, and instead of answering we nodded to her as we drove away.

'My mother, Meg, me and you . . . Shall we invite anyone else?' My father, against all expectations, had booked for Saturday at the small Italian on the corner of his road.

'I could bring Pamela?' I offered, and the more I thought of it the more the idea appealed. Pam was my best friend, and although I'd only known her since the start of college we were bound together through sheer drama. Her family lived in Surrey and I'd often been invited there for the weekend where Pamela's parents set out to soothe away the hardships of our student life. They set up barbecues, picnics and elaborate teas with instant cheesecake and cold crumbly flans. They drove us out to country pubs for scampi-in-a-basket, and afterwards, when we returned, they hovered over us with trays of cake and flutes of German wine. Pam's mother even packed us treats to take back on the train. Chocolate biscuits, individually wrapped, and fat white eggy rolls. Pam remained slim and flawless, while I, as soon as we reached home, would lie beached up on my bed, promising myself a three-day diet of grapes.

Pamela Harris was tall and blonde with permanent mascara clogged above her eyes. In the third week of college I had saved her life. We were working late, rehearsing scenes from Wedekind, when the hushed intensity of Act Two was shattered by a roar. 'PAMELA!' It was a bellow followed by the pounding of the door, and Pam gripped hold of my hand.

'PAMELAAAA!' The students standing on the makeshift stage froze with their hands over their mouths. 'I . . . love . . . you . . . Pamela.' There were cracks and fury in his voice. Marlon Brando in *A Streetcar Named Desire*, and the gold hairs stood up along Pam's arm. 'I . . . fucking . . . love . . . you.'

He was desperate, frothing, Jack Nicholson with an axe, and so I pulled her up and skidded through the building. 'Quick, hide in here.' Together we squeezed into a cubicle, shivering and giggling, wincing against the sudden shattering of glass.

'He'll kill me,' she insisted, so I helped to push her through a window high up above the sinks.

Pam stayed with me that night. She lay beside me in my single bed, trembling as she smoked, making me promise that I wouldn't leave her even to get up for water in the night. 'Of course I won't leave you,' I said, and curled against her arm, her ashtray balanced on my hip, and sank into a blissful and heroic sleep.

'Sarah! My dear girl.' It was Meg, already seated beside my grandmother, tiny and frail in a dust black dress. 'Sarah.' She got up and, both arms outstretched, crushed me against her bosom. 'Sarah, Sarah, I want you to sit next to me.'

Pam took the seat opposite my father and, with one hand still gripped by Meg, I made the introductions. My grandmother looked from Pam to me. She held her shoulders straight, her head a little lowered, and when she smiled her chin turned into a point just like my own. 'How do you do?' she murmured, and I heard the foreign strength of her old accent.

'Wine, we need more wine.' Meg hailed the waiter and began to fill me in on the details of her first husband's life, his triumphs and his failures. 'It's far, far worse for women,' she warned, and with great snorts and sighs she searched around for the names of agents, the ones whose reputations had been strong when her last husband was alive.

'Pam is studying drama as well,' I broke in. 'In fact she's the real star of our year.' Meg stopped in mid-flow to lean across and clasp her arm, releasing me to take hold of her glass. I took the opportunity to smile at my grandmother. If only I could think of one single thing to say.

'Risotto,' she whispered to my father, and he placed the order for her.

'And for me,' I agreed, hoping somehow to forge a link, but her eyes were fixed on Pam.

Pam laughed and gasped as Meg launched into a theatrical anecdote involving a deaf woman, her second husband and a dog. 'That's amazing, so what did he do?' Pam sparkled right on cue and Meg tightened the grip around her arm. My father caught my eye and made a private face and I tried offering my grandmother the bread basket.

Eventually Pam backed off towards the ladies'. There was a silence while we caught our breath and, under the guise of ordering more wine, I slipped away to find her. 'Pam, I'm so sorry.' Her feet were just visible below the toilet door.

'It's fine, I'm rather enjoying myself,' she shouted above the flush, and came out to join me. 'You didn't say your father had an accent.' She was twisting her head and fluffing up her hair.

'He doesn't.'

'He does, quite strong.'

I was indignant. 'They left Germany when he was seven years old!' And with a last trail of fingers through our hair we went back to join the table.

'Sarah!' Meg stretched out a hand as if we'd been gone for hours, but instead of me she pulled Pam down beside her. My father raised his eyes at me and, having little choice, I sat down opposite him.

'Who is this?' My grandmother looked at me confused, and my father, lowering his voice, said very firmly, 'This is Sarah.'

Meg winked at her and tousled Pam's streaky head. 'She does look like you, Mrs Linder, don't you think?'

'No thank you.' My father waved away more wine.

'So, write down your address,' Meg ordered, 'and I'll see what I can do about those introductions.'

Pam looked at me and shrugged, and, unable to think of what else to do, I handed her a pen.

A week or so later Pam brought a letter in to college. 'It would be better if you didn't come and visit us again,' it said in Meg's big, bouncing hand, 'as your grandmother seemed upset by meeting you after so long. You do look so very like her, you see.'

And my father, when I told him, had to agree. 'Well, you do look like my mother, it's true.' And neither of us mentioned that the letter had been meant for Pam.

CHAPTER 5

Fräulein Milner, the new governess, was a woman of twenty-two with long hands and pale, lifeless hair. She trembled when confronted with the contorted fury of Bina's tearstained face, but insisted privately that she would win the children round. On the first morning she sat them comfortably at the round table in the nursery, in good winter light from the window, and attempted to teach them how to knit. She gave them each a set of wooden needles and a ball of thick white cotton, holding her hands up like the conductor of an orchestra, and with forced cheerfulness began: 'Into the wood goes the huntsman . . .' She slipped the needle into the first stitch. 'Round the tree goes the dog.' She wound a loop of cotton. 'Out pops the rabbit.' The needles clicked. 'And off they all go.' She moved on to the next stitch. Bina stared at her with undisguised disdain, while Martha, tangling up her needles in the line of casting on, began to cry. Eva sailed both needles across the room and watched them land in the fur of a rug. Millie, as the children had already named her, ignored this turn of events. 'Into the wood,' she continued on a new row, and more quietly, 'Round the tree . . .' until, with half a white face flannel to her credit, she had calmed herself into a new authority.

A month later Fräulein Milner handed in her notice. The reason she gave was her mother, who had been taken suddenly ill, she told Marianna, yet the actual reason was not the unruliness of the children but a spiteful streak she found they brought out in her. She had always liked to think of herself as a soft, amusing woman, her sunny disposition making up for her obvious lack of looks, but now when she washed at night and glanced up at her face in the oval mirror she saw a meanness in her mousy eyes, and a hard thin glint around her mouth.

After three more months and a string of weeping, broken resignations by young women with the highest references, a telegram was dispatched to Fräulein Schulze requesting her immediate return. Wolf offered to meet her from the train, but Marianna refused, insisting she was quite capable of making her own apology.

Gabrielle Schulze stepped on to the platform with an ill-concealed smile hovering on her lips. She must have been grinning like that all across the country, Marianna thought, but she held out a daintily gloved hand. 'It seems we are unable to manage without you, after all,' she told her. And the woman's amber eyes glimmered with amusement. They rode back together through the city, their faces turned politely away as the stilted conversation failed. 'I hope your family are all well?' Marianna enquired, but she dreaded the ability of each question to turn back on itself, and eventually, grateful for the girl's restraint in asking after her own family, she drifted into silence.

Before setting out for the station Marianna had asked that Omi Lise keep the girls occupied, tucked away in the nursery, so that at least she could be spared the sight of a doorstep reunion with their governess. With a forced smile, she bid Fräulein Schulze hurry in to them, left her in the hall and walked quickly through to her own sitting room where, having taken her seat at the piano, she began to play a tinkling arpeggio with both feet firmly pressed down on the pedals.

Marianna had to summon up her courage as the time approached to wish her girls goodnight. They would be waiting for her, defiant if she didn't come, defiant if she did. She nodded civilly to Fräulein, who had been reading from a book of gruesome fables, and bending over each small bed, she lightly touched each forehead with her lips. 'Goodnight, Mama,' they said in turn, and when Marianna left the room her heart felt lighter, and she began to hope that, having provided her daughters with the one person for whom they longed above any other, they might forget their fury and warm towards her.

When Fräulein Schulze returned from Ulm she had a new way of putting up her hair, plaited and curled under in a ridge around her head, and during her short absence from Berlin, she seemed to have bloomed into an unnatural state of beauty. The glow of victory, Marianna called it, but she could not help noticing how it lasted on right through the spring and into summer where the colour of her face was drawn out by the warm nights and the changing auburn of the trees.

Even her husband, usually blind to the allure of other women, noticed the change. 'Something seems to have happened to that girl,' he said. 'Do you think she's . . .'

'She's what?'

Wolfgang Belgard removed his glasses. 'It's probably nothing.' He began to rub his eyes. 'It may just be the ramblings of old age, but does she spend her entire time with the children?'

Marianna left the dressing table. 'You know my idea?' She settled beside him on the divan. 'I think she may be some kind of demon in disguise. The Bonn Dragon. Or the Black Sea monster. I've heard rumours that it has recently escaped from a lagoon and was even sighted in the restaurant car of the express train to Berlin.' Wolf laughed. 'But seriously,' she pressed him, 'I wish . . . I just wish we didn't have to trust her with the children.'

'We've been through all this business before.' He sighed, sinking his head back into the cushions. 'She's probably got some secret admirer. Doubtless, my love, it can all be explained. Go to the park with her, keep an eye out for some young man, passing more than once. Suffering. Reading poetry.' He turned and stroked the loose hair back from her face.

34

'Are you asking me to spy on her?' Marianna shook him off. 'Do you think I don't have enough to do with my days?'

'All I'm trying to convince you of,' he tried again, 'is that you are unlikely to be sharing your house with a monster, foreign or home grown.'

Marianna was not so sure. 'Time will tell.' And she kicked him lightly to let him know she was not as angry as she had been.

Bina, Martha and Eva begged Fräulein Schulze that their hair be twisted up into the same smooth and coiling twist as her own. 'When you are older,' she promised, smiling, 'and when you have more hair.' Unlike Millie, who had tried to convince them that her previous charges went to bed early, in summer before the sun had even started to go down, and in winter straight after supper, Schu-Schu allowed them to stay up. They sat in their nightdresses and watched as she unrolled her hair and brushed it smooth and orange over her broad shoulders. She did not give it the energetic treatment used by Nanny on their own hair, but stroked it languorously, taking each section at a time and making partings like white maps across her head. Each night in rotation she asked one of the girls to brush the last back section that she couldn't reach, and then, dividing it into three, she taught them how to braid by allowing a race in fat red pigtails to where her hair ended just above the cushion of her chair. When Marianna came in to take her goodnight kisses, she slipped out, covering her head with a shawl, and the children held their breath to see if she would reappear like that, a mixture of Medusa and a clown, her lumpy, twisted pigtails standing out and spreading mythic shadows up the walls and out across the ceiling. When she did come back to sing them one more song, they found that in the privacy of her own room she had loosened the plaits so that her hair hung, slightly kinked, in a curtain round her shoulders. Bina, Martha and Eva snorted with complaint, but Schu-Schu hunched her shoulders and threatened to tell them a ghost story right there in the dark. She held her thumb and forefinger over the candle and threatened to pinch out the flame. 'Please don't,' they begged, their eyes sparkling, their knees rigid, and she gave them a final, warning leer as she tucked them in.

It was part of Fräulein Schulze's duty to escort the three girls to school. They went to Frau Dr Burtin's school by the castle, which Marianna herself had attended as a child. Marianna went with them on the first day and found that almost nothing had changed. There was still the same long courtyard, and behind the school buildings a large garden where lilac and laburnum grew instead of flowers. The same games were played, songs sung, and cinnamon cake was still eaten on the day of the Director's birthday. The children wore stiff white pinnies with bows at the back and a row of three buttons on one shoulder. It made Marianna sad to think of her mother, with tireless fingers, sewing her an identical apron for each school day. Six perfect sets of bows and buttons, and in the strongest, whitest cloth. But she herself had not been taught or brought up to sew and, not knowing where to begin, she had ordered the aprons from a dressmaker in town.

Each day Marianna watched as her three girls, appropriately dressed, set off with their governess for school. She had hoped when she enrolled them that they might be taught French by Dr Burtin, the headmistress's husband, who had passed on to her his tangy Alsace accent, but Dr Burtin had long since retired, and even though his birthday was still celebrated, Marianna's daughters were taught by a young Parisian, and they recited the same poems and songs, but with perfect twittering accents that made them raise their chins and pucker like young birds. They recited 'Les Hirondelles' and 'Le Souvenir de peuple' just as she had done, and they brought home the same playground games that she had played. Now they clasped each other from behind, and snaking through the house they chanted, 'I am going to Jerusalem and you will come along!' This was a game Marianna had forgotten, and stooping down she agreed to rest her hands on either side of Eva's narrow body and skip through the apartment. They traipsed along the corridor to their father's study where the children egged each other on to call out to him, 'Papa? We are going to Jer-*u*-sa-*lem*, and you *will* come along.'

Marianna urged them to be quiet and tried, by jostling from behind, to move them on. But they only raised their voices louder, 'We *are* going to Jerusalem,' and she was forced to call for Fräulein to distract them from their mission.

'I don't mind the interruption,' Wolf always said, when a scuffle broke out behind his door. But the truth was that he engrossed himself so entirely in his work that he never heard the shrill voices of his daughters until they were raised in screams of furious frustration, punctuated by his wife's calls for help and her foot stamping on the wooden floor.

Schu-Schu, strong as an ox, hoisted Eva up on to her back and, rolling the other two under her arms like puddings, strolled with them to the corner nursery, leaving Marianna quivering and alone, too angry to take up her husband's invitation to sit with him while he finished off his work. Marianna retreated to the curving embrace of her piano, lit a thin cigar and allowed her fingers to drift over the keys; smoking and playing melancholy waltzes until Emanuel came home.

Emanuel had begun to attend classes in Italian and English. He met up with a group of boys who read Shakespeare aloud together, taking it in turns to play a leading role. Emanuel always arrived home from these events flushed and soft-limbed, his head too full of fights and romance to want to enter into any trivial conversation and he often spent the entire evening dreaming in his room. Marianna suspected he might be writing verse. She had found a locked drawer in his desk and had glanced around, hoping to come across the key. She would never search for something hidden, but if her glance happened to fall across it, then surely there would be no harm in a little natural curiosity.

Marianna left the piano now and wandered through to his room. She sat down on the high-backed leather chair that he had insisted upon since he was a small boy, and picked up a pen left lying on its side. She dipped it in ink and let an oily drop gather and slip to the end of the quill until it fell on to the blotting paper. It absorbed almost too fast, evaporating between the hungry grains. She allowed herself one more drop, transfixed by the softness of the ink as it slid over the nib. She then hurriedly replaced the pen. What was she doing whiling away her time? She had letters of her own to write, and she rattled the locked drawer once more before leaving.

It took months of casual glances, but Marianna eventually discovered the key to Emanuel's locked drawer. Her hand trembled as she turned it and felt the lock give with a small unoiled click. It was much as she had suspected. Sheaves of closely written pages pressed together and bound with lengths of thin red ribbon. Marianna lifted the first pile and let the papers droop over her knees. She flicked through impatiently, unsure what she was searching for. 'Her eyes flash dark in winter light, her cheek is pale, her lips are bright . . .' she read at the very bottom in an old round hand. And between the essays and the translations there were other attempts at poetry. 'Her eyes grow pale, her heartbeat slows . . .' Marianna felt a special glow at having been right about her son. She held on to her pride and worked on it to cancel out the ugliness of spying. 'Her hair rolls bold in flames of gold.' She felt unnerved suddenly at the passion of his words and then, smiling quickly, she reassured herself that, after all, he showed some signs of promise.

Marianna heard a rustle in the corridor and quickly replaced the pages, stacked in the right order, in the drawer. She twisted the key and slipped it under the blotting paper where its small, irregular shape had given it away. Then to cover her short breath, she plumped up the pillows on the bed and folded back a corner of his sheet. She took a last glance at the desk to see that everything was in order, and stepped out into the hall. A murmur of voices drifted through from the kitchen where the cook clattered about, passing on licentious stories about the family for whom she used to work, enjoying the sight of Dolfi, the maid, blushing and covering her mouth, and knowing that on her first day off Dolfi would pass them on to her sister who also worked as a maid.

Wolf lounged on the divan, soothed by the nightly unpinning of Marianna's hair. 'Are you all right, my love?' he asked, caught by her slow movements and her arms frozen in the air above her head.

'Yes.' She smiled, starting. 'I'm perfectly all right.'

Wolf raised himself so that he could see his own reflection in the triple-sided mirror. He was watchful, since his daughters' births, for any signs of melancholy. 'You need a change of scene,' he told her, and before he had time to promise her an afternoon of walking in the countryside she turned to him and suggested they make a trip to Italy.

'You can't deny that the Schulze has the children under tight control.' Wolf, delighted by this joke against herself, found he had agreed.

'We shall go as far as Rome,' she said, and he came and sat beside her, pushing her along the upholstered seat so that he had to catch her quickly round the waist to stop her slipping off.

Italy had been the chosen destination of their honeymoon and they had always promised to return. They had travelled to Lucerne and then on to Milan where the white marble cathedral had reminded them of a cake shop in Berlin. This confession, shyly given, had drawn them so warmly together that, even though it had been February, Marianna still remembered Milan as a city of blue skies and flowering avenues of trees. From there they had travelled to Genoa with its narrow lanes and high white roads up above the sea. They stayed in a small hotel, recommended for its French chef, where all the other guests smiled and nodded to each other whenever they came into the dining room. 'Oh, no, we've been married well over a year!' Marianna protested when they offered their congratulations, but she could tell that not one of them believed her.

A week before they were due to leave for Italy, Marianna and Wolf were invited to a party at the house in the Tiergarten Strasse where they had first met. Marianna was taken in to dinner by the director of the German Bank. 'When you are in Rome,' he told her, 'you must not miss paying a visit to the Pope.' Marianna laughed, but he insisted that if she left her card with the Prussian Consul at the Vatican, she would most likely get an audience. He had done the same thing the year before. 'Make sure you have a black silk dress, and that your husband has a dinner jacket.'

On their first Sunday in Rome, Wolf and Marianna drove to the house of the Ambassador and left their card. 'Don't expect to hear another thing about it,' Wolf warned, but three days later they received an invitation, gold-embossed and at the request of His Holiness the Pope.

Marianna bought a square of black lace to cover her head, as the invitation instructed, and Wolf dressed in his evening suit. At the appointed time they took a taxi to the Vatican. 'Look at all those Roman Catholics,' Marianna whispered, as two women wearing identical lace squares over their hair stepped down from a carriage.

Wolf pinched her. 'Shhh, I know those people. They are the Goldsteins from Charlottenberg.' But before they could call out to them, a guard in gold-embroidered uniform helped them down and escorted them to their appointed place in the Pope's private rooms, where he left them standing under a painting of the finding of Moses.

Clerics in robes of blue, green and purple silk filed through the room and it was announced that when His Holiness passed by, the assembled company should drop to their knees and be ready to kiss the Fisherman's Ring of St Peter. Shortly afterwards the Pope himself appeared. He was dressed in snowy, glinting white and made the sign of the Cross before holding out his hand for the kiss, over which no one was meant to linger for more than a second. Marianna's neighbour, a French woman with a stricken face, detained him with a long lament about her sick son. 'Pray to the Good Lord,' he told her, but she snapped back that she'd already done that and with very little success. Either he couldn't understand her quickly spoken French, or he simply did not want to prolong the conversation, Marianna wasn't sure, but he moved on with only a mumbled response in Italian, which the woman couldn't understand. Marianna kissed the air above his ring and let him pass.

'Well, how about that?' Wolf laughed, when afterwards they sat with the Goldsteins in a trattoria by the Spanish Steps, and toasted with red wine to a more enlightened future where all religions might happily overlap. Marianna raised her glass and thought of the sick son left all alone while his mother made her pilgrimage from France. She let the rich red wine warm her and found her heart lifted by thoughts of her own children, healthily at home, even if, for this one month, there had been no alternative but to leave them under the supervision of Gabrielle Schulze.

It was only on their return from Italy that the Belgards learnt of the unlikely gift of Gaglow. For three generations the estate had been owned by the family of Hans Dieter, who over the years had amassed a small fortune in unpaid debts. Wolf had supplied him with grain on credit for four consecutive seasons, never doubting he would pay up, but Hans Dieter's gambling finally caught him up and ruined him and, to avoid official bankruptcy, he began distributing his assets. 'Take the house as payment,' he offered, 'the stables that go with it, the carriages . . .' and here he blushed, stumbling over himself, 'and also the fields that stretch down to the village.'

Wolf was unsure. 'Why shouldn't we accept the land?' Marianna insisted when he told her, sitting at her dressing table, skimming the waves of her hair. 'We should say no because we are Jews?' And she'd laughed a joyful laugh that stayed with him for several days.

Wolf and Marianna drove out to Gaglow, leaving one morning just as dawn was breaking. It was a journey of three hours, and Wolf, who had travelled on this road before, pointed out sights, ancient, black-beamed inns that sloped to one side, and a tree that had been struck by lightning.

Hans Dieter was not a married man and had only used the estate for summer shooting and the entertainment of his friends. It had a grey, abandoned look, but Marianna still gasped at the beauty of the house as they drove up the straight, steep drive. 'You didn't tell me it was on a hill.'

She turned to her husband, who smiled at her enthusiasm and shrugged. 'Does it make a difference?'

They wandered around the overgrown and meadowy lawns and looked down on every side at the farms with their neatly planted fields stretching out below. The house looked severe and dark, with nothing behind it but sky, and Marianna began to plan how she would plant vines along its walls and edge the cold stone window-sills with flowers.

Hans Dieter had driven out to join them. The moment Marianna saw him she could tell that he was eaten up with prejudice. He was straight and civil with her husband, but at her he glanced sideways, his eyes full of undisguised disgust. Marianna felt herself looked over, up and down, as if she were a foreigner. It made her even more determined to accept the house, and she met his gaze straight on and without pretending to return the cold smile in his eyes.

'He's a decent enough fellow, for all his weakness,' Wolf said, once they were alone, and Marianna pressed his arm, and told him tenderly that he was too good and stupid for this world.

Hans Dieter had shown them round the house, through the west wing of drawing rooms and out into the courtyard. The kitchens, he explained, were at the back and were so far from the dining room that holes had been knocked in several walls to allow the food to be passed through to servants posted in the corridors. In that way, meals had more chance of reaching the table while still hot. Hans Dieter ushered them upstairs and walked with them through the deserted nurseries, even allowing them to peer into his own private rooms where Marianna saw a bed draped with pelts, tails and claws still attached and hanging like the fringes of an eiderdown. She clenched her teeth and refused to allow the colour to rise in her face. She walked back down the wide, curved staircase, calling over her shoulder that she preferred to be outside.

The orchard was red and green with early apples and pungent with the unpicked fruit of the year before. The earth squelched and gave under Marianna's boots. She raised her arms and, clasping a flaking branch, hung from it, allowing her feet to leave the ground and swing gently through the grass. She picked a small hard apple and put it in her pocket. Then she walked round to the back of the house and let herself into the vegetable garden. It was overgrown and for years had been used only by the servants. A dark, gloomy fig tree spread against one wall, impossible to reach for weeds and brambles, and another wall bore the dried traces of vines and one surviving apricot. Only a long strip of the garden had been kept up and this was planted out with row after row of cabbages and potatoes.

Wolf stood in the doorway and called to her. He laughed as she strode across to him, her leather boots caked in mud, her palms moss green with lichen. 'It looks to me as if you've already made your decision,' he said, and he took her arm and led her back to the front door of the house where he had forms, already drafted, for Hans Dieter to sign.

Wolf and Marianna spent that night at an inn in the town. Word had spread that they were the new owners of Gaglow and they were greeted with unreserved curiosity and made to wait a long time for their supper.

'The children will love it here,' Wolf said, and Marianna

43

smiled and thought of Emanuel in years to come. 'The girls particularly,' he added, winking, and he clinked her glass with his.

Eva, Martha and Bina watched the flushed face of their mother as she broke the news to them. They saw the light in her eyes and the plans for grandeur twitching at her fingers. To spite her they remained unmoved. 'It sounds distinctly feudal,' Bina said. 'I shan't go there unless I have to.' And in solidarity her sisters both agreed.

Bina was ten. She sat up in the dark bedroom of their Berlin apartment and wondered aloud what could have happened to the poor little Dieter children, now that they had been turned out of their own home.

'But Papa would never have allowed that.' Martha was appalled.

'No,' Bina agreed. 'Papa couldn't know.'

'Do you mean she tricked him?' Eva asked.

And Bina whispered solemnly that she had. 'Schu-Schu says,' she continued, lowering her voice, 'that our mother has got far above herself.' Eva and Martha looked at her, unsure exactly what she meant, but convinced of the necessary depth of the outrage. 'Now you know,' Bina said, and having sworn not to be won over, they traipsed back to their own beds.

When Eva first saw the house, with painters swinging from the window-sills and gardeners pushing back and forth across the grass, she felt an urge to run off round it, dragging her fingers over the texture of the walls and exploring ledges and secret steps that were warmed at angles by the sun, but she caught sight of Fräulein standing, looking dismissively around. 'Just as I expected,' she seemed to be saying. And Eva stayed standing where she was.

The girls walked in an orderly fashion around the house. Bina kept up a mournful appearance, casting reproachful glances at her sisters when the length of a corridor or the man-sized tunnel of a chimney carried them away. Martha became engrossed by the winding maze of the kitchens and Bina was forced to start nodding like an old lady, muttering, 'How will they eat now, the little Dieter children, wandering the streets?'

When both Bina and Martha disappeared into an enormous pantry, Eva seized her chance and slipped up a flight of narrow stairs. She found herself on the first floor, and began walking from room to room, catching rising voices from the ballroom where her mother was ordering drapes and covers and replacements for the missing fragments of a chandelier. Eva continued up the main staircase and found herself in the nursery. She recognized the low white ceiling and the double row of sky blue windows, exactly as her mother had described. One night Eva had lain with her ears muffled by a pillow, while Marianna tried to breathe into her the spirit of the house. She had whispered about swallows and apple blossom, and the fountain, frozen in the winter, but Eva burrowed her head deeper down into the bed and forced her eyes closed with images of tangled forests, wolves, and Hansel and Gretel searching desperately for crumbs.

Eva took off her shoes and slid along the corridor from one room to the next. The floor had been planed and polished so that it felt as smooth as butter, and in each room was a large white fireplace and a row of high windows. In the farthest room, down by the skirting board, a faded, childish hand had written, 'This is my room and I love it.'

Eva knelt down to inspect the message. She imagined it might have been left there by one of Hans Dieter's children, or Dieter himself, or if, as Bina had told her, the family had lived in this house for hundreds of years, it might even have been his grandfather when he was a small boy. Eva wanted to cover up the message and keep it for herself. She looked around and, finding nothing in the unfurnished room with which to guard it, she peeled off the paper words and put them in her pocket in a strip, leaving a narrow length of exposed plaster underneath.

CHAPTER 6

'I've had another letter,' my father said, 'about the property.' He waved it in front of me, and for a moment I was surprised to see it was in German.

'Does it mention the theatre?' I asked, lumbering towards the sofa, fully clothed.

He peered over it, his glasses on his nose, translating as he read. ' "The descendants of the daughters of Marianna Belgard . . . are entitled . . . but only on agreement of a set commission." Oh, he's come down to forty per cent.' And he moved gleefully over to the easel.

'And no news of Gaglow?' I went through to the bathroom to undress. It was February, and for the first winter of my life my hands and feet were warm. My shoulders hadn't risen up to fight the cold and great flows of blood gave colour to my face. 'I feel fantastic,' I whispered to myself, and in a sudden rush of joy I unclipped my dungarees and dropped them to the floor. My vest had rolled up to my ribs and my stomach stuck out at an angle like a bean. 'Couldn't you make a bargain?' I called, standing sideways at the mirror, seeing how far out I'd have to lean to see my toes. 'If he finds Gaglow for you, then you'll consider paying his commission on the rest?'

'I'm ready,' he said instead, and I walked through to find him waiting, brush in hand, the easel wheeled round into position.

'But then again,' my spirits were much too high for quiet, 'I don't suppose it's just up to you.' As I lay down on the sofa, old springs and strips of cloth sang out with the strain.

'No,' he agreed, 'it's not just up to me. There are all my ghastly relatives.' And he set about mixing more paint.

As soon as we stopped for our first break I scrutinized the letter. 'Gottfried Gessler.' The signature looked sly, and I wondered if my father's various cousins, whom I'd never met, had also heard from him.

Pam met me at the hospital. 'Are you all right?' She held my hand, and each time a door flew open we both looked up.

The baby was due in four weeks' time and it still hadn't turned round. 'It's a big baby,' the doctor had warned, 'and not likely to move now on its own.' He'd prodded my side, feeling for its feet, and my stomach, smooth and tight as calf, lurched a little to the left.

'Apparently my doctor is the king of baby turning,' I whispered to Pam. 'He has an eighty per cent success rate,' and then, lowering my voice still further, I told her that I knew my baby wasn't going to turn.

'Don't say that.' She winced, thinking of the alternatives, but I was busy with a hot sensation of pride.

'It's you.' Pam pulled me up. 'It's you,' and at the end of the corridor a nurse was calling for Miss Linder.

Pam stood back and gazed into the swirling screen hoping for some hint of the sex. The heartbeat thundered, fast and loud, while Dr Mok bent by my side. 'I'm trying to get it to flip over like this,' he explained, and he began to knead and squeeze. The baby, as I'd predicted, dug in its heels and refused to move. Soon its whole small body was squeezed up under my ribs but its head would not slip down. 'It doesn't want to turn,' I pleaded, looking to Pam to intervene but the doctor insisted on one last go.

'Stubborn little fellow,' he huffed then, giving up, and I laid protective fingers on my baby's head, feeling its back uncurl while two small feet stretched luxuriously down to trample on my bladder.

'I'm badly in need of tea and cake,' I gasped as soon as we were out.

Pam took my arm. 'Not unattractive, your doctor, don't you think?'

'He's the worst type of man.' I laughed her down. 'I see your taste hasn't improved.'

But she only raised her eyebrows at me to show I didn't stand a chance. 'Excuse me?'

'OK, OK. You win,' and we hurried across the road towards a café.

'Pam?' She knew what I was going to ask her. I was sitting sideways in a booth, watching as our plates of strawberry cake sailed high towards us. 'Could you ... would you be able to bear it, you know, to be at the birth, if it turns out to be a – an operation?'

'You're not seriously telling me you'd be awake?' She looked down at the veins of juice marbling her cake.

I nodded.

'Are you sure you won't want Mike, after all ... or your mother, or ...'

'No.'

'But you can't stop Mike, not if he wants to come.'

'Who says he wants to?' And then, overtaken by a rush of fear, 'you haven't been in contact with him, have you?'

'Of course I haven't.' While she blew smoke over her shoulder I finished every last crumb of my cake, scraping up the pool of cream with the flat side of the fork.

'So,' Pam leant towards me, grinning, 'you still think it's a girl?'

I shook my head, my hands hovering to clamp over my ears.

48

'Because from looking at that screen . . .'

'Stop it!'

'. . . I could tell absolutely fuck all.'

I laughed. Relieved and disappointed. 'Would you really want to know if it was you?'

'Would I?' Pam lit another cigarette. 'I'd like to know now and I'm not even pregnant.'

'Pam.' I was tired suddenly. 'If you really can't face it . . . I would understand.' But she was reaching for my hand, insisting there was nowhere in the world she'd rather be.

Pam bought herself a mobile phone and rang me several times a day to check I wasn't trying to get through, 'I was on the tube for almost an hour, getting to some stupid audition,' and I felt guiltily hopeful each time she didn't get the job.

We never discussed the possibility that she might be called away. Almost every day there was another threat. An advert in Istanbul, a play in Hull, a small part in a film, which lost its backing just in time. Dr Mok wanted me to book in for a Caesarean but, stubborn as my child, I had to wait and let the baby choose its day. The midwives frowned and fussed, not wanting to be bothered with an emergency in the middle of the night, but there was nothing they could do to force me.

And then, just when I was all prepared, I had a call from Mike. I was sitting on the floor deep breathing, taking air in through alternate nostrils, when I reached over and picked up the phone.

'It's me.'

My heart thumped and for a moment I was tempted not to recognize his voice. 'Oh, hello,' I offered instead, in a cheery, casual tone. There was a pause. For all he knew I'd already had our baby and it was lying sleeping on my arm.

'I bumped into Pam . . .' he stammered, 'and she told me . . . she said the baby's breech . . .'

Suddenly I couldn't speak. Why was I sitting all alone leafing through a book of yoga poses, skipping out the ones where men massaged their pregnant partners' feet?

'I just wanted to tell you I was breech as well.' He sounded triumphant. 'I was a Caesarean, and my mother insists it's the best way by far to have a baby.'

All my self-pity dropped away. 'So what you're saying,' I lunged into the phone, 'is that this baby is already taking after marvellous you?' and winded by my rage I slammed down the receiver.

For a moment I sat cross-legged and serene, staring hard at the next exercise, and then, unable to pretend, I rolled on to my side and sobbed until the tears had mushed a soft patch on the floor and the salt against my face began to sting.

I never mentioned Mutti to my sisters. For all I knew there had been other visits, similarly disastrous, which we all kept to ourselves. But when we next met up I inspected them more closely. Natasha was the eldest. She had thick dark hair that turned wild when it was brushed and her eyes were lashed with black. She was tall, her shoulders straight and high, her nose just like our father's. Kate was only four months younger. She was fairer than Natasha with honey-coloured skin, and although they'd never met as children, the mannerisms of their lips and hands were unusually alike. Until now I'd considered myself the odd one out. I was two years younger, slight and brown, with olive eyes and a lopsided mouth. 'My little changeling,' my mother had once called me, but now with my new eye for family traits I saw that this was not the case. It was even possible I was the real Linder. 'You do look like my mother, it's true.' I hummed over my father's words, and it gave me new confidence in his heart.

*

50

A few years later, without our having met again, my grandmother died quietly in her sleep. I asked if I could have a photo.

'Of course.' My father chose the picture I'd admired of the three girls dressed in summer white, smiling and lounging on the porch. He also gave me a photograph of Eva by herself. She stood in profile, her shoulders back, her eyelids lowered and her almost perfect nose sloping straight down towards her chin.

'You look so like her!' My sisters stared hard at the portrait, tracing the bobble of the chin. 'It's amazing.'

I flushed and bit my lip, wondering why it made me feel so ridiculously glad. 'I'll order you both a print,' I offered, but Natasha said she'd prefer a copy of the sisters, Eva, Martha and Bina, lounging on cane chairs, and Kate agreed that she'd like one as well.

The photograph was still in its frame, the polish of the wood worn out at the corners, and it was tricky to remove the back. One clip snapped off in my hand and then the back came away. The smell of dust and old sweet powder made me sneeze. At first I thought the photograph was unusually thick, printed on to cardboard, but as I held it up I realized there was a second, smaller picture welded to its back. I peeled it carefully away and found the close-up picture of a man. He was dressed in uniform, the high-collared uniform of the First World War, and he looked confident and hopeful, staring straight into the lens. His hair was brushed back from his face, and his chin rested on one hand, a hand so fine and smooth I guessed the portrait must have been made before he ever went to war. 'Emanuel Belgard' was written on the back.

I showed it to my father. 'Who is this, do you know?' He turned the photo over in his hands, marvelling at the different shades of grey. 'How extraordinary.' He traced the fine inked letters of the name. 'My uncle Emanuel. My mother's elder brother.'

'An uncle, but I thought it was just three girls, your mother and two sisters?'

'No.' My father was impatient suddenly to begin work and he fixed the canvas with such a sharp look of concentration that I had to save my questions for another time.

I left the picture of Emanuel Belgard lying out, intending to find out more about him, but eventually, assuming he must have been killed during that war like so many other millions, I put him for safekeeping back behind his sisters, clipping them all shut together in their frame.

CHAPTER 7

'It's the war, it's the war,' Bina sang, when a letter arrived for Emanuel with a date and a time for him to report to his superior officer. She ran to the cupboard where his National Service uniform hung and struggled to pull it down. Emanuel took it from her and held it up against himself. The oval of his face seemed to shrink and pale above it.

'When you're home again,' Bina began, but her mother reached for the uniform and, handing it to Dolfi, ordered that it should be pressed and aired and kept out of sight until the moment it was needed.

'But when you do come home on leave,' Bina continued, 'will you bring –' But she was cut off by Fräulein Schulze who arrived in high colour to hear the news and knocked a china ornament to the floor where it cracked into three jagged pieces.

Emanuel left the room. 'Go after him, Eva,' Marianna urged, and Eva ran and caught hold of his hand, while Martha and Bina, Omi Lise and his mother all stood in the doorway and called for him to come back and join them for late breakfast.

Wolf Belgard was in Berlin, inspecting a new warehouse. Marianna sent frantic messages for him to return to Gaglow, but Emanuel followed these with messages of his own, insisting that he should not interrupt unfinished business, and that in his opinion the mobilization of men was nothing but a show of strength. The war, if there was one, would be over within a month.

Gruber dressed in his finest livery to drive the short distance to the train. He stood sweltering in gold and blue, flicking the reins with proud, tightly cuffed wrists. Marianna had a hat with flowers in its brim and she sat beside Emanuel longing to clasp his fingers in her hand. Bina, Martha and Eva sat across from her, their backs to the horses.

'Will you be fighting alongside Josef Friedlander?' Bina asked, blushing darkly.

Martha nudged her. 'Was he the one at the party with the curled moustache?'

'With the drooping ears, you mean,' Eva added.

Marianna frowned at them, and made a mental note to look up the Friedlander mother and see what kind of woman she was.

There were men at the station still in civilian clothes. They jostled and waved and shouted to each other as the train pulled in. It burst with startled faces, full of bravado, straining out at every window, and hundreds of men, sitting in the glaring light, bareheaded in the open trucks that had been attached to the back carriage.

Messages had been scrawled in great exclaiming letters across the doors, 'To Paris' and 'To Victory'. Wives and sisters had added hearts and their own private messages of hope. Emanuel recognized many of the faces fighting for space. There was the son of the blacksmith, and the boys who worked as gardeners on the estate. He smiled at them and they grinned in his direction, clearing a small space around him as he stood stiffly in his heavy jacket, the buttons buffed, and his trousers tucked neatly at the knee into shin-tight leather boots.

Marianna stood close beside him and the scent of flowers from her hat filled his nose and mouth. 'Will you write?' she asked, putting her hand on his arm. Emanuel began to move towards the train.

'Manu, Manu,' his sisters called after him. Feeling himself about to sneeze he jumped aboard and Gruber followed with his bags.

As the train pulled away he saw his mother and three sisters standing with the throng of other women, all in white ruffled high-necked shirts, and hats and scarves against the sun. Their arms waved in a fluttering sea of gloves and fingers and he had to keep his eyes fixed on the blue ribbon in Eva's hair so as not to lose sight of his own reeling family.

Marianna was silent as the carriage drove them home. From under the brim of her hat she let her gaze pass over the faces of her daughters. Today it made her smile to think how many hours of her life she'd given to worrying that Emanuel would be her only child. He had been born within a year of her marriage, and it still stung her eyes to think how delighted she had been with him. How she had dressed him and washed him and insisted that the nurse wake her if he cried during the night. 'It's all very well,' Wolf teased, 'but how will you manage when you have six sons all howling after you?' and he had placed an expectant hand on the flat of her stomach. But the years passed and with each month the familiar dragging ache in her knees signalled, yet again, that she had failed to catch the beginning of a life.

'You will have to be an only child like me,' she crooned over her son, and she thought of what her father called 'the holy trinity' of her own small family. And then, one after another, her daughters had been born.

'What are you smiling about?' Martha asked, and Marianna wiped her eyes with the back of her glove.

She considered telling them something about the life of an only child, its loneliness and quiet, but found herself remembering her friend the curtain mender who came regularly to help her mother. 'I was thinking,' she told Martha, 'about a very old woman and how whenever she reached the most exciting moment of a story, she began to stutter.'

'How very tiresome.' Bina raised her eyes.

'Not at all. She used to let me cut out flowers to pin onto the cloth . . .' But Martha was whispering some secret into Eva's ear, and Bina, rather than listen to her mother, was trying to overhear what they were saying.

Marianna sent off to her aunt Cornelia for the recipe of Tree Cake. Tree Cake had been her own favourite childhood treat. It was an exotic cake, layered in rings around a hollow trunk, with flakes of chocolate to look like bark, and to prise the recipe from her aunt was the hardest task she could set herself on Emanuel's behalf. Another aunt had been obsessed with cleanliness, wiping the handles of doors her guests had passed through, and dusting off the seats of their chairs, but Aunt Cornelia had kept the recipe for Tree Cake all to herself and moulded an identity around the mystique of its ingredients.

Dear, dear Manu,

Eva wrote before he'd hardly had a chance to get away.

I've been going over our plans for the future, and do you think, when the time comes to build our house we could make sure it's near a forest? Maybe by now you've even seen the perfect place. I suppose the one good thing about you going off again so soon is that the more you travel the more opportunity you'll have for finding the perfect spot.

Eva curved her elbow round the page to hide the letter from her sisters.

Please don't forget I want a garden with a wooden fence around it and a broad summer tree with a fork in it for a hammock. I know you plan to have two good horses, one especially for Sunday and another with a mild temperament to ride around on during the week, but recently I've been wondering how I will get about. I'd have my bicycle, of course, but maybe we should consider a motorcar. We could keep it in a special wooden house and only ever use it when we visit the rest of the family, which I imagine, occasionally, we'll have to do.

Eva looked round at the bent heads of her sisters. Sometimes the temptation to boast about her and Manu's secret plans was more than she could bear.

'What are you boring our poor brother with?' Bina asked, leaning across to seize her page, and Eva, holding on to their promise, slipped the letter out of reach and sealed it in an envelope.

Bina wrote short notes to Emanuel describing the health and escapades of the various dogs and, sealed in its own envelope, she repeated the exact same news, with a doubling of passion, to be forwarded on to Josef Friedlander, who was serving in the same regiment.

Martha, who had fallen in love vicariously with Josef alongside Bina, added poems in French and then, unsure whether she was now writing in an enemy language, translated them painstakingly into German.

'And what about Paris? For all the honeymoon couples?' Martha asked one night, as her neck was being washed, and Schu-Schu promised that the war would never come between a girl and her wedding plans. She continued to insist upon this, even after the line was formed right across France to the sea, with the collected enemy lined up in trenches on the other side. She promised that a special path could be cleared across no man's land to let the newly-weds through to Paris to see the Eiffel Tower.

Wolf returned to Gaglow for the first week of August, and as soon as he arrived the world declared war against each other like firecrackers catching. Russia, France and then Great Britain. They received a letter from Emanuel. He had been assigned to a cavalry regiment and was in daily training at a camp in Schleswig. 'It seems,' he wrote, 'that it is the small things in this war that are going to prove most difficult, and the fact that we are burning to put our lives at risk will not be of much consequence.' He went on to explain that, after a week strapped to the back of a horse, the lower half of his body was in such agony that he was virtually unable to sit down, stand up, or walk more than a few steps.

Marianna read the letter aloud, making her daughters blush and giggle. '"But, of course, our greatest problem is coming up with a plan to wean the horses off their favourite foods. They refuse everything except the choicest bread and pears, even though I tell them when they grumble that they must make sacrifices like everyone else, but I'm afraid they only snort with disapproval, turning up their noses – sorry, Papa – at the finest oats and barley."' Marianna smiled at her husband. It made her proud to think that grain passing almost through his hands was helping to support the German army.

'My dear family,' Emanuel wrote again from Schleswig, 'It's still uncertain when we set off. It is possible that we might not be fighting against the French and British, but against Indians and Japanese! How strange this will be, but I hasten to add it should not prevent us from winning.'

And when, in October, his regiment began to move into France, he wrote in a burst of enthusiasm: 'Last night we slept out in the fields wrapped in our coats against the rain, and the morale of the men could not have been higher. There are forty-eight cavalry regiments lying here next to one another in an endless line of trenches. Lions, hussars, dragoons, cuirassiers. I have an overwhelming feeling that things will turn out for the best, even though the air is thick with cannonfire. It will be hard for you to imagine but no one takes much notice, and the only real complaints are about the food. Last night the bread was so thick and full of dough we all preferred to fast.' Marianna broke off and looked towards her husband.

'The Belgians,' Wolf said, 'disrupting rail links.' He buried his head in his newspaper and refused to comment further.

'Is there really nothing you can do?' Marianna tried again.

Wolf closed his eyes and laid his hand over hers. 'Maybe,' he said, 'maybe,' and the two deep lines above his nose merged together, shooting upwards in a thick furrow as he frowned.

Wolf Belgard was one of very few who was not behind the war. It is a blunder on a massive scale, he thought privately, and as he read his daily paper he shook his head to think that not one of these thousands of men, foot soldiers, officers or generals, had ever fired a single war-time shot.

Bina reached for Manu's latest letter. She sped through the closely written words, unable to believe that once again her brother had failed to include any messages of hope for her from Josef Friedlander. 'What can he be thinking of?' She flung it away, and all at the long table turned to glare at her with a hard range of disapproving looks.

Martha took the letter. She touched the pages with her fingertips and began to cry quietly on to the paper. 'Please just win,' she whispered, and Eva, unable to sit by and see the precious words smudge and dissolve, eased it from her.

Eva read the letter through from beginning to end and still found little to satisfy her curiosity. Emanuel never mentioned the future or his plans for after the war. He only mentioned that he was being sent on somewhere else. By the time Eva had read the letter several times, searching for anything that might be construed as code, the breakfast dishes had been cleared and everyone else had left the table.

Fräulein Schulze put a hand on her shoulder. 'Your sisters are waiting for you,' she said. 'Have you forgotten? There's a trip planned to the forest.' Eva, immediately distracted, jumped up and ran to find her hat. Gabrielle Schulze, left alone, slipped the letter back into its envelope and folded it away into the pocket of her dress.

*

Bina, Martha and Eva settled into the carriage with their mother and sat back while Gruber set the horses at a steady pace. They were going to a beauty spot where they planned to meet Frau Samson and her daughters. They had not seen Angelika or Julika since their visit to the Castle, but their names came up regularly in conversation, and Bina had begun a correspondence.

'Do you know,' Bina said now, her round face creasing up with envy, 'that between them they've had seven proposals of marriage?'

'I wonder who they're saving themselves for.' Martha smiled.

Bina snapped, 'Well, they can't both marry the same man.'

'No, but it doesn't stop them from wanting to,' Martha added, and she grinned at her own cleverness in answering Bina back.

Eva, who sat opposite with her mother, turned away. I'd rather talk about the war than listen to any more of their nonsense. She tapped Gruber on the shoulder and asked after his nephew who was dug into a trench in France.

'We've had no news of him for over two weeks,' he answered.

'Oh, we had a letter from Manu only today,' Eva boasted, and sensing her mistake she lapsed into silence.

To pass the time Marianna offered to tell them about her own mother's engagement. Bina screwed up her eyes in contemplation but Martha was unable to resist. 'Please do, do tell us,' she said. And Eva turned one ear towards her.

'My mother,' Marianna began, 'a girl of seventeen, was sitting at the table with an enormous pile of socks and stockings.' 'How romantic.' Bina sniggered, but Marianna continued, 'She had only just begun to darn when there was a knock at the door. It was a cousin with her new husband. They had a carriage waiting and they planned to drive out to Französisch Buchholz. Mama was delighted, but her mother said that unfortunately she would not be able to go. She needed the stockings urgently, and there was no one who could darn stockings quite like her. So, Mama, usually very mild, insisted she should be allowed to go. She

60

begged her mother, beseeched her, until finally, after nearly half an hour, she had no choice but to relent. The stockings were packed away and, having changed into her best dress, she stepped into the carriage. It was a beautiful summer's day. The trees swayed in the breeze and the sky was blue without a single cloud.' Marianna stopped for a moment to take in the faces of her daughters, captured for once in the full flow of her own interest.

'Go on.' Bina frowned.

'Well, almost as soon as the party arrived they met up with some acquaintances, a couple who had also asked a friend to accompany them, and this friend turned out to be no one other . . .' Marianna was triumphant '. . . no one other than my papa!' It was as if she had somehow arranged the whole event herself.

'Go on,' Martha urged, an eager film of tears glinting in each eye.

'Well,' Marianna said more slowly, 'they fell in love . . . immediately, the minute they set eyes on one another . . .' She laughed, and Martha blinked, letting loose a drop of water on each cheek. 'And the following day Papa came to the house where my mother lived and asked for permission to marry her. And so,' Marianna folded her hands in her lap, 'they became a couple.'

There was a silence in the carriage and Bina squinted disapprovingly. 'Is that it?'

They were driving through thick woods along a track muffled by the first fall of leaves. The trees arched in places over their heads, splicing and covering them with branches of green shadow. Eva leant back in the carriage and looked up at the sky. 'Without a single cloud,' she murmured, and she began to count tiny wisps of white between the trees.

'Please carry on,' Martha urged, but Marianna shook her head, smiling and rearranging the fingers of each glove. She would have liked to go on, but she knew that their questions would inevitably lead to the sad fact of her father's early death, and her mother's subsequent decline. She would have preferred to tell them about her own meeting with their father, the flowers and dances and the romantic months of their engagement. She would describe for them the wedding feast, the roast gosling with new potatoes, the caviar and cucumber salad, but on this subject they refused to let her speak. She had no way of knowing that, with the help of Fräulein Schulze, they had devised their own history of her marriage. That she had been accepted entirely out of pity, and that a woman of higher sensibilities would never have allowed a man like Wolfgang Belgard to sacrifice himself for her.

It was late morning when they arrived. Frau Samson was already there with her daughters, more exquisite than ever in dresses of the palest pink with parasols to match. They set off to walk along the edge of the river. There was a narrow path dotted with jagged stones and in the distance the roar of a waterfall could be heard, crashing like an angry crowd. Angelika and Julika put up their shades, twisting them jauntily over their shoulders. Marianna and Frau Samson strode ahead.

'Have you never seen the falls?' Angelika asked, turning back to Bina. The path was so narrow in places they had to walk in single file.

'No.' Bina turned to Martha and Martha to Eva. Eva shrugged and stuck out her tongue. It amused her that the sun, which had shone so warmly earlier in the day, now continually disappeared behind a single fat grey cloud, which dodged and clung and followed the sun as if purposefully to make nonsense of the Samson parasols. But the sisters refused to take them down even when spray from the rushing stream sent shivers down their arms and their mother turned back to drape shawls over their shoulders.

The Belgard girls were dressed in white puffed-sleeved blouses and full polka-dot skirts. Bina swore it was the latest fashion, and she had had Schu-Schu pin up their hair in rolls that pulled back from their centre parting and twisted round the sides of their heads like harvest loaves. 'My three little milkmaids,'

Marianna had exclaimed when the girls appeared at breakfast, and Bina told her it was the fashion of the Dolomites and that she'd read about it in a magazine.

The waterfall was ferocious. It fell into a black pool that frothed and spun under the rocks. Marianna and Frau Samson had reached it first and were leaning on a railing that was set up especially for sightseers. Their daughters joined them, and they stood, all gathered together, mesmerized by the hissing gargle of the water as it fell. 'It is possible to climb right behind, and see it from the other side,' Julika said, and she began to lead the way along a ledge of large damp stones that stretched into a cave.

'Please be careful,' Frau Samson called after them. Marianna watched as they lifted the ends of their skirts and tiptoed nervously along. She would have liked to exert her authority and order her daughters back, but the prospect of showing up her lack of influence restrained her and she only followed them with her eyes until the bright red of Eva's skirt had disappeared behind a wall of water. Frau Samson remained silent, and both women leant against the railing and waited.

'It's completely dry in here,' Eva gasped, and her voice made a hollow sound against the back wall of the cave. The others knelt down as near to the edge as they dared, tucking their skirts under the backs of their knees. The water slid past them in a huge, moving screen, shimmering and icy.

Martha's teeth began to chatter and she edged back into the cave. 'It's pulling me forward,' she said, and the others all laughed and teased but took the opportunity to move back an inch or two themselves. They squatted in a line and held each other's hands. As their eyes became a little more accustomed to the spray and the dazzling sheet of water, they found they could make out the green shadow of trees and the shapes of birds as they flew low across their path. Angelika waved her arms in the hope that her mother might catch the pale pink spangle of her dress. And then the sun went dark behind a cloud and the water lost its luminance. It thundered past them in solid grey steel and crashed into the pool like cannonfire.

'It's horrible in here,' Eva decided, convulsed suddenly with fear, and she thought of her brother living in a world where at any moment a dead body might fall in on him. Martha, relieved and close to tears, offered to take her out. They led the way, trembling as they placed each foot on the next safe stone, and gasping for air as they filed out into the light. The others followed quickly.

'You should have come in,' the Samson girls said to their mother, but they stayed by her side, each with a slender arm clasped round the width of her waist.

They had not heard from Emanuel for nearly a month when Wolf was asked, in a letter personally authorized by the Kaiser, if he would supply grain exclusively to the army. Wolf did not show the letter to the men with whom he worked, or mention it to Marianna, but placed it at the bottom of a drawer and prayed he would not be forced to make any decision before learning of the safety of his son. He took it out at the end of each day, after checking with his wife for news, and cursed it. Within a week a second letter arrived, delivered by a palace guard who told him he was under instructions to wait for the reply.

'What is all this?' His colleagues crowded around him, and Wolf told them that he was accepting an order to supply the army with grain, but on one condition: that he did it on a strictly non-profit-making basis. He wrote out his contract with slow deliberation, signing and sealing it with a set face, and took it down to the guard himself. The officer, who couldn't have been much older than Emanuel, clicked his heels and turned sharply away.

Marianna was delighted. 'At least I can think of Manu eating good fresh bread, wherever he is.' Wolf nodded, and went through to his study without mentioning to her the terms on which the contract had been drawn up.

The following day a letter arrived. It had Emanuel's smooth, blue writing on the envelope and the sight of it sent a sigh of relief shimmering through the house.

He said nothing to excuse his silence but started straight in with rapid, rambling news.

We have just completed a backwards march across the edge of Germany without knowing why or where we were going, and without permission to stop. Eventually we crossed the border into Russia, and were rewarded – but in the most unexpected way. We stopped, we sniffed, we charged ... and there to our delight we discovered a cluster of beehives, which we immediately attacked, breaking up the combs of honey with our bare hands and cramming them into our mouths, swallowing and laughing until we were too full even to lick the last wax scales from our fingers. But, as always, we were forced to pay for this distraction. Night came on faster than expected and turned the air so bitterly cold that it was impossible to find water for the horses as everything was frozen up. We spent a particularly unhappy night, crashing about and smashing miserably at the ice. Early the next morning we set off again in the dark to travel further south to occupy a Polish village situated on a hill. By the time we reached it the sun had come out and, although not melting the thick snow, it beat down on the white landscape so brightly that it cheered us up. And it was here, my dear family, that I was responsible for the first death of that day. Yes, as all the provisions that we had with us had run out, I transported a chicken into the beyond.

Marianna stopped reading and looked round at the confused, amused and slightly irritable faces of her family. She breathed, and having recovered from the shock of such a joke, continued.

This was the first opportunity we'd had to see the Polish villages in all their misery. The houses have wooden walls and mud floors, and in practically every one there is a person lying sick. Filthy children squat on the floor and the only food is usually a pile of potatoes heaped up in the corner. You cannot imagine how happy we were to be able to sit ourselves down on those mud floors and eat potato

65

soup out of a filthy pan. But, before you rush off to try this particular delicacy, I should warn you that it can only be really appreciated after a diet of ice-cold pond water, drunk on an empty stomach.

Marianna folded the letter and smiled broadly before passing it, as always, along the table for her daughters to examine, one by one, for anything that she might have missed. It was only Wolf who trusted her, but today even he reached out for the sheets of paper as they fluttered from Bina to Eva over his coffee. 'My dear family,' he began again, and as Wolf read he sensed an icy desperation that had not been there in the light, warm tone of his wife's rendition. Wolf began to sweat. He should never have allowed his son to leave. He should have hidden him, slipped him out of the country. He should himself be standing on a soap box under the avenue of limes preaching to the people on the futility of sending their sons to war. And instead he was feeding them, fattening them up for slaughter.

'Wolf,' Marianna called to him from the other end of the table, 'what are you doing?'

He realized with a start that he was crushing Emanuel's letter in his hands, mashing and tearing at the paper. 'I am sorry.' He looked round at the startled faces of his daughters. 'I seem to have one of my headaches.' Rather than go into the office, he went through to the back of the apartment. He pulled the blinds and lit a lamp. With his head – which really had begun to ache – propped up on pillows, he started to compose a letter to Emanuel. Usually he left this to his wife, confident that she would sign his name beside hers and that any thoughts she might lovingly express would also be his own. 'My dear boy,' he wrote, and paused, his pen hovering above the page. He let his elbow rest on the edge of the bed while he considered everything that he wanted to put down, his feelings about the war, which until now he had kept to himself, and the articles in newspapers that described young men, objectors, rounded up and imprisoned for their unpatriotic views. Wolf folded his arm across his stomach, and let the nib of the pen rest on his sleeve. He closed his eyes to get a clearer vision of the finished draft and, without having written anything at all, he fell asleep.

At midday Marianna came in to bring him some beef broth. She found the letter, dated and addressed, rising and falling on his chest and, making herself comfortable at the desk, she finished it, signing it tenderly from the entire family.

Marianna had a special fondness for Kaiser Wilhelm. As a child on her way to school she had seen his father in an open carriage drawn by piebalds, and whereas the other people stopped to curtsy or raise their hats, Marianna in her excitement found herself skipping off along the street, laughing and pointing and pursued by her anxious mother. But the Kaiser, rather than take offence, had lifted his hand most solemnly and given her a private wave, so that all along that street and for the rest of the school day she had become a small celebrity.

'It is as if we had met up again,' Marianna said that night, as she attempted to urge Wolf into a celebration of his contract. And whatever he said to the contrary she couldn't shake off the belief that, in honouring her husband with such an order for grain, Kaiser Wilhelm was somehow continuing the warm and personal relationship between the families.

CHAPTER 8

'I've had rather a good idea.' My father was serving me one half of a lobster. I waited while he cracked the claws. 'It doesn't seem likely that we'll finish the picture before the baby . . . well, not unless you're very late.'

I dipped some white flesh into salt. I felt too tired even to imagine what he was going to say.

'So, I thought, we'll just have to incorporate the little squib into the picture.'

I laughed. 'The baby? Are you serious?' And I had an image of the paint all coming off as my stomach flattened and my breasts went down.

'Of course, we'd make the studio very warm.'

I sucked soft meat out of a claw. 'Does that mean there wouldn't be much point in working any more today?'

'Well . . . if you don't feel up to it.'

'I suppose all I'll be doing afterwards is lying around, so I might as well lie around here.' And the thought of my father's unreal world, full of light and turps and delicate meals, appealed to me. 'Your youngest ever model.' I laughed, and as soon as I'd eaten the last shreds of the lobster, satisfying myself there was nothing left inside the splintered legs, I walked out into the afternoon to catch a bus.

*

It was an unusually hot spring. I planted sweet pea and corn-flower seeds in tiny pots and lined them up against the windows. I pulled the sash cord up as high as it would go and wished and wished I had a garden. My bag was packed ready by the door and I spent most of my time answering the phone to say that no, no, no, I hadn't had the baby. My mother rang to say I'd been seventeen days late, and taking heart that the baby would take after me I put my due date back. I bought *Time Out* and made a list of all the plays I hadn't seen. 'It's now or never,' I told Pam, and we set off for the National Theatre.

'I don't want to interfere,' an usherette approached me as I sank into my seat, 'but would you prefer to sit a little nearer to the exit?'

'A very good idea,' Pam said, and we agreed that if the play was really awful I could pretend to be in labour and give the audience a thrill. And then, deep down, I felt a pull. Dark blood pushing, the grate and rustle of a tiny bird. I decided to ignore it. There are fifteen more days to go, I told myself, fifteen whole days, and I let myself be drawn into the story of the play in which a group of astronauts were trying to find words to describe how they had felt in space.

Half-way through the second half I staggered out of my seat. The little click was recurring low inside, pulling in and out like tide. A kitten clawing at new cloth. It can take days, I told myself, or it might even be a false alarm, and I realized that, after nine long months of waiting, I was unprepared.

'I'm fine,' I insisted, backing into the ladies', and then, on the white fold of the tissue, there was a streak of blood. My teeth shook with the shock. I stood up and leant against the door. My hands were trembling and I was freezing cold.

'Pam,' I hissed, and she swung round, shocked out of the play. 'Yes!' I nodded to her frantically, and she rummaged for our coats, making as much noise and fuss as possible, proud, for once, to draw attention to herself.

'Are you all right?' She wrapped me in my coat, and when

I was still shaking she put her own over the top. 'We'll go straight to the hospital.'

'But I didn't bring my bag.'

'You didn't?' She was alarmed, and then we both agreed it must be possible to give birth without the contents of a bag. 'What's in it anyway?' I told her about my baby book and what it said you had to pack. The list started with This Book, a Video Recorder or Camera, and Something for your Birthing Partner to Eat.

'We don't have anything for you to eat!' I wailed, and we both began to laugh.

'Pam?' But she had her hands determined on the wheel of her car and was bursting in great style through a string of orange lights. 'Thanks,' I muttered, and I closed my eyes, remembering to breathe.

'Oh, yes, we've been expecting you.' The midwife smiled into her notes and she wired me up to a chart of graphs to check on the contractions. They came every four minutes, and I watched the needle of the graph rise up to make a hill, sloping down again when it was over. 'Are you all right?' Pam clutched my hand, and suddenly I was bursting with excitement.

'So, did you bring your camera?' the midwife asked, turning down the volume, letting the heartbeat fade away, so that I could get up off the bed.

'In too much of a hurry,' Pam explained, and the midwife straightened up with surprise.

'Oh dear.'

'I could go and get it I suppose. It isn't far,' and, instead of stopping her, the midwife bustled Pam away.

It was nice to be alone. I wandered about the room, touching the furniture, flicking one side of the curtain to look out into the street. There was an armchair, ribbed in beige like a friendly hippopotamus, and I stretched back into it, feeling the pain strengthen as I tested out positions. 'Is there a dimmer for these lights?' I asked, leaning out into the outside world, and a nurse, bustling along the corridor, shook her head. The lights ran right across the ceiling in thick tubes of white. I switched them off and the room fell suddenly away, reappearing slowly in a new soft grain of grey. Street lights filtered through the curtains and I put my head up to the window and looked out. People were parking cars and walking, whistling and hurrying home, and not one of them knew that tonight of all nights my baby was choosing to be born.

Pam opened the door. 'Hi,' she whispered, hushed by the new light, and she came and stood beside me at the window. 'It's beautiful out there, warm and clear,' and I thought, It's just like Christmas when you're four years old.

At 2 a.m. the midwife came in to measure me. 'Four centimetres.' She looked disapproving. 'There's a long way to go yet, and the baby hasn't even engaged. I'll call the operating theatre, shall I? And tell them you'll be down for the Caesarean.' But another contraction came upon me and I had to roll onto my side to see it through.

'Can I just wait a little bit longer?' I begged, and she tutted and said that she'd be back.

Pam looked at me as if I must be mad. 'I'm just not quite ready.' I tried to convince her that it wasn't really painful, not yet. 'It's like being at a funfair, swooping down over the next hill.'

But Pam reminded me I hated funfairs. 'When I have a baby,' she said, 'I'll organize a surrogate mother, and then I'll just collect it, you know, after it's been washed and dressed.'

'You wouldn't,' I said, but Pam smoothed her shirt down over her waist and laughed.

'I would. Isn't there anyone you want me to call?' She had her phone, squat in her hand, her eyebrows raised.

'Let's wait,' and I had to hold onto the back of the chair, remembering what I'd learnt. 'Ohhhoooooohaaaaahhheeee.'

'It's like being back at drama school,' Pam said, and she joined me, her low voice yodelling out, 'Ooooooeeeehooooow.'

71

The midwife blinked as she came in, but she didn't switch on the lights. She laid both hands over the baby, head up, high under my ribs. 'I've booked the theatre for seven,' she said kindly, and this time I didn't argue. When the birds began to twitter, Pam lay down on the bed and I moved around the room, breathing and humming and knowing all the time that I was never really going to be put to the test. It was like a week of rehearsals with the first night magically postponed. I drew the curtains and was surprised to see it was already light.

There were too many people in the theatre. It was bright white and freezing cold. 'Pam, is that you?' My body was lost to me from the chest down and there was Pam dressed up out of *Casualty* with a white mask over her face. I was battling with terror. She held my hand, 'Just look at me,' and we stared into each other's eyes as a team of men and women, all busy with individual tasks, shimmered with steel just out of sight. 'Who'd have thought it, eh?' and, in a quick low voice, she glided through the day we met, lined up in leotards and tights while the head of the drama school strutted back and forth. ' "I smoke, you don't," ' Pam mimicked, in his over-pompous voice, and we squeezed each other's hands instead of laughing.

'What are they doing? Oh, my God!' One half of my brain was screaming while the other smiled, soothed, repeated the news that this was the most exciting moment of my life.

'You're doing brilliantly,' Pam said. And then I felt a pulling of numb flesh, the tug of hands, and out of the still air a long, strong cry. I jolted around, and there above my eyeline was the wet and bloodied bottom of my baby.

'It's a boy,' Pam whispered and someone laid him on me, just under my chin, too close to see.

'It's a boy.' I repeated. 'It's a boy, I can't believe it, it's a boy.' And everyone in the room began to laugh.

They laid him on a table, his arms and legs together like a lamb and I watched sideways as his cord was cut and he was wrapped up in a towel. Pam carried him to where I lay, walking on tiptoe like a ballerina with a glass bouquet, and at her elbow hovered a careful nurse. 'It's a boy,' I said again, and my mouth was aching with a wreath of smiles. All the people working fast to stitch me up were laughing too, remarking on the size, the strength and beauty of my boy.

'So, who does he look like?' someone asked, down by my feet, and it occurred to me for the first time that he looked like Mike.

'We'll take him off to weigh him and get him warm,' the nurse told me, and she ushered Pam out of the room.

'You see, no one in our family has boys,' I tried to explain, 'hardly ever,' but the shock of it all had made me dizzy and I closed my eyes.

Pam was waiting with my camera. As soon as I'd been lifted into bed she packed the baby into my arms. 'Smile,' and there I was, delirious with joy, gazing down into his perfect gummy face.

When I woke up my mother was beside my bed. The baby lay with his head against my arm, and she leant over to give us both a kiss. 'I can't believe I slept,' and I remembered thinking I was too excited ever to fall asleep again.

'I came straight here,' she said, and I saw a stick of Seven-Eleven flowers standing in a vase, 'there wasn't anywhere open,' and we both grinned down at the baby. '"And a child that is born on the Sabbath day is bonny and blithe, good and gay."'

'He is,' I said, 'he's all those things.' And we laughed to think that he was just a few hours old.

'So what are you going to call him?' Pam had reappeared, smelling of smoke, and she laid one finger against his hand, which even in sleep was held up quite flat like an important statesman.

'Daisy Pamela Linder.' I laughed, and we all turned to stare again into his face.

A nurse put her head round the door. 'There's a visitor for you,' she said. And Pamela looked down at her feet. 'I'm sorry . . . I got carried away.'

'Tell him to come in.' I sighed. And I pinched her on the arm. My mother stood up to arrange the flowers.

Mike shifted from one foot to the other, hovering, and then as if he should, he skirted round the bed to look down at his son. His face, amazed, filled up on the inside with a smile and he slipped one finger against the baby's palm to see if it would grip. The fingers curled shut like a flower and Mike's smile spilled out into a grin. 'He's great,' he said, and nudging each other Pam and my mother slipped out of the room.

With his free hand Mike produced a bunch of flowers. White roses with soft thornless stems, 'These are for you,' and he laid them beside me on the bed.

'Thanks.'

Still attached, he sat down on the narrow mattress, his elbow resting on my legs. I felt a small old thud of pain. 'I haven't named him yet.' I would have liked to call him after my father, but unfortunately Michael had been all used up. My only other relatives were female. 'How about Emanuel?' I remembered.

'Emmanuelle, like that seventies porno film?'

I pulled away from him as best I could. 'Trust you to think of that.'

And then the baby raised his chin and yawned. It was a luxurious Walt Disney yawn and, without opening his eyes, he snuggled down again, making small sucking movements like a cat against a dish of milk.

'Did Pamela tell you he was nearly born at the National Theatre?' And together, silently, we considered Laurence and then thought better of it.

'I hope that doesn't mean he's going to be an actor.' Mike's voice was gloomy, and I nearly told him about the theatre in Berlin.

74

'How about Bert?' I mused, but Mike was staring into the baby's sleepy, rumpled face, his hair still wet, his eyes glued shut.

'All right son?' And for the time being we decided he might as well be Sonny.

My father arrived, dressed up in a suit with brightly polished shoes. He sat formally beside my bed. My legs had thawed but I was still dressed in my pale blue operation gown with drips and tubes attached. Sonny was what the midwives called 'a good little feeder'. His mouth latched on and as he sucked my milk came in, swelling rock hard with what felt like a gallon of ice cream.

My father took a letter from his inside pocket. 'They've discovered Gaglow.' He looked as smily as a fox. 'And there is no doubt at all that it belongs to us.'

I shook my head, amazed.

'Well, usually it would be much harder to prove, but it turns out that the house was taken over by a real Nazi, some high-ranking official, and so they haven't got a leg to stand on, pretending that it wasn't seized.'

'Is he still there?'

'No, no, long dead. Apparently for the last ten years or so the house has been used as a training centre for Communist teachers.'

'Christ, what will it be like?'

And for a while we sat in silence listening to the gulping of my milk as Sonny sucked, choking now and then and having to come off for air.

'Was it very big, the house?'

'Well, I remember it as being huge. There were stables, and an orchard. Apparently all the land around had once belonged to the house, but my grandfather was forced to sell it. You know, Jews weren't meant to own land. They were only supposed to meddle around in business. But there were families, of course, that did own land, very grand and rich, who got away with it.'

'How many rooms, do you remember?' And I moved Sonny over to my other side.

My father folded the letter and tucked it back inside his suit. 'Fourteen bedrooms? There was a nursery up on the top floor from where you could see right out over the gardens to a lake.' And he drifted into silence.

Sonny was drunk with milk. His head lolled against my arm and he burped happily.

'Might you go back and look at it?'

My father shook his head and, keeping his voice low for the baby's sake, insisted he'd no intention of ever going back.

CHAPTER 9

Towards the end of February Emanuel came home on leave and during his one short week in Berlin he was inundated with visitors. The Samson girls called for him on the first day, and Aunt Cornelia, who had been unable to part with her recipe, arrived by taxi with the Tree Cake already made and shielded from the falling snow by two umbrellas.

Emanuel was ragged with exhaustion. He threw himself down on the sofa, and then immediately sat upright, swearing that he wouldn't waste a moment of his leave in sleep. His mother and sisters crowded round him, craning forward, sniffing and smiling and trying to distinguish the unfamiliar smell of him. The burnt smell of fresh air. It had darkened his skin to oxblood and his hair was dry and light. Eva put out a finger and touched the sharp edge of his new beard. It bristled in strips of brown and red, circles of distinct colour. She tried to peer into his eyes, but he closed them, swaying slightly with the effort it took to stay awake. Marianna put a finger to her lips and began to ease her son back on to the cushions. He gave in heavily to the strength of her hands and let his head fall back, but then Wolf arrived home, and Emanuel started with the slamming of the door.

Wolf hurried forward. He pushed his way past Fräulein Schulze, hovering in the hall, through the crowd of his daughters, fully intending to clasp Emanuel in his arms, but when he saw him, rising stiffly to his feet, a stranger in his uniform, he only put a formal hand around his shoulder and patted him on the back.

Emanuel stayed in uniform. Everywhere he went people stopped and spoke to him, remarking on the latest news or asking after their own heart's interest – regiments as far away as Egypt. Marianna gripped his arm and laughed. She told him how, as a tiny baby, his perfect face had made her reluctant to allow him out in public. 'It was unfair on the other mothers,' she said, and however much Emanuel teased her and protested, she would not desert her theory that he had been a child of astounding beauty.

The Samsons held a party in Emanuel's honour. Marianna would have done so herself, but her husband insisted it was in bad taste. It was to be a costume ball. Costumes, Frau Samson felt, might distract from the impossible shortage of young men. Bina, Martha and Eva had only two days to prepare. They flew into a rage of activity, quizzing, teasing and howling at the household to help them create the perfect outfit. Schu-Schu suggested a theme from Ancient Greece. She ordered metres of white organza, draping them with folds and pleats of snowy cloth, tied in at the waist with twists of gold brocade. They were, she said, to go as Goddesses of Love.

Eva had a band of winter roses in her hair. She rushed back and forth glittering with excitement while Martha waited, calm and ready, and undeniably beautiful. She had inherited Marianna's grace, the looseness in her wrists and ankles and the soft curve of her neck. Bina, disgruntled, turned to look at herself in the mirror. 'Under normal circumstances you wouldn't have even been invited to this dance,' she reminded Eva, and she cursed the unfairness of the war. Bina was sixteen and growing steadily plumper. Her round face with its round eyes and mouth displeased her. She moulded her cheeks into a more pleasing shape, pulling at her hair and pressing back her ears until she recognized a hint of her mother's graceful features, the charm and ease that disarmed everyone she met and the line of her nose, which was responsible, so Schu-Schu had often told her, for the beguiling of Papa.

'Oh,' Bina wailed, giving up. 'I look ridiculous.'

Both her sisters crowded in on either side and insisted she looked perfect. 'Spectacular.' Eva winked.

Bina saw her and struck out. She slapped her sister's ear, catching her finger on the sharp stem of a rose so that a drop of blood fell onto the white bodice of her costume. Bina let out a howl of fury.

'What is it?' Their governess appeared, and with one short diamond snip she cut out the stain. Bina stared despondently at the hole, made almost invisible by the layers of white behind it, until Schu-Schu took a needle and a length of thread and, with tiny stitches, set out to turn the repair into a delicate satin flower.

'Oh, Schu, why can't you come with us?' Eva leant against her, but she only frowned and with strong teeth bit off the thread.

'Are you quite ready?' Their mother stood, amused and waiting in the doorway. She ignored the bent head of the governess.

'They'll be right with you.' Fräulein rose, smoothing down her skirt, and the girls jostled among themselves for a last look in the mirror.

'I'll be waiting,' Marianna said, and they heard the leather of her heels tap away along the hall.

'Did you see that dress?' Bina scowled. 'So out of fashion.' And Eva agreed that red wasn't the right colour for her at all.

'And those earrings.' Martha shook her head and laughed. 'Dragging down her ears.'

Emanuel was leaning into the room. 'But, Manu, you're not ready!' Eva protested, looking at the unbuttoned tunic of his uniform. But he only smiled, laughing over their heads at Schu-Schu's attempts to twist a last curl into Bina's hair.

'Hurry now,' their father called from the front door. 'Don't keep your mother waiting.' And without looking back for Schu-Schu or their brother they rushed off in a froth of white.

The party jostled with old men and younger sons, boys of seventeen, dressed up as soldiers and talking of nothing else than that the war would last until the date of their next birthday. Emanuel arrived half an hour late. 'I wanted to walk,' he whispered, as his sisters crowded round him like a flock of doves. His face was flushed and his hair curled damply from the snow.

'Are you freezing?' Eva asked, but Angelika and Julika were waiting for him by the door, 'We need your help,' and it transpired that an artist had been brought in to arrange a *tableau vivant*, and Emanuel was to be its centrepiece.

'But not everyone's help is needed, obviously,' Bina said, as, blushing and protesting, Emanuel was led away. Very soon Angelika reappeared and asked that Eva might come with her too. Someone small and light was needed to stand with wings and a trumpet at the top of a ladder. A curtain would be drawn below so that from the audience she would appear to be suspended in thin air.

A gasp went up from the guests when the double doors were thrown apart and the tableau was displayed. It was a scene of military victory. Emanuel stood with his sword bared and the German flag fluttering above him. Actors who had been hired to play the conquered enemy lay dying at his feet, and a choir burst into song once the scene had been fully taken in. Eva stood at the top of her ladder, her wings balanced precariously, grinning, and once the sighing harmonies of the choir had faded out, she raised the trumpet to her lips and let out a long, discordant bellow. The crowd stirred, laughing and clapping and the floor was cleared for dancing.

Eva sat at the side and watched. She saw Bina glide past with a tall blond officer in squeaking boots, and Martha, graceful in the arms of a professor. As they danced Martha kept her face tilted, and her ear open to hear his version of the birth of Aphrodite. 'She was born of sea foam, after the brutal castration of Uranus, and washed ashore, naked as the dawn.' Martha paled, but he continued with details of Aphrodite's marriage and the child that she bore for her earthly Trojan lover. Martha's ear glowed pink and her ankles quivered, but it took three long dances before she could ease herself away.

'May I have the honour of this dance?' It was Emanuel who had taken pity on her.

'Oh, if you insist,' Eva said, jumping up, and it was only then that she found she had forgotten to unstrap her wings.

'Keep them on,' Emanuel whispered. 'It will give us more room.' And when she stepped on his toes during the first waltz he laughed and called her his left-footed little angel.

On the last day of Emanuel's leave, Marianna woke out of a hollow web of dreams. 'It would be less cruel not to have allowed him home at all,' she said, and the words formed in curlicues in the cold room. 'It would have been far less painful.' And, unable to bear the thought of his departure, she swung out of bed and let her toes feel blindly for her slippers. She would run through to his room and wake him. Force him to look her in the eye. Tell him that she hadn't seen him properly and that he couldn't possibly leave until, at the very least, they could reacquaint themselves. She twisted her hair as she hurried along, tucking it under the collar of her gown so that it formed a ridge down her back like the long moulded spine of a dragon.

Outside Emanuel's door she stopped and calmed herself. 'Manu,' she whispered, and when there was no answer, she eased the handle and went in. Emanuel was not in bed. She stood there for a minute, expecting to be startled as he stepped back from the window or rose up from his desk, and it took her several moments to see that the room was empty. The curtains were drawn back and, breathing hard to calm herself, she watched the snow falling in the street, swirling and catching on the hurrying figures as they went about the beginnings of their day.

And then Manu slipped into the room. He was already dressed. 'It's difficult to sleep,' he offered, and she reached out to him and placed her hand around the fingers of his fist. 'It would be easier if they didn't allow one home at all,' he said. And Marianna flushed indignantly and refused to accept what he was saying. 'You can't understand,' he interrupted her. 'Nothing has changed for you. It's as if the war were a bad smell, far off, blowing the other way.' And when she said nothing, he clasped his hands, cold suddenly and white, behind his back.

Emanuel caught the train, his pockets full of cigarettes and short cigars for trading, his bag heavy with packed food, wrapped and arranged around his kit. There were potato cakes, and scones baked with raisins, a spiralling coil of sausage and two packets of butter wrapped in muslin. His mother had tried to add tall jars of fruit: apricots and plums preserved in syrup and a pot of stem ginger. But Emanuel had been unable to imagine spooning up these delicacies in the sleet and squalor of a camp and he had refused to take them.

His father, alone, accompanied him to the station. It was at his insistence that the others remained behind and he kissed each of his sisters goodbye in the hall, taking a last good look at them as Marianna held open the heavy door against the snow. Schu-Schu stood with her hands on Eva's shoulders, and as Emanuel disappeared down the street, Eva felt her fingers tightening until she had to duck away to avoid a bruise. 'You're hurting me.' She twisted round and was surprised to see a hard look of fury on her governess's face. 'Schu?' Eva pulled her arm, and in an instant Schu-Schu had softened back into herself and was bustling the girls in out of the cold.

The two men remained silent through the shouts and echoes of the station. They strode together down the crowded platform and Wolf looked on as Emanuel found a seat, threw his bag onto a rack and opened a window for the last, gruff goodbye. They smiled at each other, wishing on and dreading the sharp sound of the whistle, and then, as doors began to slam and the wheels rocked, hissing and moaning, Wolf took his son's hand. He clasped it in his own, holding onto it as the train began to pull away. 'Your inheritance,' he whispered fiercely, and as their arms were drawn apart, Emanuel found a large warm coin lodged against his palm.

Emanuel sat amid a crowd of soldiers, new recruits and several older men showing signs of wounds only recently repaired. He did not look at them but gazed into the hot, rich heart of his gold. It was not money but a medal, carved on one side with thick ears of corn, and on the other in small print the words Belgard and Son. He smiled and pressed it in his hands. This will always be worth something, when everything else is dust, and he thought how a nub of gold would not splatter and disintegrate when caught in the blast of a shell. It may dent if fired upon but even a bullet hole through its core would not detract from its intrinsic value. And he began to think of Josef Friedlander and how during his week's leave he had avoided the subject of his disappearance, locking him out from the comfort of his home. He closed his eyes to let in the image of his friend, lit up as he had seen him last and staggering on the stumps of his legs. Emanuel felt again the explosion that had driven him back into his trench where he had lain against the warm wet body of a boy, dying on his first day at the front, and it wasn't until daybreak, when the fighting had calmed, that he was able to crawl over the ground to search for Josef, peering into the muddy and devastated faces of the wounded, and turning up the legless corpses of men. Neither he nor anyone else he knew of had ever had another sighting of Josef Friedlander, and it was concluded that he must have fallen and drowned in a waterlogged crater, one of many blown into the earth. Emanuel did not know whether or not a letter had been sent to the Friedlanders, with the official 'missing in action' written across it. But if it had, no news of it had been passed on to Bina, who stubbornly refused to let his silence stamp out her feelings for him. Emanuel had a letter from her now, folded safely in his jacket pocket, and at the top of his canvas bag lay a pair of finely knitted socks. They lay side by side with socks of his own. Dark green and knee high, with purple, well-turned heels. A present from the Samson girls whose names in cross-stitch were tucked away under the wide rim of the ribbing.

Emanuel slipped the medal into the long pocket of his trousers. He could feel it there, warm against his thigh, and he hoped it might protect him through the rest of the winter and into the spring. 'On my next leave I shall not go home,' he promised himself, repeating what he had whispered for goodbye into Schu-Schu's ear, and in that way he felt he could will, through his own impending sacrifice, an end to the war before the summer.

Emanuel opened his eyes. The new recruits had set up a card game and were laying bets for cigarettes. They nodded to him and he shrugged and joined them, laying down his cards and raising the stakes with a cigar.

Roaming in the Gaglow orchard, attempting to identify the blossom, Eva was caught in a rainstorm, and rather than run back to the house she stayed crouched under a tree. The downpour was exhilarating. She loved the rain cracking through the afternoon, spraying her face and arms. But then the sky opened up with lightning and the tree under which she was sheltering began to shudder in a low, rough wind. She heard her name called from the back door of the house and just as she was tensed to run, another rolling wave of thunder darkened the sky, followed in three short seconds by a blaze of lightning. She heard her name again, ghostly on the wind, but she didn't dare move from where she was. The rain had turned cold and the cotton of her dress was wringing. The bow in her hair whipped into her eyes and, unable to help herself, she began to cry. Her tears were warm, and the running of her nose fell hotly on her upper lip. She put up her hands to catch some of the heat between her fingers, and as she did so the brittle branches of the tree snapped above her head and the sky lit up with a crack of cold white light. Eva opened her mouth to scream when a hand reached out and pulled her into the open. It was her mother, who clasped an arm around her and, stumbling over the ruts and trenches of the orchard, ran with her to the house.

Eva was too excited to go to bed. 'I narrowly missed being struck by lightning,' she boasted, through chattering teeth. But Marianna, her lips white, her hands shaking, insisted on a fire being lit in the nursery and that Eva, once her wet clothes had been removed, should sit wrapped in rugs and be forced to drink a bowl of soup. Marianna brought it up herself. She had the cook make it clear from chicken stock and sticks of thyme, and she sat by Eva's bed to see that every last mouthful was spooned and drunk. 'I have sent for the doctor,' she said, and when Eva wriggled and protested, Marianna only tightened the blankets round her neck and put a hand to her forehead.

By midnight Eva was delirious. Her temperature had soared and her throat was so inflamed that she could hardly swallow. The doctor declared it a severe case of flu. He stood at the end of her bed while Marianna scanned his face for the diagnosis he was too afraid to give. 'Surely she has all the symptoms of pneumonia?' Marianna challenged, and the doctor looked up startled, as if she had caught him on the exact word.

He knelt down and slipped a hand under the back of Eva's head. 'We must hope she pulls through the night,' he said, giving up on the pretence, and he pushed her eyelids back to check on the milky blue of her delirium.

The doctor, who had driven over from the nearest town, stayed on at Herr Belgard's insistence. He was given a room on the floor below with a high and inviting wooden bed, but decided for the sake of his reputation to remain in an armchair in the nursery, where he could keep an eye on any change in the condition of his patient. Marianna was too upset to talk. She pulled a chair up to Eva's bedside and mumbled out a string of incoherent prayers.

Fräulein Schulze hovered by the fire. 'Eva,' she whispered, 'you should have called for me.' And unable to restrain herself, she rushed over and plumped up the pillows, adjusted the clutter of the bedside table and placed a hand over her burning charge.

Three days later, Eva woke, feeling light and dry and strangely happy. The burning embers of a nightfire smouldered in the grate and the chairs around her bed were empty. She threw back the blanket and let her feet slide to the floor. The whiteness of her skin was mesmerizing and her blood, when she ran across the room, pricked and tingled in her joints. She knelt up on the window-sill and pushed her head out between the curtains. It was her favourite time of day: the beginning of the morning when the sun has washed away all traces of the dawn. Eva unhooked the latch and let in a still cool draught of air. She let it play over her face and down between the buttons of her nightdress, enjoying the coldness of her fingertips and the shiver that ran along her spine. She could still feel the cloying warmth of the room on the soles of her upturned feet and she longed to jump out into the morning. She pushed the latch further and, twisting on the wide sill, she began to turn herself round. The slap caught her leg. It came from nowhere and stopped her breath.

'What are you doing?' Her mother's voice flew at her, and she was pulled down from the window-sill and rushed back to bed. Marianna wrapped the blankets high up round her shoulders, and then clasping her swaddled body she held her tight and cried into her hair.

Eva was mystified. 'What have I done?' But Marianna continued to hold her, muttering Bina's name through her own as she rocked her in her arms.

Eva was kept in bed for weeks. At night the fever caught her up, less forcibly with time, but in the mornings she continued to wake with an overwhelming longing to get up and run into the cool bright air. One afternoon the children from the village school came up to Gaglow to wish her well in convalescing. They trooped into the nursery, almost twenty of them, and sang songs in an arc around her bed. Eva sat up and stared at them. The girls had plaited hair and short silver lashes, with eyes that watered with emotion when they sang. The boys made fists with their hands and thumped them hard against the leather of their shorts. After several rousing verses, the village teacher led them in a poem, mouthing the words encouragingly and with expressions of exaggerated melodrama.

Marianna stood by Eva's bed and smiled down at her, glancing from her bemused face to the ruddy open mouths of the local children. It was their teacher who had insisted. 'It is a tradition of the village,' he told her, 'and so long since there was a child in the house.'

'But I don't want to be entertained by anyone,' Eva had protested.

And Bina, on hearing the news, insisted she and Martha be taken back to Berlin in order to escape this new humiliation. 'Never has anyone been so grand,' she complained to Schu-Schu, as the carriage whisked them back to the city, and they pitied Eva for being left behind, alone and at the mercy of their mother.

Soon Eva was allowed outside for short stretches of fresh air so long as she gave her promise not to leave the lawn and at all costs to avoid straying into the bad association of the orchard. Gaglow was deserted. Wolf had returned to his work, and Bina and Martha, in the company of Fräulein Schulze, had insisted on remaining in Berlin.

Through the long hours of afternoons Eva watched her mother from an upstairs window wandering about her garden, examining the restored splendour of the grounds and making small adjustments in the absence of the gardeners. Paths had been cleared from under beds of bindweed, and over their first summer at Gaglow the gold and turquoise lichen was scaled off the statue. It fell in mossy shavings round the feet of a forgotten nymph, until one morning, pale and glimmering, it appeared stone naked in the centre of the lawn. The fountain was unblocked, the pipes repaired, and floating lilies that had clogged the pond were thinned and cleared and given space to stretch their leaves.

Marianna came up to visit in the early evening when, having bathed her hands in rose water and sprinkled it on her hair, she would take Eva's fingers in her own and ask Omi Lise for her progress. In the first days, when Eva was still drained and dizzy, Marianna sat with her and told her stories. She told her about journeys she had made when she was still a child, and how her parents took their holidays in shifts. 'I always hated my summer birthday,' she said, 'because it fell on the last day of school and was a day of packing.' Each July she and her mother travelled up into the mountains, and on their return, her father set off alone for two weeks by the sea. Marianna's mother stood in for him as head of the firm. She sat at his desk and smiled down at the five men he hired to help him in his printing business, using the time to stitch monograms in coloured thread on to the table linen. 'It wasn't until I was sixteen that I went on holiday with my father, our first and last,' and she thought of the pneumonia and how, until now, it had been a curse over her life.

'Was he ill for a very long time?' Eva asked, but Marianna simply shook her head, wincing at the vision of her mother, arriving half an hour too late.

Eva had never spent so much time alone with her mother. She found herself forgetting the years of collected woes, the tiny details of deceit and treachery, and took to watching her fondly from above, her broad-brimmed hat high over her hair, and the row of cloth-covered buttons, like jewels, scattered down the front of her dress. Her face, above the stiff, fluted collar, was lost in shadow, but Eva could see her arms waving and hear her shouts as she rallied her depleted team of gardening men, pointing and explaining and plucking at her gloves as if she would like to tear them off and plunge her own hands into the earth. Once, after a short, sharp letter from Bina, full of sneers and messages of pity, Eva tied a knot in the hem of her nightdress to remind her, when it caught against her toes, whose side she was meant to be on.

Eva did not like to let her brother know about her illness. Instead she wrote,

Dear Manu,

I've been thinking how we could have a fence around our house made from rows of runner beans. In my opinion the little red flowers are prettier than anything and just think how useful it would be when we are suddenly in need of lunch. I know our intention is to lead a very simple life but I've set my heart on a bath made exactly to my measurements, so I can rest my head and stretch my toes right to the end. Let me know if you would also like one and I'll draw up plans.

Your devoted sister, Eva.

As he read, Emanuel saw her small mouth chattering, confiding the plans, the familiar dreams she insisted that he share, and he always saved her words for last. Bina's letters were packed with news. 'The facts are,' she often began, and she would search about among the things she knew to let him into something gruesome. She had a talent for disaster and would sniff it out, drawing it in towards herself, however distant. Martha spent hours, her pen in her mouth, pondering on the perfect way to phrase her thoughts. Her letters began quite formally but soon trailed, sidetracking into snatches of myth and ancient history and revealing secrets closely kept on behalf of other girls at school. She thought of her brother in a place not dissimilar to Antarctica and trusted he would be the one person capable of keeping these things to himself.

*

Emanuel received more letters than any other man in his regiment. He was teased and envied and occasionally asked to arrange correspondence for a soldier less fortunate than himself. 'They can't all be your sisters,' they nudged, and when he insisted that they were, and that they would make for baffling if not useless pen pals, they asked to see a picture. Emanuel had a photograph, the three girls at Gaglow dressed in white and lying on cane chairs in the sun of the summer porch, but he shook his head and swore there was no such thing. The other man cursed him for a liar and a cheat and slapped him on the shoulder, but as he walked away Emanuel heard him mutter that he was nothing but a Jew, and didn't deserve the honour of dying for his country.

No one except Schu-Schu suspected that Emanuel would not come home on the first day of his leave, but after six long months, despite his promise, he found it impossible to stay away.

'Would you come in and dance with us, just once?' Eva begged him, as they waited in the shade of the veranda for the first young ladies to arrive.

Marianna, anxious that her daughters' social education should not be thwarted by the war, had set up a network of dancing lessons to be carried out at various houses throughout the summer.

'I may do.' Emanuel squeezed her hand. 'But I wouldn't want to upset your partner.'

'Oh, Amalie won't mind, and anyway you could dance with her as well. She's never danced with a man. No one except old Herr Friedrichson.'

'And you, have you danced with any men?'

Eva smiled and frowned simultaneously so that her eyes almost disappeared. 'Only with you.'

Emanuel had dreamed on many miserable nights of holding the Samson sisters in his arms. Either one, or both, but now as he sat in the drawing room listening to the rolling piano and

90

the tap of the old dancing teacher's cane, he felt disinclined even to see them. But when the soothing rumble of a waltz drifted under the door of the hall, he clicked his boots together and, for the sake of Eva, made his entrance.

There were twelve girls in the room, six couples, and as each whirling partner turned and saw him, a blush spread up over her neck and face and turned the dance into a burning ring of pink. Emanuel stood in uniform by the door. He lowered his eyes and watched the feet and ankles of the girls. 'One two three, one two three,' tapped old Herr Friedrichson, nodding with his twirled moustache and sweltering in the shiny cloth of his coat. 'One two three, one two three.' As Emanuel's eyes swept the room he wished he could shake the hard sneer for all this prettiness from the corners of his mouth.

When the music stopped Eva broke away quickly from the plump embrace of her partner and presented herself before her brother, smiling up at him for the next dance. Fräulein Schulze, who was standing by the piano, rescued the deserted Amalie and they set off again, accompanied by the ponderous chords of the ancient Frau Mendel who had been almost completely deaf since her seventieth birthday more than a decade before.

As he moved around the room Emanuel watched the dancing over Eva's head. 'One two three, one two three,' he could feel her breath counting out the steps against his shoulder, 'one two three, one two three.' And he found himself longing to hiss some horrible truth into her hot ear.

Angelika and Julika danced together, their slim bare arms clasped loosely round the other's waist and their chestnut hair curled with the heat in identical cowlicks on their foreheads. They smiled at him from across the room, a turning circle of radiance, and he saw them as a two-headed mermaid, luring men ashore, with their sweet calling voices, to be crushed against the rocks.

'I shall make my excuse and go,' Emanuel swore, but almost before one dance finished another began, and his partners replaced themselves in his arms with a strange fluidity that was

91

somehow lost once the music began again and Herr Fried-richson's cane trotted out the steps.

First Emanuel danced with each of his sisters. Martha, the tallest of the three, was the most graceful, while Bina, too used to years of leading, stumbled and hit against his boots. 'One two three,' she breathed and, like a swing boat, they moved stiffly back and forth across the room.

The dancing class ran half an hour over its normal length to give each of the girls a chance to dance with the dazzling, uniformed guest of honour. Emanuel, after his very first waltz, had longed for nothing more than to slip away. He was prepared to give up the chance even of holding the delicate, blushing Julika in his arms to get back to the drawing room where he could lie in comfort among the polished dark wood of the furniture.

'Oh, Schu, won't you have a dance with Manu?' Eva whispered, when the music finally stopped, but the governess looked straight into his eyes and said she could see the poor man was exhausted and needed to be left alone.

That night dinner was served out on the terrace. There was a goose with thick crackling skin and a salad of broad beans, and as he ate Emanuel found that he was retelling, in great detail, how half of his regiment had been wiped out. 'We were running towards a village when gunmen opened fire on us,' he heard his voice, insistent as he chewed, drilling on and on, 'but instead of firing back the call went out: "Don't shoot, they are our own men retreating." This was clearly not the case, but there was nothing to be done but curse into the ground, and attempt to avoid the torrent of the shells. It was only when our own artillery appeared and began to shoot that the order was given to advance, and all without a flicker of apology.' He looked across the table at the bright eyes of his sisters and pulled himself up short. 'I shall not describe,' he said, 'the trail of dead and injured for whom we were not allowed to stop.' But he found he could still hear them calling out to him as he cut the meat in strips across his plate.

Wolf poured him a glass of wine. 'My dear boy,' he said, and unable to think of what else to add, he shambled off towards the cellar to draw out another bottle.

Emanuel spent his afternoons reading in his room, aware at times of the rustle of one or other of his sisters as they summoned up the courage to interrupt him. 'We're going on a swimming picnic to the lake,' Eva called, twisting the handle of his door, and he answered gruffly that he would still be there when she returned and would most likely see them all at supper. There was a hurt and painful silence, and he had to shuffle his papers ferociously and slam his book down on his desk before he heard her move away and take off at a run along the corridor.

'How extraordinary that so little has changed here,' he muttered, as he wandered round the house, and he failed to notice that the table was not so lavishly laid as it had been and that his mother wore the same summer dresses, with small alterations and adjustments, as she had the previous year.

Even Fräulein Schulze seemed subdued. Her red hair looked strangely pale, pulled severely from her face, and the tasks she set them were overseen without her usual vigour. 'It's so good to have our Manu home again.' Eva snaked an arm around her as they headed out over the fields to the lake.

'For one more day.' Fräulein Schulze nodded, and hardening her tone, she shouted to Martha to look where she was going. 'You'll tear your skirt if you swing along like that.' She pulled her arm away from Eva, hurrying her along, and refusing to wave to the row of poor prisoners in their red trousers hoeing the field.

CHAPTER 10

I could hear the main maternity ward from the quiet of my room. Babies wailing, women laughing, visitors parading up and down, and above it all, the constant ringing of a squat grey telephone on wheels. On the third day I was moved to a bed right in the middle. A huge man sat almost beside me. He had a spider tattooed around his neck and he held his baby up against his chest, while the new mother slipped out on to the fire escape to smoke.

A doctor came in to check Sonny's legs. They were still bent high at the hip where they'd been tucked underneath his chin and I was warned that a breech baby often took some time to straighten out. The doctor eased him from his towelling Babygro and pulled his vest over his head. Sonny didn't like it and his face creased up with alarm. 'Nothing wrong with this one.' He seemed unperturbed by Sonny's screams, pulling him up by the hands to test his grip and pressing his hips flat, until his whole head was dark red with roaring. Unable to control myself I snatched him out of the doctor's care. I wrapped him quickly, pressing his body against mine. His crying stopped. His hands clung in my hair and a great storm of love welled up between us.

'I'm so sorry,' Pam hung her head, 'but it seemed wrong not to call Mike.'

'He's coming again today.'

'And?'

It was hard to know.

'You're not going to forgive him?' She shook her head appalled.

'Well, we did say we'd stay friends. Pam . . .' I had a quick and guilty image of her on the day that we'd split up, rushing from her car with cigarettes and brandy and a bunch of bright blue flowers. 'I'm too sick to smoke,' I'd wailed, and at each end of the sofa, our feet pushed into cushions, I told her about Mike and his reaction to my news. 'He said I'd tried to trick him, planned it, was ruining his life,' and I bit furiously into toast to stop myself from feeling sick.

'You're not going to keep it?' She drank my brandy for me. 'What about your career?'

'Come on.' I didn't have a career, we both knew that. The occasional odd job on the Fringe. Someone's daughter, sister, wife. A small tour around the Lake District.

Pam topped up her own glass. 'I give up.' She raised a toast to the tiny speck of baby and knocked it back in one.

'So what are you going to call it?' she asked, snuggling down, and we lay there for the rest of the day until we came up with Daisy. Daisy Pamela Linder. And I swore I'd never take him back, however much he begged.

Mike came back the next day to collect his things. I'd considered packing them but decided it was too much trouble.

'Ruin your life? I wouldn't waste my time.' But he looked at me, superior and cool, suggesting we try and remain friends. 'Friends,' I yelled, my mouth out of control, 'who loathe and detest each other.' And he walked off, straight-backed, down the street while I lay down in the hall to cry.

My mother arrived at the hospital with a box of Portuguese cakes. 'How are you feeling?' Before I had time to answer tears were rolling down my face. She sat and held my hand. 'It's all right.'

When I found my breath, I stuttered, 'He didn't come.'

'You're doing fine.' She shook her head from side to side with little soothing tuts, and I thought of her, all those years before, waiting to see if my father would appear.

Mike had a taxi waiting. He'd come to take us home. I was dressed in real clothes for the first time in a week and Sonny had a soft wool cardigan over his suit. His eyes were open, liquid and long, and the skin of his lids was mauve. 'I bought a hat for him,' Mike said, and he stooped to slip it on. It was a pronged hat that came down over his eyes and he looked so funny in it, like a little bag of flour knotted at the top, that I had to clutch my stomach to stop my stitches pulling while I laughed. The woman in the next bed made us stop for a photograph and we stood there, the three of us in a group, just like a real family, all ready to go home. 'Here you go' – and the flash of the camera woke me up.

I was lying on my own bed, fully clothed with Sonny squashed under my arm. My sisters, not Mike, had brought us home. Natasha had even cleaned her car in honour of the drive, and when I arrived I found fresh flowers by the window and Sonny's crib set up beside my bed. They'd heaped the sofa with pillows to support my feeding arm and set out lunch on the table. There was Greek food, white bread with feta cheese, cucumber cut up into squares and a tomato salad thick with coriander seeds and olives. My mouth, acclimatized to hospital food, stung with the sharp tastes. I hope this doesn't affect my milk, I wondered, sucking specks of chilli off an olive, and I heaped my plate with more.

There had been no news from Mike, and the thought of him mingled with my exhaustion. What I hate about him most, I decided, is that just when I'm feeling really furious it occurs to me that he might, just possibly, have been run over by a bus.

I shifted a little to look down at the baby. He was on his back with his arms up by his head, his fingers, still wrinkled with loose skin, curled out like a starfish, and collected in the sweet pout of his mouth was a tiny row of bubbles. Natasha and Kate must have crept out by themselves while I was asleep because from my bed I could see a mobile of transparent shells, a present from them both pinned up against the window.

It was three more days before Mike called. 'I'm so sorry,' he started, 'but I was suddenly called away on a job.' And I could tell that he was desperate to say more.

'I don't care, there's no excuse.' I clenched my body hard against a rush of tears.

'Someone dropped out, and I had to go off without any notice. We were out on location, and when I did get a chance to phone it was always after midnight. You know what it's like.'

'I don't know, actually.'

'Look, can I come round?'

But I gripped my sweating hand and very calmly said he couldn't. 'I don't want to see you,' I explained slowly, as if to a child. And for a moment even I believed that it was true.

Sonny was two weeks old when we set off for our first sitting.

'Well, I don't suppose we'd better be late.' I strapped him into Natasha's car, and with great care we pulled out into the traffic.

'I can't believe you're doing this.' Kate leant over from the front and I tried to explain it had seemed a good idea at the time.

'You're completely mad.' Natasha was the only one of us who never sat. She'd done one picture when she was sixteen,

97

'He made me look like a cross-Channel swimmer,' and she refused ever to pose again. Kate, like me, had modelled countless times.

'He's a difficult person to say no to,' we protested.

'Your problem,' Natasha cut in, 'is you've got nothing better to do.'

'And neither has Sonny,' Kate pointed out. Kate worked as an editor for films. It was a job like mine with endless lulls. 'There's no doubt about it,' she insisted, 'this is going to be my last painting.' And Natasha said that now he had another model he could afford to let her go.

'I like sitting,' I said, and I thought of the soft light of the studio, the stories and the food, and I tried to make myself remember to ask him more about Emanuel Belgard and what had happened to him in the war.

'They never mentioned him,' my father said, once Sonny was lying beside me on the sofa. I'd had to explain he wouldn't tolerate even a minute without his clothes.

'He was a sort of black sheep, as far as I can tell, although he did have some extraordinary adventures.' And I begged him to think up what they might have been.

'Yes, yes,' he murmured, but he was too taken up with fitting Sonny in under my arm.

I had propped a pillow under my shoulder to support myself while I looked down on my baby's sleeping face. I found I could stare at him for hours, the rounded eyelids, pale purple, and the eyebrows, a tiny sketch of gold. The hair on his head was dark, a little oily fringe around the back, but with each day I noticed it was lightening.

My father stopped, a stick of charcoal in mid-air. 'Could you just turn her a fraction this way?'

I shifted my arm and rolled the pillow. 'Him,' I corrected, and I took the opportunity to brush his warm cheek with my lips, feeling for his toes which didn't quite reach down into his towelling feet.

'Do you need a break?' he asked, quite out of character, but I didn't want to waste the time while Sonny slept.

Sonny was a charcoal outline, his nose up in the air, his hands like paws, and as my father took a small brush and mashed it up with paint, I watched to see where he would start. He always started with my eyes, but I knew from glancing at other canvases this wasn't always the way. There was one abandoned mouth, a nose, a knee pressed close against another and one disembodied penis, hanging from a smudge of ginger hair. With one swift move he started on Sonny's ear. He curled the pink lip over, swirling up the colour to form the sinews of the shell.

'You're working so fast,' I said, when finally we stopped.

The paint had spread out to incorporate Sonny's mouth, blistered into coral from continuous sucking. He muttered as I slipped away, his hands flying out to catch me, but he was too full and drowsy to wake up. It made me laugh to see him at a distance, a plump green bug against the sofa flowers, and I tore myself away to make some tea.

'Do you want a cup?' I called through to my father, but he was watching Sonny as he slept, moving his head from side to side to try to measure him against the work. He hesitated, his fingers teasing out his rag, and I held my breath for him to be wiped out. 'Tea?' I said again, and he held out his hand for a cup. I'm so glad I'm doing this, I thought, as I snuggled back on to the sofa, glancing down at the rise and fall of Sonny's breath, watching while the paint built up around the ear, thickening against his skull.

'Oh, yes, I do remember one thing,' my father said, surprising me. 'My mother, when she was a little girl, gave Emanuel some bosom-enlarging pills as a present on his birthday. ' "Pilule Oriental", she said they were.' And he smiled to himself as he worked on.

It was not at all what I'd expected. I'd imagined embroidery and silk, heavy silver watches and ashtrays in carved glass. 'Was he pleased?' I wondered.

'I don't suppose so,' and we both started to laugh.

As soon as we got home, Sonny woke up and it was midnight before he was tired enough to sleep again. 'Oh, Pam,' I wailed into her answerphone, 'why did I ever agree to this?' But Pam had been cast as a suspect in a detective series set in Leeds and wouldn't be back for several weeks.

'How did it go?' Natasha called the next day, and choking on my pride, my eyes red with exhaustion, I said it had gone really well.

Mike sent a card with a cheque tucked inside it for two hundred pounds, 'Hope you're both thriving,' and there was his telephone number, quite unnecessarily printed in brackets after his name. Pam had made me promise not to call him, 'You're better off without the selfish, thoughtless bastard,' and I knew that it was true.

CHAPTER II

Emanuel refused to take the carefully prepared food Marianna tried to press on him, but packed his bags instead with books. He left hollow dusty spaces in the library where entire volumes were prised out and then abandoned, left lying in piles on the centre table. The books he chose to take were all poems and philosophy. Kleist and Nietzsche. Strindberg's *The Agony of Conscience*, from which he memorized whole passages, and Schopenhauer's *Correspondences*.

'I have been promoted,' he told his family, as he set off for the train, 'to the staff of the regiment.' But he fought off their warm congratulations, their surprise that he hadn't mentioned it before, and insisted that his predecessor had been dismissed for misspelling a word.

'Well, really, Manu, this is wonderful news.' His mother moved to embrace him, and slipping her hand into his, Eva whispered, 'But you would never make a mistake like that so we won't even think about it.'

Bina narrowed her eyes at him. 'A simple German fulfilment is the greatest thing about this war, greater than all the brilliant deeds of individuals, and it is only because of this that we are winning.'

Emanuel stiffened, and Wolf turned sharply on his daughter and asked where she found the opportunity to air such views.

'Are we really winning?' Martha asked, but Bina put her chin in the air and refused to answer.

Emanuel looked over at his father. Wolf's hair had turned from grey to silver in the course of the last year and the two lines between his still black eyebrows were held now in a perpetual frown. He knew that his father had guessed what his mother and sisters never would: that this promotion might have come to him months earlier, possibly at the end of the previous year, if he had been the son of another, more established family.

'Well, in my opinion it is the best possible news.' Wolf put a hand on his son's shoulder, and together they walked towards the carriage. Eva followed, kicking small stones with the scuffed ends of her shoes. 'Manu,' she called, but the horses had begun to rustle, sidestepping against each other, ready to be off. 'Manu.' As she turned she saw, framed in the long window above the porch, the pale figure of her governess waving in large urgent strokes.

Emanuel felt it was a mistake to have returned to Gaglow. Even though there had been little choice over the taking of his leave, he might have resisted the summer comfort of the estate and his mother's overwhelming care, and made his way instead to Berlin where the apartment was locked up. He could have lived among the shrouded furniture, surviving on war rations and preserved fruit. And if he had done this, perhaps, then possibly his punishment would not now be so great. 'I know I shouldn't complain,' he murmured, several times a day, but he could not shake off the feeling that what he was enduring was a form of torture.

Emanuel was stationed in a remote farmhouse in the Russian woods. At first he had been involved in spying missions to check on the cut and colour of the enemy's uniform, and had returned victorious after glimpsing through a thicket a straggly bunch of Cossacks, their faces obscured by beards, their coats so worn and battered as to make them almost invisible in the camouflage of the surrounding trees. But early snows had made such trips impossible, and now if any excursions were to be attempted they had to be made by sled. Emanuel was no longer able to ride out into the night to visit solitary stations stretched across the plains. He missed the satisfying glow of the sun rising as, his mission completed, he sank on to his bed. 'I should not complain, I know,' he said when, day after day, the only orders that came down to him were to teach a group of soldiers how to ski. A ski port had been built the previous year, and it made Emanuel smile to think how, even then, he would have welcomed as hilarious the chance to practise cross-country in this most unlikely situation. The men under his command had the appearance of being in the highest spirits, and they laughed continuously and bombarded each other with desperate jokes. Emanuel watched them closely as they wound their way by sled to practise every morning, and although they regularly threw each other to the ground and pelted snow into the faces of their friends, he came to the conclusion, after several weeks of observation, that they were just as miserable as he was.

He wrote in a reluctant letter home,

This great time is gradually becoming smaller. We can hardly move from the front door, and mostly I sit inside the house playing chess and marking the route of our advances on maps. I know I am in an enviable position, but really with so much time on one's hands it is impossible not to wonder – what is the point of it all? I wake up every morning with the heavy thought that I am not being used, and spend the day trying to shake off the subsequent feeling of being useless. By nightfall, having achieved nothing, I fall exhausted back on to my bed.

These letters, by the simple fact of their existence, lightened Marianna's heart. She sent Emanuel cheering, passionate replies, full of instances of his own importance, and in every daily letter she slipped in some news of the loss, by death or maiming, of the son, cousin or nephew of a family of her acquaintance, who had had the bad luck to have been posted to more dangerous parts.

I feel like Sleeping Beauty, lying here in my white world. Every day I sit and watch the snow falling on the fir trees, sealing the river with another layer of ice. From where I am, so far behind the line, even the shells give the impression of falling softly, landing with the thud and scatter of a snowball, and it is only the occasional burst of artillery that rouses me and disturbs me from my books. Sometimes I am so far away, lost in someone else's story, that I have to shake my head and look down at my patched boots to remind myself that I am in reality a member of the Kaiser's army.

Reading is the one thing I am gaining from this war, but it means I am also painfully reminded, unlike the characters I read about, that I am leading a life utterly devoid of drama. What kind of a story would my life make? A man rushes into battle, bursting to risk his life, and then remains through an entire winter with his feet beside a fire, waiting for the pussy willow to open up outside the window and signal the arrival of spring.

In the last days of 1915, Emanuel wrote home,

While hundreds of thousands of men crouched freezing in the trenches, I have spent my second wartime Christmas in a comfortable farm-house, several kilometres behind the front line. I and five other scouts sat drinking before a blazing fire in the company of our superior officers, and in order to blot out the misery of our friends we finished up our jug and drank a second. With the third our spirits rose so high that we ran out into the snow to cut down a Christmas tree. We decorated it with lighted twists of paper and watched, transfixed, as the guns battered on in a two-hundred-metre ring around it. The talk was not, as it was the year before, of Germany's Decisive Victory. There is rarely now any mention of politics or an end to the war, and as the night sped by, anecdotes concerning the treacherousness of certain skiing routes formed a breathless queue to be listened to and told. At midnight a ludicrous cartwheel competition broke out, and men whose fingers would have frozen under soberer conditions threw off their gloves and, placing their palms squarely on the ice, displayed their skill at backflips. I woke the following morning convinced I had spent the night lying on a slab of stone, and found to my disgust that

I was sunk luxuriously among the feather pillows of a high down bed. It was the gravelly voice of an officer that roused me, singing as he rubbed his face with snow. 'Si—ilent night, ho—oly night.' And I found that, despite myself, I had to laugh.

The family were out at Gaglow for the first warm week in spring when the telegram arrived. A boy ran up with it from the village, his heart beating wildly and his mouth twisted up in a frantic desire to suit the seriousness of the occasion. He delivered it straight into Wolf Belgard's hands and stopped to watch him open it. Wolf only noticed him, a small pale boy, his hand over his mouth, when he had finished studying the envelope, turning it over and over to convince himself that it was not the news he dreaded. 'Get away,' he shouted, sweeping his arms, and then, seeing the streaks of sweat like tear stains on the boy's dirty face, he called him back and told him to go round to the side door to drink a glass of water.

Wolf walked out into the garden to tear open the seal then, feeling suddenly afraid, he hurried back inside to find his wife.

Marianna was in the morning room, examining packets of seeds. Two whippets lay beside her on the sofa, wrapped against the cold in a mass of darkly coloured shawls so that only the black matt tips of their noses were visible above the rise and fall of the cloth. Wolf stood over her and let the telegram flutter down into her lap. It was light and grimy and Marianna turned to ash as she picked it up and held it in her hands. 'Let me,' he said then, regretting his cowardice. But to his relief she kept hold of it, swinging away out of his reach to break the seal herself.

The news at first lifted them both on a wave of relief and they sank against each other in a half embrace, Wolf dropping to the floor to catch his wife as she rocked forwards. They had hardly taken in this news when the sound of hurrying feet drew them apart, and the sight of Bina, her face flushed, her eyes fierce and questioning, brought them to their feet. The two dogs lifted their heads, stretched their straight legs and sighed at the disturbance. The telegram's arrival had spread with great rapidity up from the back door. News of it came through into the kitchens with the empty water cup and was passed, whispering over hatches along the dark maze of downstairs corridors. It spread hurriedly up into the servants' quarters, round the wooden rooms, from where Dolfi carried it through into the nursery with the linen. Bina assumed, from the relieved expression of her mother's face, that the news was wholly good. 'Let me,' she said, reaching for the paper, and as she read, her face became suffused with fury. Her mouth hung open in a small round gasp and her eyes blazed with outrage. Martha and Eva rushed into the room, and she turned and clasped them in her arms, spluttering out the terrible news before Marianna had a chance to get to them.

'What is it?' Fräulein Schulze was standing in the door, her red hair pulled severely off her face, her freckles standing out against her whitening skin. 'It's Manu.' Bina looked up, holding out a hand to her. 'He's . . .' But the governess did not wait to hear. A strange noise was gurgling in her throat and, hunching her shoulders to her neck, she turned and hurried from the room.

'Schu-Schu?' Eva called. 'Schu?' Having searched through every room, she sat down, exhausted, on the floor. 'This is my room and I love it,' she whispered, and, glancing guiltily into the corner, she thought she could still see a tiny dent under the smooth line of the redecoration. She turned around to peer between the dark legs of her bed. At first she could see nothing, and her heart began to pound as she ran her fingers up and along the wooden under-slats of the frame to find her box. She had hung it like a hammock, fastening it with loops of string that stretched between the boards so that it could only be reached by lifting up the mattress. Eva put her fingers round it and eased it from its cradle, lowering it like treasure to the floor and finally bringing it up to sit on the white cover of her bed. She turned the key, which rested in its lock, and let the lid fall back to reveal her initials roughly carved between the hinges. And there they were, the paper words, curled for safety in a thimble. Eva spread them across her knee and then, raising the strip of paper to her lips, she kissed them. Next she lifted out her photograph of Schu-Schu, her freckles spilling out in sepia dots against the brown tones of the image. '1911. Neuenahr' was scrawled in thin brown ink on the back, and Eva could still see her governess standing on the promenade, her hat in her hand, her head held high, while Emanuel took his time clicking and whirring with the shutter. Eva looked into her pale eyes and saw a faint glimmer of amusement in the familiar stare. At the very bottom of the box, under dusty skeins of coloured silk, she found the childish note, smudged with dried brown blood and dictated to Emanuel when she was seven years old. It swore that when she had grown up and reached sixteen, her only brother Emanuel would take her off to live with him and never, ever have another friend. At the bottom, by an oversized full-stop, the print of their two thumbs was smudged, Eva's small and oval, and Emanuel's too large for the one drop of blood so that the pattern of it faded to one side and slipped, transparent, off the page.

That night Fräulein Schulze did not appear for supper. 'How extraordinary,' Marianna said, and for once her daughters had to agree. They sat in dismal silence over a casserole of rabbit, the boiled bones sticking up out of the stew. Omi Lise tried her hardest to keep up some conversation, but the house seemed suddenly too big, shadows seeping in from disused rooms and the weight of the great ceiling pressing down on them.

That night Eva lay awake, waiting for the sound of Schu's large feet treading the back stairs. She imagined her out in the garden, wrapped up in her coat and sauntering in pure fury up and down the hill. 'Martha?' she whispered, and hearing nothing from her sister but the slow hush of her breath, she slid over to the window. It was dark, with a low-lying cloudy sky that blotted out the stars. Eva pressed her face against the glass, screwing up her eyes, but could still see nothing beyond the ice-house path. Shivering she got back into bed where, unable to sleep, she conjured up a new image for herself: her governess sitting warm in the long maze of the kitchens, talking over this important day with Gruber, Dolfi and their Gaglow cook.

It wasn't until the following morning that Bina found Schu's letter. It had been posted between the sheets, and pushed down so far that, curled up against cold linen, she didn't come across it until she woke. With a final morning stretch she nudged her feet into the outer reaches of the bed and there, between her toes, she caught the blunt edge of the envelope. She screamed and dived down to retrieve it. By the time she'd torn out the letter her sisters had collected round her.

'What is it?' Martha asked, and Bina stretched the letter out over the pillow. It reminded Eva of a will, the last and final testament, and she shivered as she knelt with Martha on the quilt. 'Do not forget what I have taught you.' The letter addressed them formally and was laid out in brown ink on thick white paper. 'Do not forget.' And there followed a rather disappointing list of hair-brushing, nail-scrubbing, neck-washing, and at what angle to hold one's head for poise, beauty and maximum effect. But at the very bottom of the paper their governess set out her most fervent wish that they listen carefully at all times to what their mother might be telling them. 'To be warned from within the heart of your own family of the evils of frivolity, the dangers of shallow feeling and of trapping a man of whom you are not worthy.' Bina read this last phrase twice in a low, gravelly voice, so that only the word 'evils' sprang out and cleared itself. Martha and Eva tugged at the cold end of the quilt and pressed their toes together.

Bina fixed them with a frown and began to read the letter again. 'Bina,' they complained, but she made them swear never to forget by twisting their fingers childishly in a cat's cradle of her own devising. In her room across the hall Nanny coughed, and in a sudden fit of terror Eva and Martha leapt from their nest at the bottom of Bina's bed and scurried back across the room.

'But where could she have gone?' they asked their father. 'Where could Schu have gone?' And he answered calmly that, in these uncertain times, she must have felt the need to return to her own family. Eva looked anxiously around. How many times had Fräulein Schulze told them it was they who were her family? 'My blood and guts,' she whispered, when they pleased her. 'My only girls.'

'In no time at all we'll find she's back.' Marianna smiled, and realized to her surprise that she hoped it might be true.

As the days passed with no more news, Bina became convinced that Schu-Schu had been sacked. 'It was the perfect moment to get rid of her, don't you understand?'

Martha shook her head uneasily, and Eva chewed her lip. 'Not really.'

'Now Manu's not here to fight for her, to get her back.' They thought of him, imprisoned by the Russians, not even knowing that Fräulein Schulze was gone. 'After all, he made Mama get her back before.'

'Yes.' Eva frowned. She'd been too young to remember, but she still knew, from Bina telling her, that it was all her fault.

Bina put her finger to her lips. 'I've been thinking,' her eyes made a quick dart across the floor, 'it's possible Mama may know where Schu is. She might even have a letter with her address. A letter to us, one that she never had the decency to pass on.'

Eva found herself doubting this last claim. But then the

thought excited her of creeping through her mother's cupboards, rummaging in drawers and letting the silkiness of pearls and amber lie against her palm.

'And if we find Schu-Schu's address, she might, it's just possible, she might know how to get Manu released.'

'With bribes?' Martha screwed up her face.

And Bina, her eyes fierce: 'With whatever it takes.'

'But whatever happens,' Martha argued, 'the Russians will let him out when the war ends, surely.'

Bina put an arm round her shoulder and drew her sister's face close in to hers. 'Typhoid, lice, starvation, torture,' she whispered. 'Does it never occur to you to read a newspaper? Yes, they'll let him out. If he's still alive.' And she released her hold.

'Then what if the war never ends?' Martha added, twisting round the argument to regain her pride. And she widened her eyes to register her point.

The three girls sat in silence. They could hear Omi Lise moving crookedly about next door. It was her sudden descent into old age that highlighted more than anything that they were beginning to outgrow their nursery. A warm streak of sunlight lay across the floor and through the door stood their three beds, neatly folded and made up.

'In normal times, I suppose I might be married by now.' Bina laughed, and they continued to sit in silence, wondering at the left fork of their lives, the waste of their unanswered prayers, and the hours and hours of waiting time.

'Julika is engaged to an officer,' Martha said, and then immediately regretted it. 'But not Jewish,' she added quickly. 'And Angelika has no one.'

It was a week before Emanuel's last letter arrived. It lay unopened on the breakfast table, waiting by Marianna's plate and as Eva looked at it she felt hot blood roaring in her ears.

She did not want to hear her brother's old, old news, and shrank away from catching him in the humiliating act of knowing less than them.

In a strange, low voice her mother read, '"The snows are finally starting to melt, and for the first time in six months I am able to get about without the use of a sled."' Marianna's fingers trembled at the bottom of the page, but she'd made her decision and was sticking to it. '"I have orders to ride out tonight to where the leader of the regiment has spent the entire winter playing cards with his toes toasting by an open fire. Even my poor bored horse is longing for the challenge to negotiate the way by moonlight. We shall be careful as always to avoid the thinning ice and stick like shadows to the shelter of the woods. When I whispered the news into my horse's ear I could swear she snorted that there is nothing she would like more than to embark on this small adventure . . ."' Eva clasped her fingers painfully together. 'It is still only afternoon,' Marianna continued, 'but the moon has already risen in the sky and is hanging there larger than seems normal. I shall take this as a good sign whether it is one or not . . .' Unable to bear it for a moment longer, Eva shook herself and, with a half-intended thrust, jolted Martha's elbow as she raised cold acorn coffee to her lips. Martha cried out as the liquid splashed across her dress and the whole table used the moment as an excuse to put the letter to one side, distracting themselves with an unnatural bustle.

Marianna refrained from asking her husband about a replacement for the governess. She detected a shrinking away whenever the subject was raised, and saw his frown shoot deeper, drawing down the thick line of his hair. 'We could send out word to Fräulein Milner,' she tried half-heartedly to draw him in. 'I hear she is still unmarried, unlikely ever to be so now . . .' But then the memory of Millie, nervously knitting in the drawing room, throwing out insipid glances over supper, dampened her enthusiasm.

'Why not let them manage as they are?' he suggested. 'At least we'll have one less person to feed.' And his words, impractical as they were, lifted her spirits. 'How old is Eva anyway? Already turned thirteen? Well, it will be the best thing for them all.'

Marianna agreed. 'After all,' she said, 'we don't want them, middle-aged and still crying out for someone to run in and wash their necks.'

'And, of course, Fräulein may reappear any day,' Wolf said, and he shuffled through to the library.

They started with her dressing table. Eva and Martha could only stand and watch while, with plump fingers, Bina drew out each drawer. 'She must keep some of her things in Berlin.' She frowned when a stack of silk handkerchiefs, shaken out, did not disgorge a single ornament. Drawer after drawer revealed only dented beds of satin and the dried, dusty needles of lavender and pine. In separate envelopes they found locks of their hair, dry and curled from childhood. There was one for each of them and two for Bina. Bina, surprised, held the two curls up before her face, marvelling at the changing texture of the hair. The first was soft and brown, and the other sprang out from its ribbon, black and wild just as it was now. 'How strange,' she muttered, 'and unusual,' but she looked pleased as she folded both envelopes away. In a secret shelf above the turning figure of a music box they came across their mother's ruby earrings. Bina held them up to her own ears and stood looking in the glass. She knew they had been a present from Papa on the day they married, and before that had belonged to Omi Josefa, the previous Frau Belgard.

'Maybe when you marry they'll be yours,' Eva whispered, understanding for the first time the hard red planes of their beauty.

'Not Bina's,' Martha said. 'By tradition they should be passed on to the new wife. To whoever is the one Emanuel marries.' And they all remembered their brother and what they had originally come here to do. Bina slipped the earrings back into their box and turned into the room.

'Come on, you two.' Bina allocated them each a bedside table, slipping her own hands into a wardrobe. Eva shivered as she stirred the private contents of the cupboard. There were books and letters and the broken strand of a necklace, so that as she pushed her fingers to the back, tiny glass beads caught below her nails. The envelopes were all addressed in a sloping, familiar hand. 'What are these?' she called to Bina, and Bina looked over her shoulder and reached for one.

'From Papa to Mama, before they were married, as if he hadn't better things to do,' she said, and tossed it back in an arc so that the sharp corner struck Eva on the chin and a slip of paper fell out on to the floor.

'My dearest love,' she read, bending to retrieve it, and at the very bottom the postscript caught her eye. 'My darling, surely you can tell me, is there a remedy for dreams?'

'How long have we been in here?' Martha whispered then, and they all turned anxiously towards the door.

'Quick.' Bina spun round. 'Eva, search under the bed, and you Martha under the divan, and then we'd better get out.' Eva pressed the letter back into the drawer and dropped down to her knees. She glanced along the floor, and with her fingers brushed the springs. There was nothing there, and just as she was about to crawl out, she heard the floorboards creak and a step outside the door. She swallowed hard, taking in some dust. There was another slow creak, a few fast steps, and then she recognized the old dry cough of Omi Lise. 'Bina?' she called sticking her nose out into the room, but she found that both her sisters had deserted.

Marianna was standing in her hat and coat, staring down at Wolf. She fixed him with a look of such severity that he jolted in his chair, rattling his paper where it drooped over his knee. 'What is it, my dear?' He reached for her hand. Marianna resisted, shaking him off, and Eva, her hand on the door, slunk back against the wall.

'Wolf,' Marianna stood a little closer so that her skirt brushed up against his knees, 'listen to me. I don't have anything at all to pay the gardeners. The stable roof needs mending. The girls from the village spent most of Easter grumbling. And much as we can let our debts build up in town, it is not so possible out here.' She swallowed and her voice rose up with resentment. 'You'll have to help me. It's impossible for me to understand how the business can fail when all over Germany people are talking about the huge profits to be made in agriculture from this war.' Wolf wearily laid aside his newspaper. Marianna bit her lip, silently restraining a curse for their Kaiser who must, she assumed, have failed to pay up when making his enormous orders.

Wolf stood and put his arms around her. He could find no way of answering her question. But Marianna only backed away and, shaking her head and sighing, she hurried from the room.

Eva heard her mother's thumbs at the piano hitting dark uneven notes. She glanced round the door. Her father was sitting exactly as before, his back bent into the leather chair, his face buried in the pages of the paper. 'Papa?' she called to him, and she hovered as she had seen her mother do. 'Papa?' But even when she passed a hand between him and the page he failed to register her presence. 'We are going to Jerusalem,' she whispered, remembering her childhood disappointment in him, and when he still failed to respond, she tiptoed out.

CHAPTER 12

My father stood in paint-splattered clothes. 'Wait till you see this.' It was a photograph, filmy with colour, and he laid it down over the rim of a cup so I could peer at it. It looked like a folly or a tiny bandstand, half enclosed with pillars. 'It's the ice-house,' my father said, 'at Gaglow.' And I looked at it again. The roof was like a dovecote with rounded, sloping tiles, and I imagined the East German teachers eating their sandwiches in there.

'Did you get another letter?' I was feeding Sonny, weighing his little body down with milk, but my father said the photo had been sent by his first cousin John. Johann Guttenberger. Or John Godber, as he likes to be known. 'He changed his name, poor sod, while he was still at school.'

'Has he been out there?'

'Yes.' He looked faintly disgusted. 'He flew to Berlin and hired a car and was there within an hour. I suppose this is a photograph to prove it.'

'It's odd he didn't send one of the actual house.'

'Well, I like to think it's because the house is too big to fit into the frame,' he laughed at himself, staring once more at the ice-house with its peeling pillars, 'but I'm probably just making that up.' He wheeled the easel round, squeaking it across the floor towards us.

'So what else did your cousin say?' I asked, once Sonny lay sozzled on my arm.

'Well, apparently after the Wall came down they decided to

use Gaglow as a centre for retraining all their teachers in good capitalist philosophy, so they did up the house, and then,' my father stopped and waved a brush in the air, 'imagine their horror to find that the whole place, the stables and the orchard, all belongs to a family of old Jews.' He laughed and dipped his brush in leaf green paint. 'They might have to be moved to some army barracks to finish off their course, and none of them are pleased.'

'So what will happen to the house?'

'Well, Johann says he offered to rent it back to them at some extortionate fee, but they weren't able to afford it.' And we laughed straight at each other, in surprised delight.

He was standing with his green brush poised, waiting to start. I laid Sonny down, cupping his head with my palm, transferring him on to the sofa as carefully as I could. I'll wake him half-way through the afternoon, I thought, but he opened his eyes and whimpered so I picked him up again to see if he would burp. My father dropped his arm. 'Sorry,' I said.

Sonny burped, and I congratulated him. My father mixed more paint. 'He should be all right now,' I said, laying him down again, but immediately he began to cry. My father tried to get a quick stroke in before I picked him up. 'Shhh,' I soothed, and I put him back on for another feed.

Dad sat down in an armchair, the springs spiralling down towards the floor. 'So what will happen now?' I asked, but he sighed to say he didn't know.

Sonny was so full now that his face looked greasy and his eyes rolled back in his head. 'Right.' I lay down beside him, pressing one arm against his back so that he didn't think he was alone, but before even one small lick of paint was laid, he'd woken up again and was mewling like a cat.

'Is he all right?' My father looked upset, and I propped myself up on one elbow and smiled as if I knew.

'He's fine, he just doesn't feel like lying down.' And I held him up against my shoulder and patted his back. All afternoon I laid him down and picked him up until my stomach ached and my hands shook with exhaustion. 'It's not going to work,' I said at last, looking at my father, his face full of suspense, standing on tiptoe with one more fresh brush in his hand.

'Is it possible he just doesn't want to be painted?' He looked quite serious, almost put out, but I felt too drained to do more than shrug.

There was a message from Pam when I got home. Sonny had fallen asleep in the back of the cab, and I left him in his chair on the kitchen table while I sat down on the floor. Every part of my body hurt and the left side of my scar where they'd pulled Sonny out felt ridged and tender. 'I'm so tired,' I almost sobbed when I got through to her. She was in a double room at the Station Hotel in Leeds.

'Why don't you just stop? Say you'll do it another time?'

But my theory was that while Sonny was so small, the picture would be finished more quickly. 'We've already done his ear, it's such a waste,' and I heard myself and laughed. 'How are you anyway?' I longed to hear about someone else's life and I could tell from her jaunty tone that she had news. 'Go on,' I urged her, 'tell me every single thing.'

'You're not going to like it,' she warned, and she mouthed the name, half whispered, of the actor Bradly Teale.

'No!' I wailed, already relishing the dreadful, inevitable course of events, but Pam only sighed. It was already much too late for no. 'I know he's famous for being a prick, but you have to admit he's incredibly good-looking, and . . . well, in private . . . he's actually quite sweet.'

'Hmm,' I glanced over at Sonny, whose sleeping face, squashed down against his chin like an elder member of the House of Lords, filled me with such a thrill of love that I felt irrationally hopeful. 'Well, maybe it will work out.' I made her promise to keep me up to date with news.

I carried the baby, still asleep, through to the bedroom and, with the telephone cradled beside me, I lay down and closed my eyes. Pam, I thought, Pamela Harris, so beautiful and bright, wasting herself on Bradly Teale. At least with Mike there had been hope. We'd had nine long months of bliss, and then a year or two of ambling happiness before things started to slide. His work had dried up and he'd begun to brood. He wouldn't make any plans with me, refused to consider a holiday or even leaving London for the day. Now when he came in from an interview he'd move over to the television and stand staring at the screen. 'You see?' he shook his head, 'What's that idiot got that I haven't?' and he raised the volume higher.

'Mike!' I'd have to stand in front of him, rip the remote out of his hands before he'd look at me.

At Christmas time we held a party, and as we loaded up the car with food – sticks of French bread, crisps and cheese – he reminded me that they weren't his friends, the people we'd invited, and that the flat we lived in wasn't really his. He'd just moved in with me, that was all. I snapped a stick of bread into the boot, tensing up my ears, and although his confession seemed to ease him, allowing his affection to shine through, I felt a sliding out of faith. He made love to me again, but in the mornings only, reaching out hungrily before he'd opened his eyes, and he held my hand in public, dropping it as soon as we closed our front door. 'This summer, shall we go away somewhere, work or no work?' I tested him, as we walked home through Regent's Park, our fingers clinging coolly, and I looked sideways at him to gather in his doom.

I didn't take Sonny to the studio for a week. 'He's enormous,' my father said when we arrived, and we started immediately before he could grow a millimetre more. 'He's only a month old.' I laughed, but it was true he'd filled out so that his cheeks looked like a hamster's. I felt refreshed and optimistic. Thank God, I thought, as the first green stroke of paint went on and the outline of his collar frilled under his chin in white. But then his arms began to wave and he turned his head from side to side, sticking out his lower lip in preparation for tears. I pushed a pillow under my arm, turned him towards me and attached him quickly to my breast. The rising purple of his face subdued and he looked at me, long eyes dark blue with joy.

'Do you mind?' my father asked, readjusting the easel, and although I didn't want my baby's head ballooned out of proportion by one enormous breast I saw there was no other way.

'Happy now,' I whispered, as, still sucking, he closed his eyes and I saw the perfect painted ear rubbed out and moved a fraction round.

The new ear wasn't quite the same. It was rougher, coiled and brown, and shadowed with the dark lines of baby hair I'd been told would disappear.

'Oh, this is much better.' My father rocked forward on his feet, and I thought of all the times he'd taken out a smile, a nose, the soft slope of a wrist for being too easy on the eye.

I pressed a quick kiss on Sonny's face and thought of how I'd always been too busy for perfection, using up my time on dreams. Once, during the last act of a play, I'd drifted off into a fantasy of romance and forgotten to say my line. 'Tssk.' It was the actor about whom I'd just been thinking, looking far from pleased. He nudged me in the ribs, and I blushed up through my costume as I spluttered out the words.

I didn't suffer over my work like Mike, sitting up all night with scripts, locking himself away, and shaking with pure terror when he went out on stage. It made me nervous certainly, but I was too easily distracted, sidetracked by the people in my life.

'Dad?' I asked. 'Have you heard anything else about that theatre?' But he only shook his head, mixing up more paint and frowning as he laid it on.

I'd told my agent I'd be up for work again when Sonny was three months old. Kate said she'd mind him if I got an audition, but I hadn't taken account then of his ravenous desire for milk. 'You should try a bottle,' Kate said, 'so I can feed him when you go out.' But the thought of brand names, teat sizes and twenty minutes' sterilizing sent fear into my heart. 'I don't have time to make a bottle,' I told her, 'I'm too busy breastfeeding,' and anyway my agent never rang.

Pam's agent, a sun-tanned, glinting head of a conglomerate, was making business calls from her hospital trolley as they wheeled her back up to her room. 'But did she have a Caesarean?' I asked, refusing to be impressed, and Pam laughed.

'You think Camilla Heston was going to waste days of her life in labour? She booked in three weeks early to coincide with Christmas and was back at work straight after New Year.'

'That's disgusting.' I felt relieved that my own agent, a timid, balding man of fifty-two, was most unlikely even to know about such things.

'That's wonderful news, darling,' he said, when I told him I was pregnant, and apart from a large and inappropriate card of animals tearing into flesh, I'd heard nothing from him since.

'Dad,' I tried again, as he clattered round the kitchen, 'what's happened about this theatre?'

He had to think for some time to know what I was talking about. 'Oh, yes,' he said at last. 'Your theatre.' A pan jumped twice as it hit the floor. 'I'm afraid we were slightly mis-led over the theatre.' He explained that it was, in fact, a grain warehouse that had been used by a nearby theatre to store their props. 'The warehouses will be sold on together as a lot,' he said. 'They're not even worth much, according to Johann.'

'Have you heard from him again, then, your cousin?'

But the subject was putting him into a bad mood. 'Oh, endless, ridiculous complications.' He turned a flame up high. 'I've said I want nothing more to do with any of it.'

I felt a sudden, irrational slump of gloom. It's Sonny's inheritance as well, I found myself thinking, and I shook my head, knowing it was easier not to think about such things, to expect nothing and then only be surprised.

My father passed me a plate of quail eggs, tipping a mound of celery salt onto the side. 'Thanks.' I cracked the dappled shells, peeling them away with the fingers of one hand. It was true he'd never shown much interest in money. His pictures he sold to his friends, who often sold them on for more, and any spare money he collected he used to lure his models with sumptuous food. He paid us by the hour, and when and if the painting sold, he always gave over a small sum.

'Will you let me know if you need anything?' he said that evening, tweaking Sonny's nose, and it made me think of Mike and how he'd mumbled the same message into my machine.

It was a beautiful blue day, spring blazing into summer with blossom giving way to fat green leaves. I walked between Kate and Natasha, the long way round to buy ice cream.

'Have either of you seen Dad?' I asked, as we walked up towards the Heath. 'I mean, have you heard the news about Gaglow?'

'No.' Natasha laughed. 'What is it?'

'It's a country house. The house where our grandmother and her sisters were brought up.'

They both looked at me, alarmed. 'How do you know these things?' Kate frowned, and Natasha burst out, 'I thought they were brought up in Berlin.'

'Yes,' I said. 'Yes, they were, but they had this place as well.' I stopped, responsible suddenly for the glories of the past. 'Dad says they may have got it gambling. His grandfather may have won it in some kind of bet, or else it was given to him instead of payment.' I remembered the warehouse full of props. 'Money owed for grain, I think.'

'Gambling sounds more fun.' Natasha crunched the end of her cornet, and we all agreed it did.

'Dad used to go there apparently when he was a boy, and once the village children came up to sing for him when he was ill.'

'I just hope it wasn't contagious, whatever he had.' Kate laughed, and Natasha muttered, 'Can you imagine, ghastly German songs?'

I stopped to catch my breath. Ghastly German songs, I thought, and I looked at Sonny asleep against my chest, his head rolled sideways, his mouth pressed open like a rose, and thought, But he was German then.

'So what about it? What about the house?'

'It's come back,' I told them. 'I mean it's ours. Well, not ours, but it belongs to the descendants of Marianna Belgard. Dad and his cousins.' And I realized that I was beaming.

'Marianna who?' They both looked cross, and I tried to explain to them, my illegitimate family, what I'd pieced together from small scraps.

'So how many cousins are there?' Natasha wanted to know. But I wasn't sure. There was Bina's eldest son, Johann, and there had been another sister Martha, who'd stayed on too late.

'Did she have children?' I looked down at Sonny and I shivered suddenly for how little we'd been told. 'I think the children survived. And there was Emanuel, their elder brother.'

'Are you sure? A brother?'

'Yes, definitely, a sort of black sheep. They never mentioned him apparently.' And for some reason I kept the secret of his photo to myself.

'Did the black sheep have any children?'

I didn't know. 'He married somebody unsuitable, I think.'

'He probably did in that case, loads and loads.'

We strode on up the hill.

'Talking of unsuitable children,' Natasha said, once we'd stepped onto grass, 'have you heard anything from Mike?'

We were heading for a large green tree, shrouded from the path by flowering grass and with a view over the lake. 'No,' I said, 'I haven't.' But the admission met with such a flurry of abuse that, overwhelmed with guilt, I admitted that he had been calling. 'I leave my answerphone switched on,' I said. 'I've told him I don't want to see him.' And, exhausted, I slumped down against the tree.

'Quite right.'

Natasha shook out a blanket, billowing it onto the ground,

but Kate looked up, perturbed. 'That's so harsh,' and she crawled across to gaze down at Sonny's face. 'You can't keep them apart, it's cruel.' She looked as if she might be going to cry.

'Kate!' Natasha glowered. 'It's got nothing to do with you.'

But already I was filling with remorse. 'We managed all right with just a mother,' I argued, 'didn't we?' But even Natasha agreed it might be different for boys.

'And anyway,' Kate smiled, 'we did see Dad occasionally.'

And it was true that, occasionally, we had.

When I got home I replayed Mike's most recent message, banked up with the others on the tape. 'Hello, you two.' His voice was strained with cheerfulness. 'Just checking in to see how it's all going. Give us a ring. I've got something to tell you, actually.' And he repeated his number slowly and deliberately, twice. I made myself a cup of tea and put Sonny in his rocker, singing to him as I worked out what to say. 'Right.' And then the phone rang, almost in my hand, splashing hot tea right up my arm. 'Pam, how are you?' I shivered with relief, and then for twenty minutes without stopping she told me what a bastard Bradly Teale was turning out to be.

'But it's hardly unexpected.' I felt her sharp intake of breath. 'I mean . . . Oh, Pam . . . so what will you do now?' And I listened for another ten minutes as she discarded plans. I glared at Sonny, cooing like a dove, blowing bubbles and for once quite happy to be sitting on his own.

'Pam,' I finally interrupted her, 'I've got to go. Sonny's . . .' I couldn't use him as my excuse. 'Look, I'm leaking down the front of my dress.' She apologized for going on. 'No, no, I'm sorry.' I promised to call her back when I had time.

My ear felt hot and itchy and my fingers ached from clutching at the phone. Right, I thought, looking at Mike's number, and then Sonny began to howl. 'You're all right.' I stroked his head, brushing his face with kisses, and then without warning his crying rose up into a scream. I scooped him into my arms. 'What is it?' But his tongue had curled into the sharp end of a drill, shrilling through me, rattling at my heart. 'Shhhh, shhhh, shhhh,' I hushed for both our sakes, and I walked him round the room, up the two steps to the bathroom, down again, round and round the tiny hall. I took him over to the window. I could see people in the street below looking round, squinting into the sun and, worried they'd locate us, accuse me of sticking pins into my baby's eyes, I pulled down the sash. My hands were trembling. I sat down and stood up, unwrapped his nappy, and attempted to distract him with his beetroot face reflected in the mirror. I turned the cold tap on and off, and then the hot, until all I could think of was to lie down with him and cry against his dark red screaming mouth. For the first time in his life he didn't want a feed and just as we lay desperate in each other's arms the doorbell rang.

'Oh my God.' We tramped downstairs, half hoping to come across a policeman prepared to take us both away. Sonny's head bobbed on my shoulder, his screams dipping and rising with each sharp step and as we turned on to the last flight down he burped and his crying lost momentum. I felt his back relax, his stiff arms soften, and just as I stretched out to open the front door he stopped.

'Hello, there.' It was Mike. He had on a white T-shirt, broad across his chest, and old trousers from a suit I'd loved. 'Is it a bad time?' I looked down at my dress, all stained and splashed, and Sonny, slippery with tears, and I held the door for him to come in. 'I'll take him, shall I?' and he scooped Sonny off my shoulder, transferring him to his own, so that I could see his face, perfectly happy as he bumped back up the three flights of stairs. I went into the bathroom and sprayed water on my face while Mike rocked his boy around the room.

'So, how's the work situation?' It was the one thing I'd planned not to say.

'All right,' he said, surprising me. 'In fact I've got a job.'

I dropped two teabags into cups.

'Starting tomorrow.'

I felt tempted to ask him if he took milk and sugar. 'How long for?'

'Six months, it's a series for television.' I nodded my congratulations, wondering why life couldn't have been easy like this last year. We sipped our tea in silence, Sonny propped up against his father's knee. 'He's enormous,' Mike said, and I looked at Sonny, for the first time at a distance. His hair was turning gold like Mike's and even his feet were wide and boyish.

'Don't be ridiculous,' I muttered, 'he's tiny. He's a tiny little baby.' And I got up and went into the kitchen. It was difficult to know quite what to do. My hands felt empty, and my arms hung light and full of air.

Mike leant against the door. 'You look exhausted.' He had the concerned look I hated most.

'Thanks,' I sneered.

But he shook his head. 'No, I just meant, seeing as I'm here, why don't you go and lie down for an hour?'

'Well, I . . .' and then, seeing I could only lose by arguing, I walked through to the bedroom and threw myself onto the bed. What if he cries or needs a new nappy? I thought, as I pulled the quilt over my legs. What if Mike runs off with him? And then I remembered it was Mike who didn't want him. Didn't want either of us, and I sighed a long sigh of relief and slipped off into sleep.

At first I dreamt about nothing, convinced I was still awake, and then black sheep crept in, nosing along and munching at the grass. They trotted along in a neat long line, their wool dusty, their faces turning white, while their hard hoofs clipped against the cool stone floor. And then I was in the country by the sea, and my grandmother, a young girl dressed in white, was showing me where I could sleep. It was a high bed mounded up with pillows and outside my window in the attic I heard the sheep bleating, the whole flock crying like a cat. I woke up and realized it was Sonny crying for his evening feed. 'He's hungry.' I stretched out my arms automatically and Mike, who was hovering in the doorway, handed him down. I unbuttoned my dress while Sonny, his nose twitching, his mouth poised, searched round wildly in the folds of cloth.

Mike looked tactfully away. How ridiculous, I thought, and once the baby had latched on and was gulping noisily I started to laugh.

'Feeling better?' Mike asked, but I didn't want him to take any credit so I stopped.

'Sarah,' Mike was looking at his shoes, 'there's something I ought to tell you about this job. It's set in Scotland, right up near Skye, on an island,' and he looked briefly out of the window before going on. 'There's a ferry that only goes over once a week, so I don't think I'll be getting back much during the next six months, if at all.'

My body hardened, sharp as knives. 'I see,' I said, adding quietly, 'He'll be practically grown-up by then.'

'You could send me photos?'

Sonny choked on an overflow of milk.

'Or, even better than that, you could turn the job down.' I raised my eyebrows into mocking curves. 'Tell your agent you'll only work in London.' Mike looked at me, alarmed, and I smiled brightly. 'It's all right, I'm only joking,' and I had to stop myself from telling him it wouldn't matter if he went off to live at the North Pole.

Sonny gulped and coughed and I took a breath, anxious that the poison of my thoughts didn't run through into the milk.

For ten minutes we sat in silence, Mike staring down into the street while I watched Sonny's eyes roll back and flutter into sleep.

'Right,' Mike said at last, 'I'd better be off. There's packing to be done.' And he came and stood beside the bed. 'Goodbye, son,' he said, 'goodbye, small fella,' and without meaning to I began to cry.

'Sarah, don't . . .'

'Go away,' I said, and repeated, 'go away, go away, go away,' until finally he believed me and let himself out on to the stairs.

CHAPTER 13

Bina had decided to become a nurse. Eva lay with her on the cool floor of the Gaglow nursery, leafing through her practical guide. There were illustrations of white-aproned women, serene and smiling, carrying basins of water over to the bedsides of lightly wounded men. The soldiers all had gleaming bandages wound around their heads, or arms slung in sashes to hold up splinted elbows, and they were all without exception startlingly handsome. Eva leant across her sister's shoulder and examined their illustrated features, the unshaven chins and pencilled hollows of their cheeks, the strong shoulders, the bright, polite eyes. She found, as the pages turned, that she was holding her breath for Manu. 'Bina, will you be sent off to the front line, to a field hospital?' she asked.

Bina flicked through to the end with irritation. 'There is all this to learn first. There are thousands of experienced nurses just waiting to get to the front. Anyway, I'm only an untrained volunteer, anyone could do it.' And she smiled and shot a look at Eva, knowing that this was not entirely true.

'Well, I expect the war will probably be over by the time you've learnt the first thing about it,' Eva responded, and she picked up the discarded letter. They had to have a letter ready to send Schu-Schu, Bina insisted, for when they located her address. Eva read slowly through the words, aware that any criticism would not be welcome. It struck her how closely Bina had picked up their governess's own tone, with lists of reasons and lightly veiled threats of what was due and owed. She shivered. Schu, she thought, Schu-Schu-Schu, and she closed her eyes, immersed in an instant by the huge enveloping of her arms, the memory of how it felt to arrive home to a house that existed completely and without rivalry for them.

'As soon as we get back to Berlin,' Bina lowered her voice, 'we'll start the search again. You and Martha might have to begin without me after school, but as soon as I've amputated a leg or two and siphoned off some poison, I'll be home to join you.' She made a gruesome face and they both laughed, shivering and gleeful, so that when Martha called to them from the next room they jumped in shock, then, catching at each other's hands, rolled over on the floor with helpless shrieks of laughter.

Martha called again, a real, terrifying shout for help, and Bina and Eva, their blood falling away, scrambled to their feet.

'It's Omi Lise,' Martha choked, and there, bent against her bed as if in prayer, was the stiff, hunched body of their nanny. The three girls approached her slowly. 'Omi?' Martha whispered, and when she didn't answer they all bent down and Eva touched her hand. 'She's still warm.'

A tiny straining voice rose from the bedclothes. 'Of course I'm still warm. You won't get rid of me that easily.' And Martha's face flooded with colour, her tears falling onto the old woman's bony head.

'Let's try and move her,' Bina said, her few medical weeks assuming new importance, and between them they lifted her light, brittle body and laid her on the bed. 'Fetch some water,' Bina ordered, and Martha brought a glass and rested it against her lips. Eva slipped her arm behind Nanny's head. She took a tiny sip and lay back exhausted on the pillows.

'I think we should look after her ourselves. Up here.'

Martha and Eva both froze with the force of Bina's words. 'Omi,' Martha leant back over her, 'how are you feeling?' But Omi Lise seemed too stunned to move her lips.

'They'll miss her at supper,' Eva said.

Bina shook her off. 'We'll send down a message for a tray and then offer to bring it up to her ourselves.'

'No,' Eva said. 'I don't know.' She looked into the creased and funnelled face. 'She wouldn't like there to be any lies.' But Bina glared at her with such determination that she found herself slipping limply into line.

'Can we get you something from downstairs?' Martha asked. Nanny's eyelids fluttered and then lay still as if she had worn too thin to tell them one more time what they should do.

The gong for supper sounded, and Omi Lise, when they left her, seemed to have fallen into a light and even sleep. 'She may be herself again tomorrow,' Bina said. 'She probably just needs a bit of rest.' But they walked down the wide wooden staircase without the usual clatter, trailing into the dining room with dark, preoccupied eyes.

Bina, Martha and Eva kept an all-night vigil by the side of Omi Lise's bed.

'She doesn't seem to have a temperature.' Martha placed a light hand on her forehead.

Bina jerked away her arm. 'Of course she hasn't got a temperature. She's not ill. She's just exhausted.' And Eva lifted up a fork of delicately prepared rice and held it, hopelessly, close to her lips.

The three girls sat in silence as the night wore on, watching for the dawn, which spread darkly red and earlier than they would have thought. With the light of a new day, Nanny's face had turned as old as parchment. 'What age is she, do you think?' Martha asked, and they spent the slow hours trying to untangle it.

'We could carry her down to sit out in the sun,' Bina pondered, once they'd given up on the multiplication, and they all leant forward to check the cool flow of blood still running in her veins. Nanny's face was traced with green, and her hair was the faded colour of a primrose.

'I think she might like some porridge,' Eva said. 'Would you,

Omi dear?' And to avoid suspicion they all went down to breakfast.

'Dolfi, could you ask Cook to make an extra bowl of porridge?' Eva caught her mother's lowered look, and to lessen the improbability of the request, called after her, 'With extra milk.'

The porridge sat congealing at her elbow as she scraped the lining from a precious hard-boiled egg. Bina and Martha had slipped away, and she was only waiting for her mother to rise and leave the table.

She began to spoon the food in a ring around the edge. Marianna looked over at her. 'What are we to do?' She shook her head and, without waiting for an answer, folded up her napkin and left the room. Eva watched her mother's shadow disappear from the doorway then, covering the dish of porridge, she pushed back her chair and ran out into the hall. She slowed on the stairs, in an effort not to slop the milk, and paused for breath on the second landing.

'Eva.' She heard her name hissed, urgent, from above and, rushing, she hit her foot on a step and the silver spoon resting in the bowl jolted out and rattled down the stairs. 'That is too much,' she muttered, using Omi's own disapproving phrase, and setting the dish on a step she ran back to retrieve it.

'Eva?' Her mother was in front of her, the bowl in her hand. 'What are you doing, rushing your breakfast round the house?' Eva looked past her, up through the twist of banisters to the round circle of the top floor. Tears came to her eyes and, without intending it, she pushed the spoon into her mouth for comfort. 'Are you hiding someone hungry in the nursery?' Marianna asked, amused, then the corners of her mouth turned down and the colour drained out of her face. She dropped the bowl, hitched up her skirts and sped up the last flight. Eva stared down at the gluey mass of porridge, jagged with bone china. She sat on the bottom step, her toes stained with little strings of oatmeal, and waited for her mother to come back down.

*

Wolf Belgard found the countryside oppressive, all the space and time that hung so heavily and the landscape empty of the men who worked it. There was no sense in it, but he found the war easier to forget while in Berlin, even with the air-ships floating high above the city and the bands of children with their banners raising private loans to subsidize the war. He wandered round the evening streets. Shops were shutting up and cafés, which had half-heartedly stretched out to catch the sun, were being tucked behind their double folding doors. There was a subdued air of calm and disillusion. A little crowd of women, all in black, stood miserably before a stand where the latest lists of soldiers killed in action had been pasted. There was talk, he knew, of banning the public display of such information, prompted by concern that the conversations resulting from these daily lists of losses, sheet after double sheet of tiny jumping names, led to unpatriotic and defeatist comments.

Wolf stopped and looked about him, trying to re-create the jubilant faces of the crowd who had, on the day that Britain turned on them to declare war, rushed through the streets, hissing and spitting and holding up their fists. He had been swept along himself, rushed about and caught up in the current, and had found himself one of many thousand, bursting with indignation before the closely guarded British embassy.

He had seen a man, professional and well dressed, jump on to the running board of an official car and, leaning past the chauffeur strike the passenger full in the face with his hat. The man, scarlet and trembling with rage, had shouted, still clutching at his eye, that he was not British but American. On hearing this his assailant had apologized, replaced his hat and offered him his card. It was claimed afterwards in the papers that pennies had been tossed from the windows of the British embassy to humiliate the crowd, and in retaliation the people had shattered every pane of glass. But Wolf had not seen any coins. Stones had certainly been thrown and the splintering and cracking had been accompanied by cheers and shouts, growls and sighs of satisfaction. Wolf had himself felt overwhelmed with the desire to join them. He began to scuffle with his feet, peering for pebbles between the legs of the spectators, and found to his surprise that the square in which they stood was paved with asphalt. 'Pfui, pfui!' hissed a thousand contemptuous mouths and, ashamed of it as he was now, he had opened his own mouth and felt the warm snake of solidarity hiss out. 'Pfui!' He allowed himself, in a surge of hot blood, to be jostled on to Unter den Linden to stand declaiming outside a hotel known to harbour foreign journalists.

Wolf stopped and looked about him. The streets were virtually deserted, and it made him sweat when he considered with what fickleness he had behaved. It must have been his childish wonder at being in the centre of a crowd that had distracted him from memories of other gatherings, made up as they were of these same people. He had chosen to forget the hostile group who, in the first year of his marriage, had taunted him, hissing and spitting and goading each other on. Marianna, pregnant with their first child, had asked him to escort her on a walk. It was early evening and Wolf had returned from work to find her upset by a lurid article in that day's paper. It was the story of a five-year-old boy, Emanuel Goldbacher, found with his throat cut on the banks of the river Rhine. The reports suggested it had been a ritualistic murder and, with no evidence against him, a Jewish butcher and his family had been taken from their home and locked up in the local prison. Wolf had folded his wife's arm in his, and attempted to soothe her with more cheerful conversation as they walked towards the Tiergarten.

It was a favourite pastime to saunter past the house in which they'd met, to look up, smiling, at the windows as if they might just catch the innocent shadows of the people they had been. They had almost reached the gates, absorbed in a teasing game of idiotic name suggestions for the baby, when a fat globule of spit sailed across Wolf's shoulder and landed on his shoe.

They stopped, still entwined and looked behind them. A crowd had gathered, up to twenty men and women whispering and muttering. A woman pushed her way to the front and, puckering her mouth, prepared to spit again. In an instant Marianna withdrew her arm from his and pulled her coat about her. She advanced upon the woman with such speed and strength of purpose that the other was forced to gulp down her attack and step back onto the ankle of a man, who swore and fell against another woman, who struck him round the head. Marianna opened her mouth wide, exposing the pink and pearly gum above her teeth and laughed at them. The hisses died away, and Wolf, in the fraction of ensuing silence, took his wife's arm and walked briskly with her through the gates into the park.

'We shall call our boy Emanuel,' she said, after half an hour of silence. And although Wolf did not entirely agree with this choice of name for his first son, he looked fondly at his wife and put up no resistance.

Eva knew before she reached the nursery that Omi Lise was dead. It was the silence that wound down to her, and through the open door she could see their nanny lying where they'd left her before breakfast. Her head propped up on pillows, her hair tapering like wax across the sheet.

Eva watched her mother as she leant against the bed. Her eyes were not fixed, as she had expected them to be, on Omi's setting face but on Bina, who was crouching pale as a statue by the door. Bina's lips were white and thin, and as Eva tiptoed in her sister shot her an appealing glance. Eva turned away and knelt down by the bed. She blinked and wiped her eyes, and in a horrible transformation she saw Emanuel, his arm bound up, his forehead cold and clammy from his fever.

'Hadn't we better get the doctor?' she had asked.

'Yes, call the doctor,' Bina and Martha had agreed.

But Schu-Schu had shaken them off, ordering instead basins of hot water and bowls of disinfectant. She cleaned the wound carefully and dressed it, bound up the poisoned arm with skilful fingers, and mumbled prayers in her own south German drawl. She organized Schwabish songs in rounds and through two days and nights she set up a rota of willing hands to cool Emanuel's neck and forehead with cold compresses of her own devising.

And then, almost a week early, their mother returned from Rome. 'Bitten by a dog?' She reared up on the doorstep and, knocking strings of flowers and iced flannels to the floor, she had fallen on Emanuel. 'We wanted to look after him ourselves, isn't that right?' The governess attempted to explain the absence of the doctor, appealing to the three girls for their support. But Emanuel had saved her by opening his eyes, stretching his healing arm above his head and insisting he was cured.

Eva knelt down and touched the fingers of Omi's clasped hands. The difference was that Manu had been saved. Omi's hands were cold and, as she pulled away, she heard Bina shuffle to her feet. 'We wanted to look after her ourselves, that was all . . .'

'That was all,' Martha added, with an echo like a sob, and the four women stood unmoving in the room.

On the first Thursday of September, when Herr Baum came to roll their mother's hair, Martha and Eva began to search the Berlin apartment.

'Why in here?' Martha asked, as they slipped inside and closed the door. 'There's not likely to be any trace of Schu in here.'

Eva looked over at the large, leather-topped desk and wondered how it was possible for Emanuel to disappear so completely. 'You'd think he'd be allowed to send one letter out,' she said, 'wherever he is.' And she sat down on the high-backed chair and, picking up his pen, dipped it in the jar of ink. The ink had thinned and hardened with disuse and she had to pierce a thick film with the nib to reach it. Then she set the soft side of the pen against the blotting paper and let it crease a dark dent into the weave.

'Why don't we just stay here until Bina gets back from the hospital?' And Martha stretched out on Emanuel's bed, lying back against a bank of pillows. 'After all, we're not likely to find anything.'

'Yes,' Eva agreed, 'you're right.' But, despite herself, she began, one by one, to pull open the deep drawers of her brother's desk. There was nothing much in them. Notes from studies he had made and the dissected bones of poems pulled apart and examined line by line. There were no hidden envelopes, no scrawled addresses, and as she pulled it, each drawer opened smoothly in her hand.

Martha rolled half-heartedly off the bed to peer beneath it. 'Why would Mama even think of hiding anything in here?' Having reassured herself of this, she settled down in comfort, folded her arms and stared stubbornly at the ceiling.

Eva found a small iron key in one of the inbuilt compartments of the desk. She tried it in the lock of each drawer and found that it turned with a smooth, identical click. How unlike Emanuel not to have a secret, and she frowned in disappointment as she thought of her own elaborate hoard of treasure suspended safely in mid-air. She let her fingers run in and out of the tiny range of boxes, all dusted and clear with polish, pulling out small objects as she came upon them. A penknife, a faded pebble, and in one, a heavy red and yellow rose picked while still in bud. Eva held the rosebud in her hands, staring into the oval mouth of leaves, and thought of the thin petals she had sent to him in letters, glued so delicately to the borders of each page. Would he be wearing them sewn into his clothes, laced against the Siberian winds with ink and faded flowers? She shook her head and replaced the rose.

Martha had drifted off into a fitful sleep, her feet twitching back and forth to the rhythm of a waltz. 'One two three,' her mouth moved sleepily.

Eva shook her shoulder. 'Come on, we must look in one

more room before Baum drinks his schnapps and Bina arrives home.' Martha sat up, and wiped a tiny trickle of saliva from her cheek.

They closed the door with careful fingers and tiptoed off along the corridor. 'Ssh,' they hissed, stepping lightly over carpets, 'ssh.'

Then Eva stopped and, with an amused smile, took her sister's arm. 'Why are we whispering?' she whispered. And they both began to laugh.

'Stop acting so suspiciously,' Martha scolded her in turn, and they were about to go more noisily on their way when they heard the twittering voice of old Herr Baum call out from behind the drapes.

'Can it be the charming Fräuleins Belgard?' He swung open the door, a brush in his hand and a cluster of pins rustling in the pocket of his apron.

'Come in for a moment,' Marianna called, 'and say good afternoon to our dear friend.' Seeing no way to avoid it, the two girls stepped inside where they resigned themselves to lingering for another hour while their mother's hairdresser regaled them with local news and gossip, all sweetly and discreetly wrapped, interspersed only with a regular shower of compliments thrown over their two heads.

It was after six when the apartment door banged shut and they heard Bina's footsteps in the hall. Herr Baum peeled the cloth from Marianna's shoulders and folded it carefully before placing it in his bag. 'How fortunate. I shall have the opportunity to greet yet another of my favourite ladies.' He gave the gleaming head of his most regular customer one last, loving glance.

Marianna escorted Herr Baum to the door and Eva and Martha trailed along behind. 'Good evening.' Bina came politely forward, flashing searching looks over his shoulder. Eva and Martha dropped their gaze. 'Well, most likely we will see you again next week.' She turned away from him in an attempt to catch her sisters as they backed hastily along the corridor.

'Next week, then.' Marianna rested her hand on the latch of

the door, and as Eva hurried away she heard Herr Baum shuffle his feet and mumble something uneasy and apologetic about a small matter of outstanding credit.

'So?' Bina caught them in the drawing room, lounging on the sofa. Eva held a cushion against her for protection. 'There's nothing there,' she said. 'We've made a thorough inspection of the whole apartment, and there was nothing there.'

Martha glanced from her to Bina, and decided to avoid a fight. 'Mama isn't hiding anything,' she agreed, and Bina, furious, sank down beside them.

At first Bina insisted on reading Schu's last words aloud at intervals throughout each week. She kept her sisters cold and shivering at the far end of her bed, hoping to intensify the letter's contents, and to cancel out the presence of their mother, who still came in to wish them all goodnight. But it was not long before Eva led Martha in a small revolt, in which they lay like hedgehogs under down and pretended to be asleep when Bina called to them.

'Of course we won't forget her.' They sighed, huffing and struggling into their mother's choice of clothes, and they glared at Bina behind her back for holding out so little faith in them.

'It is very modern not to have a governess,' the other girls at school insisted. 'We're doing everything we can to rid ourselves of ours.' But the Samson sisters wrote that they were quite shaken by news of Fräulein Schulze's sudden dismissal, especially in such uncertain times, and that they couldn't imagine what Frau Belgard could be thinking of.

Marianna watched her husband, nodding and frowning over his newspaper, and had to stop herself from wondering who he was. 'Do something, why can't you?' she muttered, through clenched teeth, her head trembling with the effort not to shout, and although at times she caught the unfairness of her thoughts, she couldn't find it in her to forgive him.

'I think, if you don't mind,' he mumbled, 'I won't be home for lunch today.'

Marianna caught her cold eyes in the mirror, waiting for a further explanation. 'If that suits you, of course,' she agreed, when nothing more was said, and she freed a coil of dark brown hair, letting it spring out of its comb.

She turned to him. She held out her hands, palms upwards, and opened her eyes wide. 'Soon there won't be any lunch to come home to. Have you any idea what it costs to find enough food to feed this family? I can't survive indefinitely with so little money. I don't see what you expect me to do.'

Wolf looked at her without an answer. He was quite convinced she knew that small amounts of gold had been removed by him each month from the safe behind the airing cupboard. Four squat boxes, one for each of their children, which had been growing in the dark, birthday by birthday, relative by relative, over the years.

Marianna sighed, and Wolf felt tempted to dig into his pocket for the key. He could skim it at her across the carpet and let her remove the next few coins herself. 'I will do what I can,' he said, and he reached over for the corner of her dressing gown, rubbing his finger down frayed satin and twisting it round his finger like a ring.

The Samson sisters arrived one afternoon to ask after Emanuel. Bina was on duty at the hospital and Martha had gone with the maid to queue for butter. Eva brought the girls into the drawing room where she'd been laying out new plans for her and Emanuel's dream home. She'd laid foundations for the ground floor and was working on the bedrooms. She'd split the attic into two and given them a bedroom each with no room for any guests. People may visit, they'd both decided, but only for an afternoon.

Angelika and Julika sat opposite while Eva shuffled her papers out of sight. 'There is still no news,' she told them quickly, hoping to get the subject over with. And the two girls smiled and nodded, while, Eva felt sure, suppressing some new, exciting news about themselves. She couldn't think of anything to say. She ran silently through stories, old or overheard, that might pass as her own to entertain them, and then just as she was sure they were about to burst and tell her everything, she heard her mother step into the hall.

'How are you?' They both rose in one sympathetic gesture, and Marianna set down a jug of bitter-smelling coffee. She poured it out with an apology, and as they sipped, another silence grew.

'Mama.' Eva turned towards her in a flash of inspiration. 'Mama, could you tell us about your gambling days?'

Marianna blushed. The gambling story was a favourite of Wolf's and until now she'd never been called upon to tell it. 'It was so long ago, you can't be interested?' But both Samson girls set down their cups expectantly folding their hands as they prepared to listen.

'Well, it was when my mother was still alive,' Marianna told them, 'and let me say, it was only one gambling day. At Monte Carlo.' She settled into her seat. 'I was eighteen when I set off on my honeymoon and at every hotel on our route there was a letter waiting from my mother who was most concerned about me. She even wrote to one hotel to request that the room be heated to fourteen degrees for our arrival as she did not want her only daughter, or her new son-in-law, to catch a chill. But for all her forethought we were still shown into an icy room – which I noticed had the number fourteen marked clearly on the door.' The sisters laughed, their eyes floating into the future.

'When we arrived at Monte Carlo there was an extremely frantic letter full of descriptions of men whose lives had been ruined by gambling at the casinos. She had read these reports in the paper. One man, apparently, had lost his entire fortune and was found hanging below a bridge, while another became so embroiled in debt that he never dared return home and was thought by his family to be wandering like a tramp through Switzerland. "Please, my dear Marianna, I beg you, use your influence to keep Wolfgang away from the casinos."

'I showed this letter to my new husband. "Read it very carefully," I urged him. "It does seem worrying." But Wolf laughed and said he'd already made plans for us both to go that night to the most famous casino in the town. "It's all right," he reassured me. "Everything of value is locked in the hotel safe and the money I'll bring with me, I shall be quite prepared to lose." He told me to put away my mother's letter and to get ready for that night.

'By the time we arrived at the casino I was very excited and longing to see inside. "Do you have a passport with you?" the manager asked, having taken a note of our names and address. No, we didn't have passports. "Do you have any proof of your identity?" Wolf searched through the pockets of his jacket. No. We had nothing to prove who we were. "Well, I'm afraid," the manager informed us, "we will not be able to allow you to come in."

'"But we are on our honeymoon," Wolf protested. "My wife has been looking forward to this for several weeks." But the manager only looked at us sadly and repeated the rules of the casino. Suddenly I remembered my mother's letter. It was in my purse where I had folded it away. I pulled it out and showed it to him, "Herr and Frau Belgard," he read, and in an instant we were inside, walking up the steps to the roulette tables where Wolf won enough money to buy me a white feather boa and a parasol.' Angelika and Julika leant forwards, smiling in perfect joy. 'And with the rest of the winnings we bought my mother some Swiss chocolate, and for years after she insisted it was the best she'd ever tasted.'

Eva watched her mother's laughing face. 'Can I pour you

another cup of this disgusting coffee?' Marianna asked, but the girls stood up to go. They left messages for Bina and Martha and, without having had a chance to commiserate at any length over Emanuel, the Samsons walked out into the street.

CHAPTER 14

My mother was the owner of a tiny garden, two floors down and reached through someone else's hall. There was a plum tree in the centre and a small polythene pond. While we talked she pulled up stems of elder, tugging at the roots with her bare hands.

'Well, I hope Mike is contributing.'

'Yes,' I said. 'He sends me money every so often.'

A root cracked out of the earth and almost shot her backwards. 'You should insist on something definite, a regular allowance.'

'Oh, Mum.'

'Take him to court.' She was fuelling to be angry. 'Force him to pay you proper maintenance.'

'It's only been three months.' When she sat down beside me, rubbing the dirt from her hands on to her shorts, I argued, 'I don't remember you taking my father to court.'

'Of course I didn't. That's why I'm concerned.' And with one muddy finger she lifted the corner of her grandson's hat. 'I was young and stupid,' she said.

'Well, now I'm young and stupid too.'

'No,' she insisted, 'you're not allowed to be.'

'Oh, Mum.' She was right. Twenty-seven wasn't young. 'It's just so difficult . . .'

'It's always difficult.'

'Well, you know . . . with him not wanting to have a baby, being so clear . . .'

'You think your father –' And she stopped herself in time. 'Well, let's face it, he wasn't down on his knees begging for another child. And now,' she tried not to look hurt, 'he sees more of you than I do.'

'Oh, Mum, that isn't true.' For a while we sat in silence, squeezed together on the tiny patch of lawn. 'It's just you work so hard.'

'Yes.' She smiled, indulgent. In the last few years my mother's life had been transformed. She'd given up the part-time jobs, the cleaning and childminding that had seen us through, and had learnt how to lay out artwork on computers. She spent weeks bubbling and absorbed, laying the flowers she'd always loved to draw one upon another, swirling them round into patterns, and always with another commission looming up.

'How's the painting going?' she asked eventually, and I told her that Sonny had almost outgrown his Babygro. The more he grew the less there was of me. 'It looks finished but, of course, I don't like to mention it.' And we both laughed, glad to have something to share.

There was a painting that still hung on my father's wall. It was of my mother, her limbs waxy and white, her hair like silk along her back. 'You were lucky,' I told her, 'to be immortalized before realism set in,' and I thought of my thick legs, blue-veined and raw around the knee. 'Even Sonny looks as if he might be going in for the Middleweight Championship of Great Britain,' and I glanced at the uncurling fingers of his fists.

'Oh, let me hold him,' she said, and I moved the bundle of his body over to her lap.

'Anyway,' I stretched my back and arms, 'Dad is paying me to sit, and I just got a repeat cheque for that advert I did last year.'

'Goo goo goo,' my mother wasn't listening, 'who's a beautiful little boy? Who's a gorgeous little dote?' And she squealed with delight when Sonny opened his gummy mouth and smiled back at her. 'Isn't he clever?' she exclaimed. 'Isn't he extraordinary?'

And I had to remind her through my pride that all babies smiled at around six weeks.

'And there might be some family money, you know, on Dad's side.'

But she was playing peekaboo with Sonny's bonnet, leaning him up against her knees and beaming victory each time he laughed.

'Dad.' I rang the bell again and called to him through the door. I'd brought Sonny over on the bus, enjoying the admiring looks and the repeated questions from old ladies. 'Is he good?' 'Oh, yes, he's very good.' I beamed down proudly at my boy.

It wasn't like my father to be late. He rarely left his studio except to shop for food, and then usually he went out in the early morning before any of us would sit. I rang the bell again just to be sure, and as I turned, a car slowed in the street. I saw my father, small and nervous, leaping out. 'I'm sorry,' he mouthed to me as he slammed the door, but the driver of the car had rushed round on to the pavement to intercept him. He was a small, plump man with round Mongolian eyes, and as he talked he nodded earnestly, making elaborate gestures with his hands. I stayed watching as my father backed away, giving out answers of a word. The car was double parked and people began to hoot and jeer behind them. 'All right then, fine,' I heard my father say, and with a quick shake of his head the man ran back to his side of the car and slipped into his seat.

'I'm so sorry.' He drew his keys in a long line from his pocket.

'So who was that?'

My father rolled his eyes. 'My cousin Johann.'

'John Godber?' Now I wished I'd gone over to be introduced. My uncle, I wondered, or my second cousin, and I tried to recall with more detail exactly how he'd looked. 'Was that your Aunt Bina's son?'

He winced. 'The terrible Aunt Bina. You know she made my mother's life a misery?'

'How come?'

'Just pettiness and jealousy.' He had to think for a minute. 'Yes, when my grandmother lived with us in the house in London, my mother had to pretend to hate her.'

'But I thought you said she did dislike her. They all did.'

'No,' he said, 'I don't think I meant that. But certainly my awful Aunt Bina really loathed her. Well, really, she disliked just about everyone.'

'And Johann's father? Who was he? She must have liked him for five minutes at least.'

My father, with an eye for gossip, told me he'd deserted. 'He got as far away as he could – Lapland, I think he may have settled in.'

'That's ridiculous.' I laughed, and watched him while he changed his clothes. He was wearing the suit he'd welcomed Sonny in, grey, with the same black, polished shoes, and as he slung it over a chair, I noticed rainbow welts of paint across his legs. He put on workman's trousers, stiff with oils, and an old shirt, one sleeve torn around the cuff.

'So what did he want, your cousin?' I moved Sonny to my other breast as he wheeled the easel over.

'That bloody house.'

'Gaglow?' I found myself offended. 'Not Gaglow?'

He cranked the handle up to bring the picture into line. 'I should never have got involved.' He stamped hard on a tube of white to force out the thick paint.

'What's happened now?'

'Well . . .' He was eyeing Sonny with his head on one side. 'Johann wants to sell it.' He began mixing new white into green. I noticed for the first time how the towelling of the Babygro had faded with the wash. 'And the maddening thing is that all sorts of people have to agree. Someone wants it rented out so it will be worth more in ten years, and there's one old bat who thinks we should just donate it to the Germans so they don't start thinking badly of us again.' He gasped in open-mouthed amazement. 'Of course, Johann, who must be nearly seventy, would prefer the money now.'

'Is there no one who wants to keep it?' I asked. 'We could use it as a sort of time-share holiday home.' But my father was laying new strokes of thick pale colour and didn't even take the trouble to look up.

'The maddening thing is,' he said, after a while, 'Johann wants me to go out there. There are certain things that need to be sorted out, apparently, although really I can't think what.'

'Can't he go himself?'

'Well, he's already been there once, and he runs some waste-disposal empire, can't always get away.'

He worked on in silence, and then he said, 'After the war, when I was seventeen, Germany had to make reparations to all the children whose education had been disrupted . . . I remember saying to my father then that I didn't want their stinking money, and I have to say I feel the same way now.'

'But, really, it's not their money –'

'My father said, "Look, if you don't take it, all the more for them."'

'And did you?'

He didn't answer.

'I suppose you could take it and then just give the money away.' I thought of myself in a cottage in the country. I would choose one without too many stairs with a flat lawn on which Sonny could play. We could have a tree for climbing and a fence around a deep, cool lake where, once a year, we'd skate over the ice.

'Yes, that's what I thought. I took almost all of it and put it on a dog. Well, the rotten thing came in, and so with the winnings I went out and bought myself ten boxes of the most expensive paints.'

'You tried,' I told him quickly. 'What more could you do?'

'Yes, and anyway I made sure to use only the winning money

on the paint. The rest,' he said, after a minute, 'I just let dribble away.'

I kept my head down while he worked on and on, and thought of our three mothers, who wouldn't have cared one way or another where the reparation money had come from.

'You have to understand that I was very young,' he said, as if he'd heard me, and he stamped hard on another tube of paint, stooping to catch the thick sludge with his knife.

Pam was back in London. She came round on her first day off, radiant in a rose-patterned dress. 'You're looking great,' she told me, grazing my cheek with sugar-candy hair. 'You've lost all your baby fat.'

'It's the stairs,' I told her, 'and rushing round after the great Lord Sonny.'

She looked at him, his wrists and ankles braceleted with fat, his skin thick apricot. 'I can't believe he's yours.' She laughed.

We both peered into his face. 'His eyes could still get lighter,' I said hopefully, and in silence we both wondered about Mike. 'So,' I caught her grinning, 'things are looking up?'

She told me that Bradly Teale had had a change of heart. 'He's really very special,' she said, and I tried to suppress a groan.

We went out for a walk and every twenty yards she stopped to check that her mobile phone was working. 'I thought that was just for me,' I joked, half-heartedly, and she tried to link her arm with mine.

We walked up into Primrose Hill, and just as we stepped on to grass the call she was expecting came ringing through. She turned away from me to talk. 'Of course,' she breathed, 'I'd love to,' and her legs and arms twined and twisted like a colt's. 'No, absolutely that would be fine,' and she murmured on and on seductively for fifteen minutes using a minimum of words. Prickly and hot with irritation, I lifted Sonny out of his pushchair.

'Tonight at eight fifteen, the Ivy,' Pam breezed, and just then I felt a cool wet trickle as Sonny was sick over my shoulder. Pam threw herself down beside me on the grass. 'What now?' But I was dabbing at my shirt with a wet cloth.

'Just wait a minute.' I laid the baby down to change his nappy.

Pam looked on appalled. 'It's non-stop, isn't it?' She lit herself a cigarette.

'Well, it's not as if I've anything else to do.' I rubbed cream on to his bottom. 'My love life's over and so is my career.'

'Don't be ridiculous,' and she reminded me she'd just wasted a month of her life in Leeds, careering round the streets in white high heels, taking orders to keep her hair out of her eyes and not to blink so much. 'At least you've got something real, something permanent.'

'Yes.' I breathed in a trail of her white smoke. 'A job for life.' I looked at Sonny in his clean striped vest.

'Cheer up,' Pam said, forcing me to take her cigarette, and after a few quick puffs I gave in and asked about her man.

'So, come on, is he really awful?'

Pam, thrilled finally to be asked, spent the rest of the afternoon telling me exactly how hopeless he was turning out to be. 'And Mike?' she asked, just as we were parting for the day, but I was much too tired for Mike, so I shook my head and told her I'd heard nothing from him at all.

'I've got some rather creepy news.' It was Kate. 'Guess what? Our mothers have been meeting up regularly for supper.'

'Christ.' It seemed almost incestuous. 'I don't think you should mention it to Dad.' I heard Kate laugh, as if she might just save up the information.

'But, then, maybe that's what they think about us.' It had

never occurred to me before. 'You know, us all being such good friends.'

But Kate insisted it was different. 'We're related, you idiot.'

'Yes, but, then, in a way so are they,' and it suddenly surprised me that they hadn't become friends before.

Natasha rang later, and we had the same conversation, giggling like spies, until it occurred to us that we should have a supper party of our own. 'You'll have to come here,' I said, 'because after nine at night I can't face getting back up my stairs.' It was arranged that on the Thursday after next we'd meet up for a rival supper.

'Can I come?' Pam asked, when I told her, and I tried to explain to her, an only child, that she'd be welcome on any other night. 'Still no news from Mike?' she asked, as if to pay me back, so I told her that actually I'd had a card from him that day.

'Where from?'

I glanced over at the mantelpiece. 'I'll give you a clue,' I told her. 'There's a picture of the Loch Ness monster on the front.'

'He's not in the new series of *Kilmaaric*?'

I wasn't sure.

'I'll find out,' Pam insisted, 'I know a make-up woman whose friend is working on it,' and she rang off.

'Dear Sonny,' Mike had written. 'It's beautiful up here, all purple and blue and smelling of heather. By the time I see you you'll be as big as King Kong, if not my old friend Nessie,' and he'd put two kisses beside the word Dad.

'It's from your daddy,' I held it up to Sonny's face, but the word coiled up inside my mouth and made me blush. Sonny flailed his arms for it, so I put it safely with the others on the mantelpiece.

'Dear Sarah,' Mike wrote the next day, 'Here's something to keep the boy in nappies. The job has all the usual problems, but you know me, it's nice to have something real to complain about. I'd ask you both to come up, but . . .' here he'd scratched something out '. . . you know what these places are like.' And there was some more money, slipped into the paper fold. I lay awake that night, wishing that Mike would stay away for ever, sending sweet-smelling cards while I lived on and on in hope.

'Is there much more to do?' I was unpicking the seams of Sonny's Babygro to let his toes stretch through. The picture was thickening and bending, taking on new meaning with each layer of paint. 'That's better,' I murmured, as his legs eased through and I saw my father eyeing the unused feet. 'Oh, no, don't start adding anything new.' But I raised my voice to turn it into a joke as I saw his shoulders stiffen with intent. He cut a knot of old paint off his palette and flung it to the floor, rinsing off the wood with turps and mixing up a soft fresh mound of oils. 'This suit really is only going to fit him for a few more days,' I protested, 'even without the feet,' but I trailed off as he began to work.

Sonny seemed to have come round to being painted. As soon as we arrived he curved his face towards me, nuzzling my shirt, expecting to be fed, so that I had to sing at him to keep him happy while I took off my clothes. Sometimes while he sucked he looked up at me and smiled and then, very slowly, his eyelids fluttered shut and he sank into a sound, gluttonous sleep. It was almost as if he knew, while we lay there against the flowers, that for hours and hours he had me to himself.

'Apparently,' my father said, 'my mother's brother . . . What was his name?'

'Emanuel?'

'Yes, apparently he was taken prisoner by the Russians. I think he may even have worked in their mines during the war.' He paused, and it occurred to me that he was trying to placate me for these endless extra weeks. 'Anyway, I remember hearing that while he was on a train being transported from one place to another he tried to escape by climbing out of a window. He was just slipping through when the guards caught hold of him.

Instead of pulling him in and punishing him they trapped him there, left him caught up in the window all night, so that his legs were damaged horribly.'

'How terrible.' I shivered at the thought of him hanging head down over the rails while the bone and flesh all buckled up.

'When he did eventually come home he was a broken man.'

'Yes.' I imagined him on his ruined legs, limping through the city of Berlin.

'What do you think?' He stepped back from the easel, and there were two tiny feet, bursting like a strong man's through the cloth.

I sat up to look.

'No,' he shook his head before I'd had a chance to decide, 'it was better as it was.' I lay down again and watched while from memory he tucked the feet back up into their towelling socks.

'So when did he get married?' I asked, when the last pink toe had disappeared from view. 'I mean Emanuel.'

'I think he met some fallen woman roaming round the streets. All I know is that his sisters, well, my mother certainly, never forgave him for the betrayal.'

'Was there someone else he was supposed to marry, then?'

'I don't know. '

'So surely it should be his children, or grandchildren, Emanuel's, who inherit Gaglow?'

'That was the whole point. They didn't have any.'

'Why not?'

'It was her only weapon. The prostitute's. You see, because they all despised her and disapproved of her she vowed never to have any children. I think it was to punish his mother for not giving them a proper wedding.'

'How very strange.'

'Yes,' he had to admit. 'It does sound unlikely.' And he wondered where he could have overheard the story.

'If she'd really wanted children, nothing would have put her off,' and I laid a hand on Sonny's golden head, thinking of all the babies in my hospital. There had been an overflow of boys, fourteen in one weekend, and not a single girl. All the midwives were laughing and exclaiming over it, as each new boy was bundled in, and Pam had hoped, for their sakes, that some of them would turn out to be gay. 'I hope it doesn't mean there's going to be a war in eighteen years,' I'd wondered, and everyone had looked at me alarmed.

CHAPTER 15

Eva lay on the sofa, wrapped in rugs, writing a letter to Emanuel. She couldn't think where to start. Everything that came to her was not to be put down and after half an hour she was still sitting with a blank page and a streak of ink along her thumb. It didn't seem very cheerful to bring up the impending marriage of Angelika Samson to an officer, or their hopeless attempts at finding Fräulein Schulze. Instead she decided to describe the Gaglow gardens, the frostbitten vegetables, dug up too late, and the frozen orchard. She detailed the development of each of the five dogs, and told him how Marianna had brought them back with her to Berlin where she encouraged them to lie under the table, warming her feet and ankles over supper. It was lucky they were such skinny little beasts or their neighbours might be tempted to stew them up for soup, but as it was, she was sure there were few dogs, English or not, that looked less appetizing. She used her bicycle now instead of getting the overcrowded tram to school but was not sure how she'd manage once the roads iced up. She did not mention how their father went in less and less often to the office and how once she had opened the door to his study and found him sitting, hunched in his overcoat, staring into space. Poor Papa, she thought, poor, poor Papa. And something half remembered made her smile.

'What are you writing, you comedian?' Bina nudged her, and Eva tried to slip the letter through her arm.

'It's private.' She proceeded to illustrate the border with small pictures of their future house, joined by smoking chimneys and an inky chain of flowers.

Equal amounts of money had been lifted from the girls' three boxes, and until now only Emanuel's, heavier through time than the others, had remained intact. Marianna slid it to the front and opened it. Inside lay a mass of overlapping coins, glimmering up at her like smiles. Some she recognized. The gold her mother had presented on the Sunday of his birth and then the ten-mark piece given by Wolf's father a month before he died. She dipped her hands against the metal, letting her fingers choose a medium-sized coin, searching for one whose source was not so sacred. Marianna picked out the most recent addition, presented by relatives on Emanuel's last official birthday, over two years before. She held it in her palm and thought of all the extra food and clothes that it might bring him if she wired the money into the unknown. But then, at the last moment, she slipped the coin back in and, without allowing time for any thought, she opened another box, nearest to her elbow, and scooped up two gold pieces. She glanced at them as she banged shut the safe and saw, to her relief, that they were not of any real sentimental value but had been a present from Aunt Cornelia the week Bina passed her exams.

As the days grew colder the girls began to congregate for comfort on their governess's old bed. This narrow room was the easiest to warm and if they shut the door into the nursery they could heat it with their breath. Martha had found a basket of old wool, stuffed years before by Fräulein Milner into a top cupboard. She had chosen four short needles and begun a rather lumpy sock. Eva glanced over as it grew, white and lopsided, with dropped stitches and laced with ropy ladders where she had not seen to pick them up. 'Into the wood goes the huntsman' and she thought of Millie and her thin lips mouthing the lines over like a prayer.

'Not on a level with a Samson sock.' Eva was unable to resist mentioning that it looked a little draughty.

'Well, just you try,' Martha sulked. 'I'm taking important time out from my studies to do this. Making an effort for the war.' In the same instant, both Bina and Eva lunged for the basket where several other sets of needles were buried. The wool was mainly white but a few strands of green and red had become entangled in the skeins and Eva scooped them out and wound them into balls over her hand. Martha had to cast on for each of them but soon they were sitting in a row, their feet wrapped in eiderdowns and chanting out the Rabbit Song to the clicking of their needles.

On her way through to her own bedroom Marianna stopped to listen at the door. The sound of their three voices striking out on a new row made her feel so lonely that she hurried back to find her husband. She had left him slouched over the table, his grey head on his hand, but now, just when she felt able to offer up some words of comfort, she found that he had gone.

On Christmas morning Eva woke early. Her stomach ached with hunger and she crept out of bed, intending to pull on her coat and boots and slip out for a walk to pass the time till breakfast. She padded down the corridor in the socks in which she'd slept and pulled open the door to the airing cupboard. Out of habit she still kept her outside clothes in here, although now instead of finding them warmed through and dry, they were as cold and damp as when she'd slung them in the day before. The airing cupboard was a tiny room, which housed the boiler. It had no window but a slatted bench for sitting down to tug off boots, exchanging them for the slippers that were stored in racks below.

Eva reached up for her coat. She pulled it on, shivering from the clammy lining and then, as she turned, feeling for her hat, she stumbled against a shoe. A black and polished shoe that did not slide away as she'd expected. Eva froze. She could sense someone, hunched, not wishing to be seen, and with a gulp of courage she looked up into her father's face. He didn't turn away or move, but continued to sit, his knees pulled in, his hands hanging in his lap. He looked large and broken, broken just above the hip. Without changing his expression, he dropped his eyes again to a worn place on the floor.

Eva backed out and closed the door. She stood rigid in the hall, unable to stop herself from worrying how she'd find the courage to go back in and get her boots. Eventually she wrapped her shoes around with scarves and stepped out into the street.

The morning was still dark and her feet sank into a soft new fall of snow. People passed her in the gloom like ghosts, only their bones and shadows taking shape, and a bicycle, the spokes of which picked up the moonlight, whistled by. If only the airing cupboard had been warm, she could make more sense of it, and as she walked further and further away from home she wondered if she should go back, place her mittened hand in his, kiss the bent mass of his head and urge him to come out.

It was light when Eva arrived home, breathing cold air and with a red circle on each cheek. The family were up and drinking the remains of real coffee that, by some miracle, Marianna had managed to gather up for Christmas Eve to eat with poppy seed and almond cake. Wolf sat at the head of the long table, a hand cradling his cup. He looked up as she came in, and nothing in his face betrayed him.

'Eva,' her mother frowned, 'don't come in here with your damp clothes.' With a falling heart Eva trudged back to the airing cupboard and inched open the door. She unwound her shoes and placed them neatly in a box, avoiding the corner where her boots still sat and running her fingers along a row of gloves and scarves that dangled unevenly from pegs.

*

For almost a week Wolf did not leave the house, and Eva, having little else to do, kept a low eye on him. She sat and watched him read his paper, nodding into nervous sleep behind it, and saw that rather than becoming large he had actually, in recent months, begun to shrink. When he finally went out, Eva found that, without intending it, she was following him. She watched him pull on his heavy coat and a moment after ran to slip her own feet into boots, dragging on her hat and scarf and darting out into the street where she had to slow her pace so as not to overtake him. He headed at first in the direction of his office, nodding and smiling at his neighbours, but instead of going in he passed right by and walked towards the Tiergarten.

Eva followed in a lonely circumnavigation of its paths, noticing as she walked behind that her father kept his arms stiffly by his sides and never raised a hand to wipe away the snow that blew into his face. She imagined it banking up against his eyebrows and the rough hair of his upper lip; when he turned suddenly and she caught sight of him, she could only see a white shape between his collar and his hat. At first Eva made an effort to keep her distance and to hide herself as much as possible from view, but she soon realized that his mood was one of much too much absorption to notice her and she began to walk quite openly behind.

Once, he stopped and, without stooping to wipe the wood, sat down on a long, snow-covered bench, crossing his arms over his chest, and stared blindly forward. Eva could not follow him in this. It already made her shiver to think of the slowly melting snow seeping into his clothes and the chill that must be travelling up his spine. She lowered her head and walked miserably past. She left the Tiergarten, with the intention of going back in half an hour to check on him, but as she walked out onto the street she passed a woman whose figure made her start. She did not catch her eye but from a heavily cloaked shoulder and the smooth, freckled side of her face she had been startled into thinking she had seen Fräulein Schulze. Eva stopped and wiped the wet snow from her nose. All the warmth, collected in the lining of her clothes, had drained away, and without looking back, she began to run, skidding and slipping through the streets.

When Eva arrived home she found the apartment deserted. Everyone was always busy now, except for her, and for company she lured the dogs with tiny drops of bread, and helped them clamber on to Schu-Schu's old bed. She wrapped them up in folds of eiderdown, tucking in their velvet paws and making towelling cowls for the moleskin of their ears. Once they were all settled, she decided against picking up her half-finished sock, and instead started with fresh needles and her own design to make up an extra thick wool helmet, a balaclava in double stocking-stitch, with only the smallest slits for mouth and eyes. She started on the neck in mossy green and decided that if the thing became too menacing she could embroider a thick smile around the mouth and place two small rosebuds on each ear.

Marianna continued to send Emanuel small sums of money. She took gold randomly from any box and had it wired through to the bureau for the welfare of prisoners of war. She never heard whether he received the funds and sometimes in a desperate hope of shaking news from him, she sent twice the amount.

Marianna had an overwhelming desire to return to Gaglow. She knew it would be impossibly cold and closed up now in February, but she thought at least she would be able to make a wood fire in the grate and let the starving whippets out to search for food. She looked at Wolf, undressing in slow motion, and decided against asking him. Her children, she supposed, would refuse to go there with her, Bina on principle and Martha, caught up in her own world, would be incapable of taking such a decision.

Marianna put her elbows on the dressing table and smiled as she remembered Eva, tiptoeing about the house, darting into rooms, ducking out from behind doors and always with her mouth pursed and her eyebrows raised as if convinced she must be going about unnoticed. Surely Eva would not mind being taken out of school. She often complained about the point-lessness of going now that so many classes were massed together in a single room. Sometimes, it seemed, there were so many different groups that everyone was attempting to learn some-thing quite separate and the teachers spent their time conferring on quite how they should proceed. When the first freezing weather hit them, Eva had been asked to take some fuel with her to school each day, and Marianna watched her walk out into the street with a lump of coal like a potato wrapped up in her hand. But recently the caretaker had refused to allow her any more, and she set off now, like most girls of her age, with only books and a morning snack of dried white apple rings stuffed into her satchel.

Without mentioning her plans to anyone Marianna began slowly to prepare. She would have to take the train and find someone to drive her to the house. Gruber, although nearing fifty, had gone off to the war. He'd been put into the same regiment as his poor nephew, dead over a year, and it made Marianna wonder when they would come looking for her husband. She intended to live at Gaglow as much as possible in secret. She would not contact the village girls who usually opened up the house, dusting and beating and clattering through the kitchen. She would manage as far as possible to take care of herself, and conjured up a happy vision of the summers spent with her own mother, living alone for two whole weeks while her father took his holiday by the sea.

Eva's eyes narrowed when Marianna told her, and she twisted round quickly to see if they were being overheard. 'We'll go off, just the two of us.' Marianna lowered her voice and Eva, finding they were alone, gave her a smile of such complicity it opened up her heart.

Eva was left with how to break the news. 'Do you know Mama is planning to desert us?' she said one evening as they lay curled together in their usual place, their hands too cold for knitting. Martha shook her head and gasped incredulously, although she'd heard a murmur of the news from Dolfi.

'She hates us all, I always knew it.' Bina laughed.

Martha added, 'Poor Papa,' simply out of habit.

Eva took on a thoughtful air with her head a little to one side. 'What can she possibly be planning?' She closed her eyes in an attempt to fathom out the mystery. Bina tapped her nails against each other as if she almost knew.

'Maybe . . .' Eva started. She could feel the others looking at her. 'Maybe I could find a way of going with her.' There was a pause and then, to shake off any lingering suspicions, she added, 'Mama could hardly refuse, and if she does, well, then, we'll know it's something really serious.'

Eva had never seen Gaglow at this time of year. It was a crystal palace with intricate designs of frost chiselled across each window, which gave the rooms inside a magic feel as if they were encased in gingerbread, each square frame latticed with angelica and laced between with water-sugar panes. She cupped her hands over her mouth and blew, watching as the moisture cleared a space on the glass. Outside, the lawns were rolled in snow and the heaped banks of the garden looked quite plain against the intricate designs of frost.

The five dogs circled round, still nervous from the journey. Their mouths hung open and large gasps of steam rose curling from their tongues. Marianna led them through the house, past the draped piano and the covered rugs, and let them out into the corridor where the marguerites had shrivelled from neglect. Their claws rattled as they ran, growling in excitement, lifting up their ears as they caught a glimpse of Eva spinning, with her arms outstretched, back and forth across the tiled hall. She kept her face tilted to the octagonal ceiling only remembering from time to time, as she passed the open door into her mother's study, to dart her eyes inside.

Marianna laughed, and patted the cool coats of the dogs. 'Come on,' she called, and raced with them to the back door where they streaked out into the snow to hunt for rabbits.

Marianna built a fire in her study with branches of damp pine. It took an impossibly long time to catch and in her effort to encourage it she tore page after page of carefully stored dates and figures from the notebook on her desk and crushed them into kindling. The fire smoked and sighed and then the flames licked into the dry centre of the wood and, sizzling with shooting sparks, roared up the chimney in a burst of colour.

'Eva!' she called in her excitement. 'Quick!' And she ran up the back stairs shouting urgently for her daughter to come down.

Eva dropped the treasure box she'd brought with her from Berlin into the string cradle underneath her bed, and, with icy fingers, pulled the covers down on either side. Her mother's voice was high and full of hurry, and Eva almost tripped over her own feet as she clattered down the stairs. 'What is it?' She burst into the study.

Marianna pointed to the hearth. The flames were tulip-shaped, leaping up around the sticks of pine, and as they watched the fire cracked and sprinkled into stars. 'Isn't it beautiful?' she gasped, and Eva saw that she had two streaks of soot across her face and that she was smiling like a child. 'Come and get warm,' Marianna urged, and Eva dropped to her knees and held up her hands to the heat.

'It's warmer in here already,' Marianna said, and she pushed two chairs as close in to the grate as they would go. Eva sank into one and uncurled her frozen toes. She stretched her legs and, resting her heels on the ridged back of a dog, fell almost immediately asleep.

*

Eva and Marianna spent most of each day foraging for food. There was still a quantity of old supplies stored in the kitchen cupboards, and they set out together through the icy maze of the ground floor to select a jar of pickled beetroot and to wonder and discuss how it might transform itself into a meal. Eva had never seen her mother look so well. Her eyes glowed with the purpose of each day, and the pallor of her face was livened by their forays and the daily shovelling outside for food. They found a hoe leaning up against an out-house and while Marianna dug into the ground Eva turned it over, chopping it and occasionally rolling out a frozen turnip or the blighted mess of a potato. Sometimes they would lurch excitedly upon a piece of stone or the root of some forgotten tree and then, unable to control themselves, they would lean, convulsed by laughter, and howl over the wooden handles of their spades.

Eva wrapped herself in furs to climb the back stairs to the nursery. She rifled through the contents of her wooden box, sorting and inspecting her most recent treasure – the skeleton of a leaf and the high white dome of the first snowdrop. She perched on the window-sill and, looking out over the frosted garden, she began to write.

Dear Manu,
I am learning how to cook and build a fire so that we won't need any servants. Maybe just someone for the laundry, unless the river curved right in beside the house and we could peg the clothes with rocks and let them wash themselves. I'm enclosing drawings of the top floor of our house and as you can see we have three long windows each, with a bath under one and a bed below the other.
I've been wanting to ask you for some time, do you remember when Bina was first born. Did she have soft brown hair, and if so, how did it change? Slowly so you'd hardly notice, or overnight?
Your devoted and impatient sister, Eva.

*

162

One morning Eva woke to find the frost had thawed and warm sunshine glinted on to stone. The dogs twitched and snuffled in their sleep and when Eva stirred they raised their noses at her. 'Come on,' she whispered, not wanting to wake her mother, curled comfortably in her chair, and she held the door for them as they filed politely out. They ran through the slippery grass to see if, after one warm night, any of the seeds they'd dibbed into the earth were showing signs of sprouting, carrots, spinach, and a spiral of radishes, which Marianna said were the easiest things to grow. She noticed that the oldest dog was running with a limp, and she had to keep stopping to let it catch up. They trotted through the orchard, past the empty stables and round the side of the house until, exhausted and unfamiliarly warm, she lay down on the bench that curved against the ice-house wall. 'Poor hungry dogs,' she crooned, helping the last one to climb up on to the bench, 'living off mashed bread and apple cores,' and she let her hands droop over their tapered waists. She began to think of things that they might like to eat. Liver and bright red cuts of meat and, as she closed her eyes, a bowl of chocolate heaped with cream swam into her view. She stretched out, her face tilted to the sun and fell asleep dreaming of a mountain made from soft white rolls so that her stomach rumbled noisily and sharp juices pulled and stretched her jaw.

When she woke, the dogs had wandered off. She sat up and tried to catch the images she'd had of peaches, bright orange and the colour of Fräulein Schulze's hair. 'If you don't want them, I'll eat them all myself,' she'd shouted. And then the fruit had turned into a bowl of marbles and she was swallowing them while Schu-Schu spun round and round the room.

Everywhere the frost was melting, and the sound of trickling water made her desperate for a drink. She was about to run back to the house when she remembered where she was. Jumping up she pushed the heavy door into the cellar of the ice-house and, packing down the insulating straw, felt for the pick that hung against the wall. Another door forced the passage back upon itself, and a third was divided into sections so that Eva had only to lift the centre panel to slip through to the store of ice. For all the freezing weather the ice was low, and she had to climb down into the pit to get at it. It lay like boulders moulded together with fine cracks and, careful not to trap her fingers on the sticky surface, she splintered off a piece and, juggling it in the folds of her skirt, backed out into the warmth, sealing the doors as she passed through them.

She sat picking straw out of her clothes and dripping the ice against her mouth. She could see her mother shaking rugs by the back door, her hair covered by a scarf, and she wondered what the local children would think now if they could see her. She was making use of the first spring day, beating and dusting and hanging out their clothes to air, and as Eva watched she had an idea for a treat. She'd have to work hard and start immediately but she could make her an Easter present out of ice. She'd carve an ice sculpture, moulding it into the figure of a dog and present it to her as a centrepiece for supper. She'd need to hack one large block for a trunk, and she was sure if it was possible to form the curved neck of a swan, it must be a simple matter of patience to chisel a whippet's spindly tail.

Eva had been working hard for several days when Bina and Martha arrived. They stepped down from their cart in a cloud of city air, and when Eva and Marianna ran out to greet them they were stopped short by their astonished looks. Eva glanced in confusion at her mother and noticed for the first time how her hair, piled under a fur hat, was ragged with loose strands. There were spider's legs of silver running through it and the thicker width of these white hairs gave her a dishevelled look.

'How's Papa?' Eva asked, terrified to see he wasn't with them, but Bina only leant over to stare at the tattered ribbon hanging from her matted plaits, pursing her lips as if she hadn't heard.

'Shall we go inside?' Their mother smiled, and turned away as if nothing in the world had changed. She picked up the limping dog like a warm basket of sticks and, with the others prancing excitedly before them, they walked through the closed up and deserted rooms.

'What's wrong with her?' Martha whispered, and Eva explained how her back legs had stiffened with old age, forcing her to shuffle like a rabbit.

'No, you idiot,' Bina cut in. 'Mama.' Eva, unsure what she was after, hurried on in silence. 'Where are we going?' Bina protested, flapping after her and grumbling that it was far colder in this monstrous house than it ever was outside.

'Mama, where are you taking us?' Martha asked, when they had reached the octagonal hall. Marianna didn't answer but instead threw open the door to her study. A roll of smoke curled out, clearing to show the table lit up with a row of candles and the best plates carefully set out.

Marianna had spent the entire day preparing. With Eva's help she'd rolled her desk into the centre of the room, had packed the pens and blotters to one side and spread it with a dark green cloth. They had worked together to push the chairs out from the fire and packed their clothes below the window-seats. The ragged blankets of the dogs were shaken out and folded and then placed neatly round the room as little oblong mats.

'Good God,' Bina snorted, 'just look at this place.' And Eva noticed her boots ranged before the fire and a string of drying, smoky vests and handkerchiefs hanging from a beam. Martha sneezed and her eyes were turning pink around the rims.

'I suppose it is a bit smoky in here,' Eva agreed and she stared down at the heaps of soft white ash piled beside the hearth.

Marianna turned her back on them. 'I can offer you fried potatoes cooked with rosemary,' she said, lifting the lid grandly off a cracked tureen, 'or fried potatoes cooked with thyme,' and the others, eager for this luxury, stopped staring and settled round the table while Eva reluctantly opened a window, letting in a fresh cold stream of air.

*

Eva had almost turned blue in her efforts to perfect the statue. She'd started off with great success, welding on ears with salted drops of water and chiselling a perfect snout, but the legs were causing problems, so long and thin, and suddenly so many of them, and the tail had proved virtually impossible. After each attempt she wrapped her work in reeds and laid it on the diminishing pile of ice. It was waiting now, its tail alongside it, to be presented to her mother.

'Where are you going?' Bina asked, as she jumped up from the table, but Eva slipped away without answering and ran out into the garden before it grew too dark to see. She opened up one door after another, and it was only as she squatted over the clear ice body, attempting for the last time to weld the tail, that she remembered she should not be showering gifts upon her mother.

'Eva, Eva,' she could hear her sisters calling, 'where are you?' In a sudden panic she threw the unconvincing dog back on to the ice and, shaking the reeds and straw out of her skirt, ran back towards the house.

'So what have you found out?' Bina asked, once they were ensconced in separate beds up in the nursery.

'Found out?' Just in time Eva remembered the point of her extended stay.

'Poor Eva,' Martha murmured, her eyes still red from the clinging smoke, and Eva turned over on her side to face them with a martyred air.

'It has not been easy.'

'Well, as for us, we haven't heard a word,' Bina hissed, and it took Eva a moment to remember whose words it was they'd spent the winter waiting for.

Eva curled up, clasping her knees and pressing them against her chest. She tried to re-create the comfort of her chair. It had seemed unnatural to retire after supper and leave her mother on the stairs. They'd exchanged shy smiles and nodded a goodnight, and Eva had been bustled off to hear the news and gossip of the last two months.

The next morning Eva found her mother sitting on the ice-house steps. The door to the cellar was wide open and the hinged panel behind it had flapped down. Eva brought her hands up to her mouth, remembering.

'It's all right,' Marianna insisted, before she could confess. 'I'm sure it's only children. They won't mean any harm. Just children from the village.' But there were new deep lines around her mouth and the brightness of her eyes was strained. 'I hardly dare look to see what they've done to the vegetable garden.' She sighed, and then as if to herself she murmured that she'd never felt completely welcome here, not really.

'Mama.' Eva felt she must explain, but Marianna stood up and, clicking her tongue for the dogs, strode off towards the house.

Eva could hear the ice melting even before she reached it. The rocks had thawed on contact with warm air and, like a spring, it seeped and dripped into the ground. The reeds in which she'd wrapped her dog had uncurled over the surface, and there was the whippet's tail, broken into pieces and returning to a mush of snow.

Bina was greatly excited by the news. 'Vandals from the village! Smashing in the door!' And she hugged herself and shivered.

'But couldn't the rest of the ice be saved?' Martha asked. 'If the doors were closed immediately?'

Bina pointed out to her that rubbish had been thrown into the pit. 'Reeds and straw and God knows what else and now the ice wouldn't be worth having.'

'It's her own fault,' Bina kicked at a trail of loose straw, 'for being so high and mighty. Pretending to be some kind of baroness and allowing the local people to come up and entertain her.'

'Schu-Schu always said she shouldn't have made Papa take the house,' Martha remembered. 'She always said it was bad luck.'

'And she wanted him to keep the land – imagine,' Bina added.

'Couldn't it have been the wind that blew open the door?' Eva asked, loyalty pushed down in her chest. 'I'm sure I was woken last night by some kind of storm.' But Bina only scowled at her, shaking her head in mock exasperation, and asking what other patriotic German woman gave up her own food for a crowd of English dogs.

The vegetable garden was in perfect order. Eva found her mother pulling tiny radishes to make a soup. 'We should be thankful,' she told her, and Eva found herself genuinely relieved to see their rows of shoots all lying undisturbed.

CHAPTER 16

'I wonder what they're saying now, our mothers?' Kate poured the wine, and I sipped mine as I tested the spaghetti.

'Do you think they're talking about us?'

'They're probably wondering where they went wrong.' She smiled. 'You know, all three of us heading towards thirty, unmarried, still not settled down.'

'Hardly,' Natasha said. 'And, anyway, I have settled down. I've got a job with a salary, however small.' Natasha worked long, hard hours as a nurse, and she used her full employment to make fun of us.

'In any case,' I pointed out to Kate, 'I'm sure Patrick would marry you tomorrow.' Patrick was her long-suffering boyfriend, hanging on just by his nails for years.

'I'd like to go away,' Kate sighed, 'have some kind of adventure,' and to weigh her down I heaped her plate with food. 'Maybe we could all go?' She sucked a long strand of spaghetti up out of her sauce.

'Go where?' Natasha was adding up her scant days off.

'Oh, somewhere different. Chile or Mexico . . . Or where's that place practically no one has ever been – the Yemen?'

I looked at her and saw a speckling of sauce over her nose. 'The Yemen?' Just then Sonny woke up and yelled. 'Look,' I told him, 'I didn't put you down for a ten-minute nap. It's bed-time, night-time, understand?' But he looked so pleased to see me, the tears flicked back from his eyes, the roof of his mouth all pearly pink.

'The sweetness of that boy,' Kate said, as he rode in on my arm. He was passed around the table while we took it in turns to curl spaghetti with one hand.

'I don't suppose it would be impossible.' Natasha was coming round. 'Sarah could leave Sonny with her mother and we could go off, the three of us. Even just for a weekend.'

'Or we could bring Sonny with us?' Kate held tightly on to him while she stretched over the table for cheese.

'It depends when.' I felt a tiny stirring of excitement. 'We've never been anywhere together, the three of us, have we?' And we drank more wine and dug out hard helpings of ice cream.

'Even if we just went to the country for a day.' Natasha waved her spoon, and I could see Kate closing up with disappointment.

'No,' I insisted, 'we'll have to make it special,' and I remembered I'd forgotten all about the strawberries, which would be leaking through newspaper into the bottom of my bag. 'To somewhere special,' I raised my glass, and the others joined me, making Sonny chuckle when they cheered.

The next morning Sonny woke at five and then again every hour until I crawled out of bed to get away from him. The kitchen smelt of wine and cold spaghetti, and I opened the window where my cornflowers had grown into a mass of long green shoots, dark and dusty and in desperate need of thinning out. The sweet peas were trailing half-heartedly round sticks. 'I need a garden,' I mumbled into the jumble of backyards, and it suddenly occurred to me that we should visit Gaglow. 'Gaglow, it's the perfect place,' and I rushed through to my framed photograph and smiled at the far-off faces of the Belgard girls.

I rang Kate first and then Natasha, but both were either still asleep or out. 'We are going to Gagalow,' I sang, 'we are going to Gag-a-low,' and then, like a shock, it hit me. I stood in the middle of the floor, my nightdress limp, my hair all straggled on my neck and looked down at my feet. I'm lonely, I thought, and I crawled back into bed and rested one arm across my baby's body where the breath drew in and out under his vest.

'Pam?' I knew she'd still be asleep, but I didn't feel I could wait any longer. 'Pam?'

Then with a click and a whirr she cut through her machine. 'Hello?'

'I'm sorry, did I wake you?' I tried to sound surprised, and already I could hear her in her smoky bed, the creamy pillows denting while she searched round for a light.

'No.' There was a cigarette between her teeth now. 'What time is it?' A match hissed into the phone.

'I just wondered, did you ever find out anything about Mike?'

She took a deep inhalation and lowered her voice. 'Yes, as a matter of fact I did.' And she talked right on through her smoke so that I could almost see it drifting towards me down the line.

'You do realize, don't you, that Mike's not just in *Kilmaaric*. He *is* Kilmaaric. He's the lead.' And my ear felt hot with fury. No, I thought, not like that. Something bad, something real and nasty, but instead I listened as she carried on. 'Apparently they're all really excited about him, think he's going to be the next Big Thing,' and she stopped to take another drag and say, 'I hope he's sending you lots of money.'

'I don't care about the fucking money,' and I thought about my tulip dress, flowered in blue and white, and bought with the whole contents of one cheque. 'So he's not having an affair with anyone? Not sleeping with the producer? Come on, Pam, there must be more? I'm going crazy.'

Pam paused. I could feel it pained her to admit it, but she didn't know. 'I think Carol would have mentioned if there was any kind of intrigue. Why? What have you heard?'

'Nothing.' I sighed. 'Pam, you don't fancy coming up this way for lunch?' But she settled back against her pillows and said she was having lunch with Brad.

'Brad is it now?'
And she promised to call me later with more news.

'So what are we going to do?' Sonny had woken and was looking at me sideways. Outside our window was a long, hot, empty day. 'I suppose we'd better get ourselves dressed.' Then I remembered that once a week in Primrose Hill there was a baby-massage class. 'I don't suppose it can last long.' I eyed his dimpled arm and packed a towel, some almond oil and a sheaf of extra nappies.

The streets were gritty with ice cream and the sticky pips of fruit. I clacked along in my new dress, avoiding chewing gum, and stopping every now and then to adjust the shade above Sonny's head.

A mass of pushchairs was already in the hall, and upstairs, in a long bare room, babies were laid out naked on a semi-circle of mats. They lay white against the green, like water-lilies or slivers of lychees, and their mothers knelt above them rubbing oil into their hands. The babies mewed and twittered, coughed and cried while vital information was swapped back and forth from one woman to the next. The whole room hummed with their voices and the baby-massage teacher, a young, lean man with close-cropped hair, sat waiting to begin. 'All right, ladies,' his voice, soft London, cut through the noise, 'let's start with the right leg,' and I fumbled with the sticky tag of Sonny's nappy to pull it off in time. 'Lots of oil, that's right, then take the leg and ease it out, hand over hand.' Sonny was looking at the baby on his right, a tiny oriental girl with a shock of fine black hair. 'And now the other leg.' I eased oil into the creases, feeling the soft ligaments, like squid, behind each knee and the dense cool ripples of a thigh. There was silence in the room. 'Now knock those heels together for good humour,' and each woman smiled as she felt the soft pad of her baby's feet spring back into her palm. We rubbed their tummies with our fingertips, eased out each hip and let their short soft arms slide through our hands.

'Now turn them over,' and they flipped and slipped like seals on to their fronts while we smoothed along their backs with quick warm strokes. My shoulders were tight with concentration and then one baby began to cry. 'Pick him up,' the teacher said, 'if he's not happy.' And as if on cue another wail went out. Soon the room was fretful with demanding cries and a great array of breasts and bottles was ushered out to soothe them. I wrapped up Sonny in his towel and cuddled him against me. His face shone silkily with oil and his hair smelt bitter as a nut.

'He didn't used to like being undressed,' I told the teacher, as if to explain why I'd not been to his class before, and he bent knowledgeably over Sonny, papoosed in a yellow towel, and said that no babies liked to be naked when they were very young.

'You might find he drops off to sleep after he's had a feed,' and he moved away between the mats to magic one fretful baby into silence with a special sideways hold.

Sonny was still asleep when we got home so I laid him like a pat of butter on the bed and went to run myself a bath. There was a message from my mother asking if I'd like to come and have lunch the next day. 'We could have a picnic in my garden,' she enthused.

'I'm sorry,' I rang her back, 'but I've already arranged to sit for Dad.' And she laughed brightly, trying not to sound too hurt, and said we'd have to try another time.

There were three large windows in my father's studio, folding half into the roof, and the sun streaked in as thick as paint. Together we pinned sheets against the glass, hopeful of some shade, and then we had to twist them back to lose the shadow. I watched my picture from the corners of the room. I'd been looking at it too closely, and now, from the right distance, I could see exactly how it fell into place. Each stroke, each ridge of oil, was smooth and dense and lively, and I wondered that my father never felt the need to step back while he worked. I pulled the loose folds of the dressing gown around me. I'd grown thin again, my stomach flat against the pale pink scar and, without noticing, I'd stopped longing for him to whittle down my legs, paint away the veins, or soften the high flush of my once pregnant face. 'It's beautiful,' I murmured, and in place of my domed stomach there was Sonny curved in profile up towards my breast, 'I love it,' and I felt the edge of sharp delicious tears.

'Yes,' he was looking thoughtful, 'it may be nearly done.' And we stood admiring it in silence for a full five minutes.

Sonny lay waiting, his hands in fists above his head. He had a nappy on and nothing else. 'He does look wonderful like that,' he said, stepping in for a better look, and I quickly draped the stretched and faded Babygro across him before my father allowed himself a new idea.

'It's too small to go on at all now,' I explained, and I slipped into the lump and dent of the old sofa and smiled up at him to carry on.

'Dad,' I asked after we'd worked in silence for a while, 'does your cousin still want someone to go out to Gaglow?'

'I wouldn't know.'

I left him alone for another minute.

'It's just . . .'

And he turned to me, his eyes severe, his brush sharp in his fist. 'I want nothing more to do with it.' I didn't have the courage to complain.

'So what's your idea?' Kate wanted to know. She'd got my message about going away.

I hunted round for something else. 'I thought we could drive down to Devon, have a few days by the sea . . .'

'Hmmm.' Kate sounded uninspired. 'I'll talk to Natasha.'

'Or we could get the train?'

'Anyway,' she said, 'I might have an editing job that goes right through till Christmas.'

'That's great,' and I thought of her whiling away the summer, half underground in a windowless room. 'What is it?'

She said it was some Scottish saga, set up in the Highlands near the Isle of Skye.

'It's not . . .' My head began to thud. 'It's not *Kilmaaric*?' And I imagined her and Mike together, separated only by a bank of screens. She'd see him before I had the chance, and day after day she'd edit him out.

'Sarah, are you all right?' And then I heard that she was laughing, low down in her throat, waiting for me to guess it was a joke. 'It's a big documentary series, you idiot,' and she promised to let me know as soon as she had her dates.

'Devon!' Natasha sneered. 'You can't imagine I'd want to go to Devon.' And in great and gruesome detail she reminded me of a weekend she'd once spent with some regrettable man. 'That whole coast is ruined for me for ever, I'm afraid.'

I rang my mother and invited myself round for tea, accepting that for this summer I'd have to make do with her plum tree and her tiny patch of lawn.

'Maybe we could start something else now that this is finished?' my father murmured, as I lay lulled by heat against the sagging sofa.

'Hmm.' I wasn't giving in too easily, and to collect time I fingered the frayed leg of the discarded Babygro, unravelling and streaked with paint. 'You really think we're finished?'

'Could be,' he mused, adding minute touches to my ankle and stepping back at last to take in the whole thing.

Sonny was unrecognizable. He'd lost the dark fringe of his baby hair and his eyes had faded finally to a middle-Europe blue. I looked at the breadth of his stomach and his lamb-cutlet legs, and knew he was too big to go on drifting in and out of sleep. My father began turning over canvases. He had them leaning up against his walls, knocked together in their wooden frames and painted over white. I saw him eyeing Sonny as he measured one frame after another with his arm.

'Actually, Dad, I think we might be going away on holiday,' I cut in quickly, and he let the light white canvas fall back against the wall. 'I'd like to try and get out of London, just for a while,' and I smiled optimistically as he stood fidgeting away his mood.

'Where might you go?' I could see he was trying to be polite.

I told him I was arranging things with Natasha and Kate. 'Somewhere in the country, we just can't decide where.' He nodded, wiping his hands against his trousers before wandering through to the kitchen to prepare something to eat.

'Would the baby like anything?' He was peeling sharp fins of haddock on to plates. 'I've got . . .' but although at four months I had started him on carrot and ground rice, there was nothing childish enough for him to taste.

'He's all right.' And I kissed the soft top of his head.

'Dad?' He was making me a salad, rinsing leaves under the tap. 'Why do you never leave London?'

'I used to. When I was a child we used to spend summers in the country.' He laid the salad on a sheet of linen to let the water soak into the cloth.

'You mean Gaglow?'

'No, no.' I could see he meant his real life. 'Norfolk. We went there in the holidays.'

There was something in the way he said it that made me want to laugh. 'Did you hate it?'

'I didn't like it much.' And he searched among the cups and bowls and papers on the table for the flask of olive oil. 'Maybe it was because it was so flat. However far I went, wherever I hid, my mother always knew exactly how to find me.'

'Sometimes I think Sonny's first words will be "Mum, get off!"' I nibbled his cheek while I was still allowed.

But my father's eyes had cooled right over and I noticed the shooting line between his brows. I remembered him telling me how his mother didn't ever let him alone. She settled her attention on him like a vice. 'Once when I was about twelve,' he'd told me, 'I went to call for a friend. "I don't know where he is," his mother said, and I thought, the luxury of it. My mother never lost track of where I was. She knew more about me than I did myself.' And I thought of his kiss, remote and tender on her dying hair.

Simply out of habit I kissed Sonny's head again, glancing up guiltily with a shiver of defiance. But Sonny was cooing, low down, like a dove.

'We rented the same house every summer,' he went on, laying out a cardboard box of cake, 'somewhere by the sea,' and I realized it was the house I knew. The house I'd dreamed about. There were washing lines and hawthorn and I could see the garden now, the lawns all tufted up with seaside grass. My grandmother was there, leaning on the gate, listening to her summer neighbour telling her in detail about a girl that could be me.

'I tried not to go there if I could help it.' He cut me a thick wedge, slicing through the jellied tops of fruit.

'I wish I'd been brought up in the country,' I said, and I had a bright image of Sonny running off across the fens.

It was past midsummer and the evenings from my top-floor flat were long and light. Sonny was asleep, and I circled round the room, trying to adjust to the rare sensation of this time alone. I lay down on the floor, stretching out my arms and back and legs, trying to find a part of me that didn't ache. I breathed in deeply and then right beside my ear the telephone quivered into life. Two fierce, demanding rings before I pounced. 'Hello?'

There was a muffling and a choking and a broken gulping wheeze. 'Pam.' I held my heart out to her. 'Pam, what is it?'

She had to let out three long sighs of pain before the words came through. 'The bastard!' she flailed eventually and I knew that she was going to be all right.

'Where are you?'

She had folded up again with sobbing. 'I'm on my way round.' I heard a car somewhere behind her swerve away with a long loop of its horn.

Ten minutes later I saw her running towards me through the strained light of the evening, clutching cigarettes and a flat hard paper bag. She'd left her car half out in the street, and she looked more beautiful than ever, mascara streaked in dirty washes down her face. I ran downstairs to meet her. It was hard not to smile. 'Oh, God, Sarah.' She hugged me, and the ends of her hair, split white and smoky, smelt of vanilla essence.

'Come up.' Together we attempted to climb sideways, arm in arm, to the top floor.

Pam sank onto the sofa, kicking off her shoes, and I snuggled down opposite her, pushing my feet into the seams. Our knees knocked warm and brown against each other. 'At least this time you can have a drink with me,' she said, and broke the gold tin seal.

'Oh, Pam,' I cut in, as the woefully familiar tale of Bradly Teale swept on and on, 'oh, Pam,' and every now and then she broke off for another hot gulp of her drink and another cigarette. There was something inoffensive about the way Pam smoked. It curled and caught up in her hair, drifting over her like angel cloud, and even first thing in the morning she smelt like a sugary advert for Silk Cut.

Beguiled, I tried one and, as always, the bitter oil of it settled on my tongue so that I had to swill the taste of it around with brandy. 'So that's it, then, over?' And a small disloyal gleam sprang up in me to think I'd have her, for a short while, all to myself.

'I hope I never see the loathsome creature again.' She leant out for the bottle and her furious gaze caught the long arrangement of postcards, tartan, heather and misty Highland skies spread out over the mantelpiece. She arched her eyebrows at me, 'Excuse me?' and, reinvigorated, she jumped up off the sofa and went over to inspect them. 'There are two here the same,' she said, 'but then again I don't suppose there's a limitless amount of choice.'

I could tell that it was paining her to keep from flipping over to the other side. 'They're all to Sonny.' She took that as licence to lift one down.

'They're love letters,' she screamed, and even as I protested she snatched the others and spread them face up over the cushions. '"My dear sweet little boy, I hear you're cooing like a dove and blowing bubbles." You've been writing to him?' And she kicked me hard with one bare foot. '"So avocado is your favourite food? You lucky lad. All we get up here is haggis and jam tarts."' She turned over a pale pink sunset. '"I've bought you a blue and purple tam-o'-shanter, big enough to fit you in the autumn when your daddy . . ."' I knew that daddy had been crossed out. '"When I'll be home." Christ, what's got into him?'

'Distance makes the heart grow fonder, I can only assume.' And I topped up both our glasses, wishing she hadn't read out the secret, shameful word.

'So when will he be back?' There were thin grey tears still streaked across her face.

'Not for ages. November, I think. And you know how these things run over. Pam,' I bundled up the postcards, 'you don't fancy coming on holiday with me?'

Pam looked startled. 'Where?'

'I don't know. Anywhere.' I'd ruled out East Germany and Devon.

'Maybe.' I could tell she wasn't keen. I'd probably mentioned too often how Sonny woke five times a night. 'It's just that I did tell Camilla I'd be in town if any work comes up.'

'You bloody actors.' I had my chance to kick her now. 'You're all the same. Just think how well you'll feel when you get back.

How much more employable you'll be.' It was strange not to include myself.

'Yes.' She sighed. 'It might be good to have a holiday.' But I could tell she was only thinking about Bradly Teale and how glorious it would be if he rang to find her gone.

'My editing job has been brought forward,' Kate told me. 'I start in just over a week.' She had come to look after Sonny while I took her bike and cycled up to Hampstead for a swim.

'Oh, Kate.' I realized I'd hardly see her now.

'You should go somewhere with Natasha,' she said, 'even for a few days.'

'Yes,' I said, but I didn't want to be alone just with Natasha. We needed her to smooth things through. I picked up one strand of her honey-coloured hair and let it fall again.

'Go on, if you're going,' Kate urged. 'We'll talk when you get back.' I could tell that she was nervous.

I took one last look at Sonny and kissed his fingers.

'Go *on*,' Kate hissed at me, 'while he's still asleep,' and without looking back I fled downstairs. I pushed the bike out into the street and spun the pedals. It was the first time I'd left him. My throat felt heavy with alarm as I lurched out into the traffic.

The journey to the ladies' pond on Hampstead Heath was subtly and gradually uphill. My thin dress stuck to my body, and occasionally I felt the tug of cotton as it twined up in the spokes. I wrenched it out and carried on. I had to get off and push the last hundred yards and then I was on the Heath, gliding past the men's pond, with a field packed like a beach, and up past the ice-cream van. The lane here was gold and gritted over and I let the pedals fly as I sailed down towards the gate. The entrance to the lake was cool with shade. Back wheels of bikes overlapped along the fence and the grass behind the trees was thick with bodies, reading, eating, talking, bathing up the sun, and all stripped down to the waist. There were tattooed women with nipple rings and pale, long-legged Camden girls studying for school. There were old women and large women, some beautiful, some pocked and veined, and others you would never see naked in any other public pool. I ran into the changing room and pulled on my old costume. 'I thought my life was over when my husband died,' a woman, well over seventy, was chatting to a friend, 'but since then I've taken a psychology degree and taught myself to swim.' I followed her out of the changing room and watched as she dived into the lake.

There was a ladder and I lowered myself in one rung at a time. The water was breathtakingly cold, but then, steeling myself, I pushed away and ducked my head. The water closed silk brown above me and I thrashed and swam, arm over arm, until I came up warm. I ducked onto my back. A dragonfly buzzed beside my nose and three small birds skidded to a stop. It was impossible not to smile. The thick brown water slunk around my waist and as I stretched and turned, rolling over weightless, the warm smell of watermelon drifted towards me on the breeze. I hovered on my back and stared up at the sky. It's like being reborn, I laughed, and I struck out and swam in strong, long breaststroke right up to the other end where beds of yellow and blue iris made a natural bank. There were sudden patches of cold water, mysterious swells shadowed from the sun and as my feet caught one I suddenly remembered Sonny. I hadn't thought about him for nearly twenty minutes – for the first time in five months – and it amazed me that he was possible to forget. And then suddenly I was cold, and tired, and it seemed a long way back to land. Will he be all right, waking up to find that I'm not there? The whole strength of my body dragged behind each stroke.

There were beards of mud around my legs and chin and I had to stand under the one cold shower to smear them off. I dressed myself and then stood for a minute, tingling in the sun, calm again, and looking out over the lake where slow swimmers floated on their backs. I had intended to lie down beside the sea of women on the slope of grass but instead I turned the bicycle round and headed home.

Kate looked startled as I burst into the flat. 'Are you back already?' I could see that Sonny hadn't even woken up. 'You've been gone less than an hour.'

I threw myself into a chair and laughed out my relief.

'Well, obviously, any time, it was no trouble.' Kate folded shut her book, and it occurred to me that I should go straight out again while I had the chance.

'It's a shame that we couldn't take him with us,' she said. But the sign by the lake gate ruled against children, dogs and men. 'All the annoying things in life,' Kate laughed, 'and all the fun ones.'

I took the opportunity to ask her about Patrick. 'Fine.' She shrugged and smiled and I knew I wasn't likely to get more.

'You know where you could go? If you do still intend to go away?' She thought for a while before speaking.

'Where?'

'Well, you know Dad's parents used to rent this house in Norfolk.'

'Yes?' I wondered how she knew.

'Well, apparently it's still there. Someone I know stayed there quite by chance. The family name was in the visitors' book summer after summer.'

'Really?' I imagined him receiving this news, cool and uninspired. Asking how they'd ended up in such a flat and dreary place.

'Apparently it's really lovely.'

We sat in silence for a while.

'D'you think he'd mind?'

'Why should he?'

And I thought of all the trouble he'd taken to throw his family off.

'Why do you think . . . ?' I didn't know how to say it. 'Why . . .'

'I suppose,' she said, following my thought, 'he didn't want to be one of them. Refugees huddling together.' And we smiled at the big wide gaps he'd made between us.

CHAPTER 17

'Oh, Papa.' He came out into the hallway to welcome them. 'Oh, Papa.' They crowded round him. 'Have you been working much too hard?'

Even Marianna was unable to pretend that he looked well.

'Such important work,' he said, 'buying and selling, storing and rationing. And all for the highest price. No, no letters,' he was forced to admit, and by mid-afternoon he had sunk into a seat in the drawing room and let his head fall forward into that day's news.

Eva sat opposite him playing solitaire, glancing up occasionally at the unchanged expression of his eyebrows. She let the marbles drop into their cups, staring hard at the board and attempting to remember the trick for winning that Emanuel had taught her. It was a matter of order and routine. Clearing the game in triangles, jumping over one marble at a time and picking off small sections. It was vital to resist the trap of striking out too fast for the pure pleasure of seeing the defeated marbles swimming round the edge, clinking against each other as they mounted up. But however often Eva played, and in whatever order, there were always four obstinate glass balls glinting up at her, winking and stranded on the board. 'Papa?' she asked, picking up the game and holding it above his sheet of paper. 'Do you remember the trick of this?' But Wolf raised his eyes to hers with such a wearied expression that, after a second of dazed silence, she carried it carefully back across the room and set it down.

Bina, Martha and Eva sat huffing and sighing over the appropriate way to congratulate the Samsons. Julika had become officially engaged as well as Angelika and it was possible the girls might share a double wedding. Eva felt her shoulders tense as she tried for her next word. 'Why isn't Papa at his office?' she asked, when Dolfi bustled in to tidy up around them. 'Isn't he needed there any more?' But her sisters shrugged as if there was nothing unusual about their father spending the whole day bent over in his chair.

'You can ask him yourself.' Bina looked up and there he was, teetering in the doorway. 'Papa,' she whispered, and she realized she'd never seen him cross the threshold of their room.

His face was powdery, his eyes focused far away. 'Papa?' But instead of answering he tilted forward and, like a boat sinking in the graceful distance, he up-ended and crashed down towards the floor.

'What is it? What's happened?' Eva scrambled desperately over furniture to get to him.

Dolfi bustled, a smile forced on her face. 'Come on now, Herr Belgard,' she coaxed, and with some help from him she heaved him up. He stood reeling as if even he had been surprised, and with Dolfi's arm around his waist they shunted off together from the room.

Bina and Martha remained motionless, their heads bent low, and just as Eva was about to turn on them she noticed their fingers both white against their pens. She walked over to the window. Her hands were freezing and she held them up against the panes, waiting there until the sun sank below the level of the street and Dolfi, with a bright new face, came in to switch on the light.

*

One afternoon Eva met her sister outside the hospital. She had a small bag of dried apple rings and a wilting bunch of leaves. 'Can I really visit him?' she asked, when Bina came out in her nurse's uniform, and Bina looked her over and took her back inside.

Bina had befriended a young soldier, whose leg was shattered at the knee. It refused to heal and almost every day there was a check on it to see it wasn't turning gangrenous. 'Don't mention anything about it,' Bina warned, as they hurried through the ward, but once they arrived beside his bed, Eva felt her eyes travelling compulsively towards his leg to check that, in the short time Bina had been absent, a decision hadn't been made to cut it off.

'Ernst Guttenberger.' Bina hovered over him. 'Ernstl, this is my sister.'

Eva noticed that he and Bina looked alike. He had the same round mouth and eyes, short neck and sloping shoulders, and she longed for a chance to examine his feet to check if they'd been bound up in another life, like Bina's. Instead Eva stood and looked at him in silence, pushing down the flood of amputation stories that sprang into her mind.

'And your other sister?' Ernst asked, and looked expectantly around as if Martha were likely to stroll out from behind a screen.

'My other sister,' Bina blustered, 'is too busy studying.'

Eva couldn't think of a single thing to say to him. She looked unhappily at her sister and found her involved in a silent but absorbing communication of minute facial gestures, small frowns and smiles and crinkles of the eyes that passed silently between her and Ernst. Eva sat down on a chair beside the bed and absent-mindedly began to eat the apple rings.

'Dear Emanuel,' she wrote out in her mind, 'I've been thinking I'd like to have a pair of fat white ducks and see their yellow bills chattering first thing every morning. We could eat their eggs, and I'm sure they could be trained to get on well with a dog and I know the horses wouldn't be bothered by them for a moment. Do you know, instead of a car I've been wondering if it mightn't suit you better to get a motorcycle. Then I could climb on to the back and we could cut paths through the woods without worrying about the horses' shoes.'

Eva looked up to find a pair of vexed expressions staring over at her. 'Eva,' Bina patted down her uniform in shock, 'you've eaten Ernstl's apple rings.' Eva looked into the crumpled bag and saw that it was true.

A charity had been set up in Berlin especially for governesses who'd fallen on hard times. Over the last year, Bina had managed to convince her sisters that Fräulein Schulze had most definitely been sacked. 'She may have gone there to seek refuge,' she insisted, and set out to investigate. But the charity, it transpired, only catered for young women who'd been foolish enough to take work in England before the war, and they had never heard of Gabrielle Schulze. Martha thought it possible she might have put herself into a convent. The others laughed her out of this and together they decided she was more likely to have found a place with some aristocratic family. The wife of a baron or a prince. They looked out for her in photographs of the reported weddings of the Kaiser's sons, hoping to get a glimpse of her between the heads of officers, screwing up their eyes for maids of honour and trying to identify each grainy smile. Eva watched out for her as she cycled through the city, steering round the endless queues for food, and staring instead through the long windows of the Esplanade Hotel or at the people milling about before the theatre.

She took to wandering through the Tiergarten, listening to the patriotic tunes of the old orchestras and watching men on leave sitting straight-backed under shades, while women used communal fires to brew up jugs of watery green coffee. She no longer saw her father on these walks and once when she thought she caught a glimpse of him, she quickly turned away. She watched him in the mornings, leaving for his office, and nodded to him when he returned at night, but she refused to be the only one to notice his decline and prayed that it would not be her who witnessed its next stage.

The newspapers were full of Russia, men giving up, marching away from battle, and the Cossacks, who were under orders to shoot down any deserters, refusing to fire. 'It looks as if the war might soon be finished on the Eastern Front.' Marianna turned to Wolf. 'Think what this could mean for us. For Manu.' Wolf did not reply. Marianna stood and watched him. Then, unable to keep the sharpness from her voice, she said, 'Do you intend going in to work at all today?'

'Of course.' Wolf lowered his paper and, like a sleep walker, began to move towards the door.

'My dear,' she called after him regretfully, but he didn't turn, and a few moments later she heard a shuffle and his steps out in the hall.

Marianna opened up the safe to look into the girls' three boxes. The coins were thinning out now, and she wondered whether any of the money had ever reached Emanuel. His box was dense and heavy with untouched gold, and in a fit of guilt she considered making some small adjustment in favour of her daughters. She moved one coin tentatively over, and then another, and then, as if to redress the balance, she ran to her own room to find her ruby earrings, returning to drop them hastily into the new narrow space in Manu's box.

Martha was not allowed to visit Ernst. Bina insisted it would be too much for him, the excitement of a stranger, and Eva, who was free to come and go, felt proud and then a little vexed that she was considered so unthreatening. She glanced more often into the hall mirror. She was almost as tall as Martha, with the same straight hair, but the last years of rationing had thinned her face so that her ears stood out and her eyes were shadowed by a permanent sleepy blue. She looked better if she stepped up close but at a distance, in the gloom of the front hall, she had the air of being half invisible.

Ernst had lost his leg above the knee. Bina remained loyal, explaining regularly how much worse things might have been if it wasn't for her extra special care, and insisting that nothing between them had altered. But Eva could see that Ernst was fading. He no longer responded to her sister's special signs, her eyebrows raised and the tiny language of her hands, but lay submerged in a world all of his own.

Eva sometimes sat and talked to him about Emanuel. She broke her secret promise and told him about their plans. The house they intended building, once she was sixteen, the garden and the lake, the forest, and how it was simply a matter of finding a forked tree a certain distance from the house, so that she could lie dozing in a hammock and still smell supper just before it burnt. Ernst Guttenberger listened, sometimes with a smile and more often with his eyes fixed on the lopsided hillock of his sheet. He didn't have the energy or interest to remember what she said, and even when she came to ask him what could have happened to Emanuel, now that the war was finished between Germany and Russia, he still only glanced towards her with a polite smile and asked her to repeat the question.

'Typhoid, torture, lice, starvation.' She remembered Bina's words when Emanuel was first taken prisoner and wondered if news had spread into the far reaches of Siberia that the war was over.

Eva rose early to queue with Dolfi for their food. Prices had been fixed to every allocated portion but it was still possible to find an egg or two or an extra pat of butter. Women shuffled forward in the early morning, tightening their lips against a smile when, after hours of patient waiting, they were rewarded with a little heap of cabbage.

This morning Dolfi shook Eva awake with the rumour of a goose. Around the country supplies were still smuggled regularly, despite the humiliation and the chance of being caught. Eva had once seen a lady forced to open her suitcase on the station steps. She'd glimpsed the snout and hairy ear of a pig before the crowd closed in, demanding that the animal be divided up and sold right there in equal shares to all the starving people.

It was still half light when Dolfi found the street and slipped along a lane between two buildings. There was a busy trade in the small yard and large sums were being handed over for eggs and milk and syrup. A little crippled man lifted, packed and handed goods out of a shed, shouting orders to a woman who moved about behind. Eva stood back while Dolfi fought her way through the people, the housekeeping money secured in the inside pocket of her coat, and listened to the murmur of voices as they insisted, one against each other, on getting what they needed most. From time to time she glanced back towards the street for anyone suspicious and it wasn't until Dolfi called her to hide a jar of sugarbeet syrup in her clothes that she caught sight of the woman. It was her hands she saw, bare above the wrist, passing the goose out through the shed door, knocking its lolling neck against the wood. 'Schu-Schu?' she had to cough to find her voice. A woman pushed in front of her and Dolfi, having wrapped the goose in a scarf, began to bundle her away. 'Wait.' She twisted round to catch the woman's eye, but there were the heavy shoulders and bent head of a stranger and the freckled wrists had disappeared from view.

'Quick, Evschen, come along,' Dolfi called and, with the swaddled goose under her coat, they hurried off.

One late afternoon Marianna was walking in the Tiergarten when she saw the Kaiser. He was strolling in a little group of men, his hand clutching at a cane and his head bent as if he wished he were alone. She stopped and bowed, smiling over at him, hoping to make up for her childish impudence so many years before, when she remembered how her feelings for his family had changed.

The people around her stopped and stared and a murmur hissed from mouth to mouth, a savage wonder that the Kaiser dared to show his face. A special store of hatred was brewing up against both Kaiser Wilhelm and the Empress. It was the relentless good health of their sons, all six remaining year after year unhurt, while every other family in the land was mourning. Marianna had heard it said that until they let one go, sacrificed just one of their own children, they had no chance of finding any favour with the people.

Marianna stood back and watched him pass. His burly frame had stooped and there was something fragile in the steps he took. She shivered as she watched him wind along the path, his back bent like an old woman's, and she couldn't quite find it in her heart to blame him.

The Samsons' was the first smart wedding since the beginning of the war. Private balls and parties had been banned, but now, with the general air of cynicism, entertaining had crept back into fashion. Marianna stared at the expensive lines of the invitation and felt a stab of pain as if her son had been thrown off right there in front of her. 'Wolf?' she called, running back through the apartment, glancing into rooms. 'Wolf?' But he seemed not to be there. She saw Eva wandering sleepily towards her, wrapped up in a blanket. 'Have you seen your father?' Eva stopped and placed the flat of her hand against the airing-cupboard door. 'He's hardly likely to be in here.' But despite herself she followed Eva in.

The little room was cool and musty. The rows of boots and hanging gloves gave off a mouldering smell. 'Papa?' Eva called, as if he might have camouflaged himself among the coats and scarves. 'Papa?' But no one was there.

Marianna had a sudden overwhelming sense of doom. 'What would he possibly want in here?' she said, closing her eyes against the locked door of the safe, and Eva, seeing that the room was empty, shook herself and said she didn't know.

The Samson wedding was extravagant beyond all expectations. There were ten bridesmaids, all dressed in pink and carrying bouquets of matching flowers. Bina looked on, incensed not to have been included, as each perfect girl swayed by. 'They're all members of the family,' Martha pointed out. 'Cousins and second cousins.' But Bina did not want to be placated.

'And, of course, where is Mama when we need her?' she scorned, knowing that Marianna had chosen to stay at home in mourning for her dog. The day before, she'd found her favourite whippet stretched out and cold, her dead back legs as brittle as old sticks. Her eyes were open, soft as prunes, and her perfect ribs strained hard against her skin. 'Bluebird,' she crooned. She wrapped her up, a corner of the cloth over her ears, and held her in her arms.

Marianna looked out of the carriage window. The rain was falling, slanting lightly past them and scattering away into the earth. She could see the cornfields unfolding with relief, straightening and opening after weeks of cold, dry wind. She closed her eyes and pictured Wolf, almost driven to distraction as each dry day through June had threatened to destroy the harvest. The potatoes came to an abrupt end and, with the blasting wind, the vegetables lay stunted in the ground. He had withered, shrunk, predicting slow starvation for anyone who'd escaped the war, and turned grey and silent in his grief.

But the first warm drops of rain had pulled him up, opening his limp face like a plant and, with a great explosion of renewed faith, he began to spend each day and most of the night in working out just how each ear of corn could be most valuably distributed. 'Of course you must go,' he insisted, when she suggested taking the girls straight on to Gaglow, and he set off for his office with an energy she had hardly seen since the beginning of the war.

'Did you know,' Martha whispered, squeezed in opposite her mother in their third-class carriage, 'that every soldier at the Samson wedding was called back to the front?'

'That night? Even the husbands?' Eva asked, and Bina smiled. 'They'll have to wait now for their honeymoon.'

'The telegram arrived just after the service,' Martha sighed, 'and by now, for all we know . . .'

'Martha!' Marianna frowned, and the three girls looked quickly round the carriage full of soldiers.

Marianna thought what it could mean. Another offensive? The push that would finally break the line? She started to count the men in uniform. How many, she thought, expected even to come home? She wondered that it didn't break their hearts, the fat Americans all new and ready for the war, to see these worn-out men, half starved, half dressed, staggering towards them through the mud.

It was still raining when they arrived at Gaglow. The lawns were wildly overgrown and, as Marianna paid the driver of the cart, Eva stood between her sisters staring up at the house. The paint was peeling and the tiles of the roof had slipped. The outbuildings in their hollow to one side were crumbling with disuse.

Eva knelt down in the grass and pulled off both her shoes. She spun round, her knees catching on the husks of flowers, and raced away across the lawn, whooping and calling and spreading out her arms. She looked back once to see her mother unbuckling the four remaining dogs, trembling on their whippet legs and the faces of her sisters staring after her. They looked half thunderous and half amused, and she had a sudden memory of Fräulein Schulze glancing disapprovingly around as she held her charges steady in a neat, neat line. The grass was slippery and wet, tangling between her toes with clover, and she held out her tongue to catch the tantalizing drops of rain, fine against her face. She ran right round the lawn, past the fountain and the lichened statue, through the beds of trailing flowers and, finding she was quite alone, she threw herself against the soft slope of the ice-house path and stared up at the sky.

The row of attic windows cut soft grey shapes in the roof and, in a lazy attempt to stare up into the nursery, she remembered her treasure box in its string cradle underneath her bed. It had been sitting there all winter, quite forgotten, and in an act of guilt she reached around her for a pebble or a twig to mark out the important points of her collection. There was her photograph of Schu-Schu, which had a knack of rising to the top. Next there was the coil of wallpaper words, hidden in their thimble, and with a leaf as a reminder she lifted out Emanuel's oath. The thin veins of the leaf were perfect for his purple blood, and she saw him pressing down with his thumb, sealing the promise of their future. There were the straw stars for the Christmases he'd missed, and the dried head of the first snowdrop. As she was laying out these lesser treasures she thought she heard a whistle. She turned quickly and searched the edges of the lawn, the swaying trees and the little structure of the ice-house. 'Eva,' she heard then quite distinctly, and she swivelled round to see Martha standing at the back door, peering out into the rain. 'Evaaaa,' Martha called again. Looking down at her scattering of twigs and leaves, Eva jumped up and, throwing out her arms, she ran dripping towards the house.

Eva lay in bed, holding her breath for what had woken her. The moon was still high in the sky but the first light, shadowy and red, was seeping in over the sill. Straining past the shallow noise of her sisters' combined breath, Eva thought she heard a shuffling. The sound of steps slapping hard over the flags. She slipped out of bed, twisted a shawl around her shoulders and ran down to the first landing. She listened on tiptoe and, hearing nothing, traipsed slowly down into the main hall, taking in the smell of stone and the dust from husks and heads of flowers that lay like soup in a great bowl. The front door clanked as she pulled at it so, not wanting to risk waking the whole house, she trod softly through the drawing rooms and let herself into the stone corridor that led to the back door. Shadows collected here in the arches of the roof and spread through half-open doors into empty, unused rooms. Eva kept her head down, hurrying towards the tiled hall, and with relief pulled open the back door.

The rain had stopped and the garden stretched away, warm and friendly, the lawns waist high with hay and bordered by the waving arms of roses that had overshot themselves. But then, as she turned to shut the door, she heard a noise. A hoarse whistle that could have been the wind. She swung round, freezing with fear, and there, staring out between the pillars of the ice-house, was a man. A dark, bent figure, who backed away as her hands flew to her mouth.

'Papa?' she called, but instead of answering, the man sent out another whistle. 'Manu.' She ran towards him, her bare feet catching against grass, and as she ran she practised little grunts and smiles of happiness. But when she arrived she found that it was Gruber. He was old and grey and battered to a stoop. His jacket gave off a sour smell, and as she stared at him, appalled, he backed away from her, hovering into the shadow of the ice-house.

'Can't you come into the house?' she asked, once she'd recovered from the shock. They were crouching in the underground chill of the cellar. Gruber shook his head. 'Is it very dangerous?' she asked.

'Only for me,' and he asked her to keep his secret to herself. 'I'll bring you food,' she promised, and she also thought she'd bring him a gun. He could take it out with him in the dead of night and hunt for roebuck and wild duck, and they could eat together over a fire, stewing up the remains for soup. 'I won't tell,' she said, and Gruber pressed her hand.

When Eva went in to breakfast she felt self-conscious and afraid, and the sight of her mother, straight-backed and pale, fending off the hungry dogs, made her unsure.

Gruber had managed to escape the army. He'd made his way out dressed as a peasant, pretending to be deaf and dumb. Eva, peering at his worn and muddy clothes, wondered if he was still in his disguise. Had he seen Emanuel? she asked, knowing as she spoke that it was hopeless. Gruber put up a trembling hand and asked her kindly to keep her voice low.

'But I'm sure they wouldn't send you back to fight,' Eva said, 'even if they found you. They couldn't make you ... could they?' She was looking at his fragile face and the thin bones of his shins. But Gruber insisted that less robust men than him were at this moment on their way to France.

Carefully Eva followed her mother through the garden, slipping after her as she went in to inspect the vegetables. They found the old arched door hanging from one hinge, and the garden, abandoned through the spring, quite gone to seed. The spears of leeks were waving at her, nodding the bobbles of their heads, and the bony skeletons of cabbage stood at gnarled intervals in an indistinguishable row. Marianna bent down to clear the leaves from a bed of strawberries, faithfully emerging in a dark green line. She hoped to find at least a few ripe fruit, protected from the birds, but as she scanned each plant she found that every last berry had been plucked away. She searched the trees for fruit, apricots and peaches softening against the wall, but there were only stalks and shreds of unripe flesh pulled away too early. Children, she thought, remembering the melting ice, and she saw Hans Dieter's lip, curling coldly at her. The only thriving thing was a great striped marrow, lying under a fan of prickly leaves, and it made her feel a little more forgiving of the birds, who must have dropped the seed while eating Eva's beans. The garden was knee high with weeds, and nettles had taken over one whole corner, disguising what had once been a bed of kale. Marianna found the spade leaning against a wall and, grabbing at it in a sudden fury, she began to beat them away. The handle squelched between her ungloved hands, and as she stamped, tears stung into her eyes.

Eva watched from the doorway, half hidden by the poles for her beans. To her surprise she saw her mother stop and press her head against the handle of her spade, her body shivering in long, sad sobs. Eva froze. She felt incapable of scrambling out unseen and the thought of being caught backing away was unacceptable. She hardly dared breathe. She spun out songs and half-remembered verses to keep herself still until she saw her mother wipe her face, slice the spade into the ground with new determination and begin to dig again. She shifted with relief and, making more noise than was necessary, she bustled into view. The tangled mass of marrow nearly tripped her up.

'What are you doing?' Marianna called to her, and Eva wondered if there wasn't a way in which she could let her know about Gruber, and how it was he, most likely, who'd been living off the garden. Instead she followed the trail of knotted stems until she came across the marrow, green and yellow where it lay against the earth. A trailing bed of stalks lifted with it until it snapped into her hands. 'Eva, it isn't ready,' Marianna called, striding towards her. 'It needs at least another week.' But Eva, cradling her find, ran across the garden and out on to the lawn, wildly hoping that her mother might suspect and follow her.

Marianna turned back to her bed of nettles, dragging the spade over the ground, remembering how different things had been when it was just the two of them.

*

Eva sat with Gruber on the ice-house steps and watched him as he ate. It was dark but she could see him as he let the marrow juice dribble round his chin. She had also brought him out a little portion of dried beans, boiled up with precious oil, and now she found that she was hungry for them. 'Tell me some of your adventures,' she asked, hoping to distract herself, and when he refused to speak she told him how in Berlin it cost over a hundred marks for one pair of leather shoes.

Eva had been unable to find Gruber a gun. She'd let herself into the stone corridor where the marguerites were dying of neglect. They stood, their little flowers shrivelled, grizzling in their pots and Eva plucked at them as she went past. She had glanced into her mother's study and was surprised to see her there, hunched over the remainder of her thick white book. She stepped a little closer, craning her neck, and saw that she was building toppling towers up and down the page, squares and lines of calculations, and as she worked she crossed off each row of figures with a sharp sweep of her pen. Eva backed away unnoticed and continued on, glancing into the abandoned rooms and hoping to come across some hidden store of weapons. She had an image of a row of rifles hanging from one wall, their thongs attached to nails, like geese against the sky. Eva pushed open the door into another room. The windows here were shuttered, and through the slats of light she could see giant cobwebs meshed and growing in the dark. The walls were rough and empty and only a few discarded pieces of old furniture were heaped, waiting to be used for fuel. In the last room there was a row of pegs, lower than she remembered, and hanging down was an old corn dolly, half chewed away by moths. Eva stood and stared, wondering if she'd dreamt the gun collections, the knives and whips, left by Hans Dieter to remind them of his reign. She remembered Schu-Schu insisting that Dieter was a good man, simply down on his luck, and that it had been their mother who had turned his family out. 'Where will they sleep now, the poor little Dieter children?' she heard Bina hissing through the house, and although she had since discovered that there weren't any Dieter children, not officially, she still shivered with the thought that someone had been turned out of her sunny attic room.

The following evening, Eva went up to bed with the rest of the house and only when she was sure that her sisters were asleep did she venture out again. She arrived with smoked meat and a little portion of dried peas. 'Gruber,' she whispered, but when she pushed open the door into the ice-house cellar she found that he was gone. His coat was gone, his small pile of possessions, and even the leaves and straw he'd gathered for a bed were kicked into the ground.

Eva backed out in alarm, convinced that the soldiers had come for him, but as she soothed herself with the unexpected extra food she realized he'd been simply passing through.

Sometimes at night Marianna imagined she heard whispers, light steps out in the dark, and she checked to see that her dogs were in. Even on warm nights they liked to burrow under cloth and she made a quick inspection of their ears and tails, checking the black edges of their smiles. Another of her dogs was sickening. Its blood was slow under the thin skin and a sour smell seeped between its teeth. She'd read last winter in the paper about a family of Schleswig princes who'd been forced to kill their kangaroos for meat. They'd kept them as pets on their estate, breeding them for over twenty years, and now they'd all been eaten. She squeezed herself between the folded legs of several dogs and, lifting one long nose on to her lap, she stared into the little bulge of hooded eye and gave thanks that there was so little meat on them.

Marianna followed every piece of agricultural news. She became an expert on the forecasts, heaving sighs and saying prayers for each dry day, and swapping news with anyone who came up from the village. Relief settled with the harvesting of crops and now the late potatoes had come through safely. But then, towards the end of August, the farmers were caught out by rain and the precious cut corn began to sprout, too wet to be brought in, and Marianna, worried for her husband's sliding spirits, prepared for an early return to Berlin.

Wolf was smaller than ever, with a glitter in his eye, and so thin that his trousers hung in hollows round his knees. He put an arm around his wife and kissed her warmly on the ear. 'How are you, my dear? Not changed at all, I see.' He took one of her rough brown hands in his.

Eva watched him as he described the city, the shortage of food, the absence of all meat and how if the war lasted even for another month there was unlikely to be any livestock left in the entire country, 'But I shall say no more.' Lowering his voice he told them that now, after four years of war, Hindenburg had ordered only hopeful conversations to be held.

Marianna wouldn't let her daughters leave the apartment. She had been to Wertheim's to look at comforters, with no real hope of buying, and found the shop half empty. 'Laid up with the *grippe*,' a sales assistant told her, promoted in this crisis to the job of manageress. She leant across the counter and whispered, 'In the last week we've lost nearly seventy of our girls.' Marianna put a hand up to her forehead. It was cool and even. 'They say it's much, much worse in the countryside,' the manageress continued, crossing her arms against her chest. 'In some villages whole families are dying out within a day. Women,' she said, 'who've waited patiently for four years for their men are burning up with fever, carted off in furniture vans before their young men even have a chance to ask for leave.'

Marianna shrank away from her, and the woman smiled and shivered and turned to help a customer, using gloved fingers to ensure that his pass allowed him to buy his wife a vest.

*

On her way home Marianna met the wife of old Herr Baum. She darted across the road and whispered that she was going to the bank to hand over her jewels, 'Pearls given to me by my dear husband on our wedding day.' Slipping one arm out of her muff Marianna glimpsed a string of pink, like tiny sausages, wound around her hand. 'If you need a place to hide when the revolution comes,' Frau Baum put away her pearls, 'living right there by the royal palace, come straight round to us.' And as they parted Marianna thought she caught her staring sharply at her hair. '*Guten Tag*, Frau Baum,' Marianna waved and watched as the other woman hurried up the steps, pushing open the heavy doors into the bank.

Eva wrote a letter to Emanuel. She used only one side of the paper so that if he needed to he could use up the rest.

Dear Manu,

  I won't say anything at all about the gloomy state of things here in Berlin because it has been ruled that anyone with a bad word to say could end up with five years in prison. Bina has gone back to the hospital and when I visited her there I saw soldiers with arms and legs as thin as sticks. One man told me how he advanced from trench to trench for five days with nothing to eat at all and his friends who weren't killed just fell down with exhaustion. This man survived by jumping down into an enemy trench, where he found biscuits and a cigarette!

Eva read through this letter and decided she should start again.

Dear Manu,

  I think we should paint the walls of our house green so that we can imagine at all times we are in the garden. The ceilings could be blue, and wouldn't it be nice to have a room without dark curtains? I shall throw out any cerise rugs or drapes in burgundy, and we'll have bowls of floating leaves on all the tables.

She sealed this letter and, without any clue as to his real address, stored it tightly with the others in her box.

CHAPTER 18

'There's something still not quite right with the painting.' My father rang first thing one morning. 'I think we'll just have one more go.' It took me half an hour to find the scrap of Babygro, bundled out of sight into a cupboard. I considered bringing toys to keep Sonny transfixed. I could hold a string of plastic teddy bears above him while he posed, but the idea of the studio, its silence broken by the tinkling of electronic Brahms, decided me against it.

When I arrived someone was ringing the bell. I could see him leaning on his finger, determined, and even from behind I recognized the rounded figure of my father's cousin John.

'Hello.' He straightened guiltily. 'I'm Sarah . . . I'm Michael's daughter.'

He was looking at me, his eyes round with surprise. 'Sarah.' And he began to nod and smile. 'How very nice to meet you.'

'And this is Sonny, my . . . Michael's grandson.' John's smile quivered, as if more than one new relative might be too much to take in in a day.

'He doesn't appear to be there.' John looked up at the house.

'No,' I agreed, but thought I caught a shadow stepping out of sight against a wall. 'Was it important?'

John shuffled and turned to look at his car, waiting neatly on a meter. 'There was something I wanted him to sign.'

I offered to take it in to him, sitting on the flat top of the gatepost to show that I was quite prepared to wait.

As soon as John drove away, beeping as he turned the corner, my father appeared at the door. He looked out, nervous as a bird, and grinned over at me. 'I thought he'd never go away.' He took the clean brown envelope that John had given me, tucking it under his arm as if he'd been expecting it.

I had to help him find his glasses. We trawled through magazines, searched under towels and found them in a saucer of dried paint. Sonny started to grizzle. I held him up to the mirror and watched him beam into his eyes. 'Now you see him,' I swept him away, 'now you don't.' He gave a throaty chuckle, like a rude old man. 'Now you see him –' But I was interrupted by my father scrabbling and cursing as he began a new search for a pen.

'What's it about?'

'The same old thing,' he muttered, plucking up a biro with a splintered side. 'Gaglow.' And I watched, delighted as he set his signature, scrawling across the blank space for his name.

By the time we settled down to sit, the sky was clouding over. It was a thick August afternoon with warm fat drops threatening to fall, and Sonny, whose sleep had been delayed, sank heavily against my arm.

It was impossible to imagine what more there was to do. I had a slanting view, too close and harsh, but even from there the picture looked quite finished. My father stared at it, a brush clenched in one hand, and I waited, the breath short in my throat, for him to come to some decision. He looked from me to it and then to Sonny, his face all strained and burrelled up with pain, and then he stood back, nodding. He mixed new paint in a flurry of activity, and as he stepped forward, raised up on his toes, I saw that he was working on the yellow plaster, uncovered, just above my head. Sonny only sleeps for forty minutes now, I wanted to tell him, but I kept quiet, tense with concentration, feeling my part in the way the paint went on. 'Is it warm enough?' he asked, as the rain splashed sideways against the glass, and two lights had to be switched on above our heads.

I nodded and tucked the towelling corners tight around the

baby's feet, feeling his padded palm for warmth. I loved the rain. The sound of it thudding against glass and the day-time gold of the electric light mixing in with grey. I could lie like this for ever, and then I remembered that in another ten minutes my hip would start to ache, and by the end of the afternoon I would be wrung out and miserable with trying to keep still. Natasha had shrieked with triumph when I said the painting needed one last go. 'What if you had a life?' she teased me. 'What would you do then?'

And Kate had taken pity on us all. 'Sarah and Sonny are the only ones he has left, now we've both retired from the modelling world.' And she laughed and said, 'So he does need his family, after all.'

I closed my eyes and waited, resting while I had the chance, and when I glanced back at the picture I saw the plaster wall exactly as before. There it was, pale yellow, but now I could see into it, behind it. Green and gold and blue. I could even tell that it had been there for a hundred years. I smiled and wondered what I was going to do if I held firm against another picture. I'd written notes to call my agent, week after week, but had never managed to pick up the phone. It didn't seem worth leaving Sonny for a three-month tour of *Don't Forget Your Trousers*. Even if I was lucky enough to get a part.

I lay so still and waited for so long that eventually my father had to suggest a break. It was something I knew he hated to do. He liked to hold up his strength against yours and win. I pulled on the dressing gown quickly to show I was relieved.

'Did I tell you about the Belgard curse?' He had gone through to the kitchen and was peering into the envelope to check the papers were still there.

'No.' I was half listening out for Sonny, sleeping through the break. 'What kind of curse?'

'The woman my uncle married, the prostitute, she was so incensed about the wedding not being grand enough, not taking place at Gaglow as she wished, that she put a curse on the family.'

I felt a small electric shiver run under the skin. 'For some reason she turned on my grandfather, Wolfgang, blaming him particularly. Not long afterwards he died.'

'Wait one minute,' I said, and raced into the studio to check that Sonny hadn't rolled off on to the floor. He was awake, staring at the window, watching squashed drops of water rolling down the glass. I scooped him up and brought him through. 'How did he die? Was it immediate?' And I imagined the long crook of her finger, striking him down.

'It's possible she was a gypsy or something,' my father said, 'or she came from the South. But I'm not quite sure how he died.'

'So she wasn't Jewish?'

'God, no.'

I laughed. I'd always assumed my father had been the first to look outside his faith.

'What I've been meaning to ask,' I remembered quickly while he was in the mood, 'is, tell me about Bina.'

'The loathsome Bina?'

'Yes. I mean, was she really so terrible?'

My father thought for a while. 'Absolutely.' It was how he liked things to be.

'But why? There must be some reason.'

I expected a sharp look, a warning to cut out the cod analysis, but he was nodding, mulling over some forgotten news. 'You know the story about Van Gogh?'

I wasn't sure. I imagined I did, assuming it was the ancient one about his ear.

'Well, there was another Vincent who died when he was very young, beautiful, perfect, a blessing to his parents in all ways, and so of course the new Vincent Van Gogh was meant simply as a replacement.'

'Poor thing. He didn't stand a chance.'

' It happens surprisingly often. Well, that's what happened in my mother's family. There was another child, who died after six months. Also called Bina. But, of course, it didn't work. I think when the second Bina was born my grandmother, Marianna, went into a decline, went off to a health spa, could hardly look at her. She was brought up by some governess or other.'

'How terrible.'

To my surprise he put the kettle on for a second cup of tea. 'I don't think she ever knew.'

'Really?'

'My grandmother told my mother, right at the very end, just before she died. I remember them crying together, holding hands.' The kettle whistled as it reached the boil, and as if remembering himself he switched it off and ordered us back to work.

The remainder of the afternoon turned into a struggle. Sonny had woken up refreshed, wanting to be entertained. He wanted to be rocked and kissed and played with, shown the view and taken for a walk. I sang to him as he lay beside me, introduced him to his toes, and wondered why we were needed there at all while layer after peeling layer of plaster went on above our heads.

When we finally got out, the rain had stopped. The clouds were thin and scattered and the sodden heads of flowers lay strewn across the street. I noticed the first fallen leaves burnt brown against the puddles and, breathing in the city smell of raspberry, hot against wet walls, I walked on past my bus stop. Shrubs and bushes were bursting out on to the street, cleared of their dust, and I brushed them with my shoulder to shake the last glass drops of rain against my face. And then the sun came out, streaking the pavement pearl, and the glint of it on the curved roof of a postbox reminded me of the Gaglow letter I'd promised to post. Without slowing I rummaged for it in my bag, hoping to slide it in as I walked past, but the envelope was too wide for the slot and I had to stop and curve it round to make it fit. I could bend it carefully so that it might unfurl in the wide inside without creasing, but as I stopped to free up both my hands I noticed the address. It was a street above

Camden Town and I realized that simply by staying on my bus for several extra stops, I could deliver it myself. I pushed the envelope back into my bag and, glancing behind me to check I hadn't been observed, walked quickly on.

The door was answered by a woman. She had soft grey hair cut into a square, and fragile arms and legs. 'I have something to give to Johann . . .' I glanced down at the name '. . . John Godber.'

'John,' the lady called, 'John.'

He trod slowly through, ignoring her urgency, and only startling when he saw me. 'I'm sorry to bother you,' I held out the envelope, 'but I was passing so I brought you this.'

'Of course, how kind,' and he insisted, as I'd hoped he would, that I come in.

'This is Sarah.' He opened his eyes wide at his wife. 'Michael's daughter.' I could tell from the angle of her head that she'd been told.

Their house was cool and comfortable, and he laid the envelope on a table of dark wood. 'This is my wife, Elisabeth.' John introduced us, and she clucked and kissed the air at Sonny as she went out for a tray of tea.

We sat in silence as the pot was left to brew.

'So you live nearby?' John asked, and I nodded, saying quickly that I was taking the baby to look at other children on the Heath.

'Do you have children?' I asked, and he told me eagerly that they had three, two sons and a daughter, and together they began counting off grandchildren proudly on their hands.

'And this is your first child?' Elisabeth asked.

'Yes, my first.' I knew that my ringless finger had been caught as I came through the door, and it made the questions stop up politely in their throats.

'You do look like your grandmother.' They turned to each other, relieved to have found a subject on which they both felt safe. 'Very like dear Eva.' Agreeing, they spent the next ten minutes nodding over it while I kept my head lowered so that they might see the uncanny similarity of our chins.

'And as for this little fellow,' Elisabeth stretched out her arms to him, 'he looks . . . ?' We all stared into the wheat and cornflower of Sonny's smiling face.

'Just like his father,' I explained, and they both laughed, accepting that I had found a civil way to introduce him. 'He's an actor.' It seemed my duty to explain. 'Working away.' And I smiled, twisting my mouth against the sudden knot of pain. The envelope was lying where I'd left it, smooth and brown across the swirls of polish. 'Is everything nearly sorted out?' I turned the conversation, and without meaning to I stumbled. 'My father tells me you went back to Germany, to Gaglow.'

John frowned as he took a long swallow of tea. 'Yes, yes.'

'We both went,' Elisabeth said, and she laid a hand on his arm.

I lifted Sonny onto my knee. It gave me confidence, having him in my arms, and quickly, before the moment passed, I asked John, 'Do you think, before the place is sold, I might go and visit?'

He looked surprised. He turned and pulled the envelope towards him. 'Of course.' He flicked quickly through the contents. 'After all, it was Eva, your grandmother, who loved it best.'

'What . . . how would I go about it?' I asked, as I stood up. And he wrote down his telephone number and said that I should call him when I'd decided on the date.

'Thank you so much.' I smiled. 'It was nice to meet you.' They both waved at me as I pushed Sonny off along the street.

In order not to cheat them I walked up on to Parliament Fields, stopping to watch the last children prancing, like small horses, back and forth across the bright blue paddling pool. The sun was sinking, dusty again and hot, and the grass on the great swoop of the Heath had turned to hay.

I walked slowly up under the avenue of trees, pushing against the path, avoiding bicycles and joggers, whole families laden down with rugs, and then with one last open stretch of hill I came out on the top. A small cluster of people, panting and amazed, were all looking out over London, identifying the Post Office tower, the green dome of St Paul's. I stood with them, taking in the still, high air, and then I turned and looked the other way. The hill dipped down and up again to a thin circle of pines, and in the distance I could see the reedy edges of the row of lakes. There were no buildings here and no sights, nothing to break the view, but in the distance, just below my breath, I could still hear the roar of city noise.

'Pam?' I had to call out to her through the shield of her machine. 'I know you're there.' And, breathless, she picked up the phone. 'Pam...' I started, but she hissed at me that it wasn't a good time.

'I'll call you later.'

'Pam.' I tried to warn her, but she didn't want any of my words, and still whispering my meaning, I was cut off.

I didn't hear from her until the next day. 'Don't tell me, I don't want to know,' I said.

But she was adamant that the news was good. 'Listen, he's not an actor.'

'Not ... an ... actor?'

'Can you believe it?'

'Not really. What's the catch?'

There was an ominous pause. 'He's an accountant.'

I couldn't think what she meant.

'He's wonderful,' she said. 'Every morning he wakes up at eight and goes straight off to work, and when he's finished he's all happy and lighthearted and wants to meet up for a drink. It's quite amazing.'

'But, isn't . . . isn't he . . . ?'

'What? Boring?' she answered for me. 'I'm forgetting, you never met Bradly Teale.' And we both laughed, relieved that he was over with.

'Listen,' I said, once she'd calmed down, 'have you thought any more about our holiday?'

I could tell she hadn't. 'How would you feel about going to Germany? You know, just for a few days.'

'Germany?'

'There's this house there, in the country.'

'The country?'

And before I'd even explained about the attic bedrooms and the lake, the rose garden and the steep, straight drive up to the porch, I knew that she'd lost interest.

'The thing is Alan might be going away on business.'

'Alan?' And I pretended Sonny had been sick right down my dress and that I'd call her back when I had time.

'Oh, Mum.' I lay prostrate under her plum tree while she sat with Sonny, introducing him to her fish. 'I haven't got anyone to go away with.'

'What about Kate? Or Natasha.'

'Yes.' But neither of them had a break coming up for months and I needed to go now.

'I'd come with you,' she said, fluffing Sonny's hair into a spike, 'but I'm going to a conference about websites, and then I've got a great build-up of work.'

'It's such bad luck,' I said sulkily, looking up into the sticky branches of the tree. 'Maybe I'll just go off on my own.'

'You should,' she said, 'it'll do you good.' And she handed Sonny back.

*

When I left the travel agent I was trembling with the shock. I'd used one of Mike's cheques to buy the ticket. A four-day return to Berlin and a slip of a ticket for Sonny at a fraction of the price. I would have liked to go for longer. If I was on my own, I told myself, but I knew that if I'd been on my own I wouldn't have had the courage to go at all.

That night I sent off my passport to have the baby added. I marked the envelope Urgent, and explained that I was leaving in ten days' time. I danced around the room with the tickets in my hand, wondering whom I could tell. Sonny was sick of hearing about it. He lay on his back with his legs in the air, looking with amazement at his toes. And then I thought I'd better call John.

'Mr Godber? Hello. It's me, it's Sarah Linder.'

'Oh, yes.' He sounded distant, as if he only just remembered who I was.

'I've decided to go, definitely. The week after next. To Gaglow.' And it was only then that I stopped to ask if I'd called at a bad time.

'It's just my wife,' he faltered. 'Elisabeth. She's unwell.'

'I'm so sorry.' I held the phone too hard against my ear, desperate for the words. 'I'm so sorry to have troubled you.'

'It's all right.' He sounded vague, as if his strength was all used up with worry.

'I'll call back another time.' I heard him fumbling to replace the phone.

I sat with my head in my hands. 'I don't have to go,' I told myself. 'I don't have to go.' But somehow I felt I did.

CHAPTER 19

Eva and Martha agreed that someone should force Kaiser Wilhelm to put an end to the war. But Bina was adamant, insisting that every surviving man be called upon to force a great last fight. 'I thought you longed to have a revolution,' Eva taunted her. 'It's what Schu-Schu would have wanted.'

'A revolution.' Martha was flushed and afraid, and she recounted how a group of officers, returning to the front, had been forced out of their train and made to return home. 'The soldiers threatened them with hand grenades,' she said, biting hard into her lip. And she wondered if it could really be true that the Emperor of Austria had run away, taking with him the Crown Jewels and followed by eighteen buses full of furniture.

'It's true, it's true.' Eva stood up, 'I heard it in the street.' And then, remembering what she had also heard, she sat down again. 'There are people breaking into the big houses,' she whispered. 'Raiding them for food. Some families are slipping off in the middle of the night, taking anything that they can carry.' And she had a sudden image of the Samson girls balancing a crate of soft white rolls between them.

'Well, they won't find anything at Gaglow,' Martha said sadly.

'No, they won't find anything, not even ice.' And Eva wondered how Manu would escape if he was hiding, like Gruber, in the ice-house cellar.

*

It was Dolfi who came in with the news. 'The Kaiser has abdicated!' Her face was bright red, her mouth delighted.

Marianna found that tears were in her eyes, but Wolf jumped up and struggled to pull open the window. He leaned out into the street and watched the stream of people marching solidly, the gold of girls' uncovered heads bobbing in the sun. Soldiers carried long red flags, and in the bright November sunshine children played, whooping on the fringes of the crowd. Wolf looked quickly at his daughters and, touching his wife's hand to let her know, he slipped away. 'Wolf,' Marianna called, but the front door had slammed, and instead they hung out of the windows to try to find him in the crowd.

Wolf marched, lightfooted with the revolution. No tears were falling here for Kaiser Wilhelm, the Empress or their six surviving sons. Lorries packed with soldiers honked and cheered, and sailors, waving flags, stirred up the people with songs.

The young men in the trucks, many of them not old enough for more than a small taste of the war, scanned the crowd for officers, ordering them to pull off their insignia and, if they refused, taking great delight in ripping them away, hurling the badges up into the air as trophies for the children.

Wolf was swept along, down the Linden and into Pariser Platz. The Brandenburger Tor was teeming, small black figures clinging to its surface, and as he stood, craning his neck, a long red flag was hoisted, unfurling from the centre of its arch. The afternoon had turned and in the cold half-dark of dusk the crowd began to swell. The pale women in their shawls were shouting, and men raised their fists and shook them at the palace. The Emperor's motorcar bleated its way out of the *Schloss* and a great roar of delight rose up from the crowd. Wolf was pressed back and forth, and forced on to the bosom of a grocer's girl, still in her overall and smelling of apples. 'Excuse me. I'm so sorry.' He struggled to step back a pace, but a truck rolled by, packed full of Russian prisoners, the men reeling with their sudden freedom and each one with a red cockade, like a little patch of blood, over one eye. The grocer's girl was pushed sideways in the scuffle and Wolf was almost thrown under the wheels of the truck.

Dolfi came in and out all afternoon with news. 'The royal palace has been broken into,' she told Marianna, 'and they are removing all the silver plate.' Then they heard the trumpeting of horns that, until now, had led them to expect the appearance of the Kaiser's motorcar. All four women jumped and Dolfi had to stop herself from racing back out into the street.

It was dark and Wolf was still not home. Marianna insisted that they sit down to an early supper and then, as if there was no such thing as a revolution just outside their door, she ordered them to bed. There was a firmness in her manner that made it hard to argue and the three girls retired to the small back room, sitting in a row and listening to the muffled noises of the night, broken up by shouts and the stray hot racket of a bullet.

Marianna was still waiting up for Wolf when a volley of machine-gun fire burst above her head. She had been dozing, picturing her husband in his soft black hat, sailing on the ripples of the crowd, when the force of the explosion shook her to her feet, pounding round the building, rumbling in a well of noise. Dolfi appeared at the door, her face white, her hands over her ears, calling to Marianna to get down, and then Eva rushed in and pulled her mother to the ground. They crouched together in the dark, tightly holding hands. The room had filled with smoke, the fumes from guns seeping in between the bricks. Eva began to crawl towards the window.

'Eva,' Marianna called, 'come back.' But Eva put her fingers on the sill and eased her body up. She could see small groups of soldiers, clutching their red flags, and an occasional figure as it sped away along the street, running to the safety of a house.

'Do you see Papa?' Martha called, shivering with Bina by the door, but as Eva peered out, she was knocked back into the room by a fresh blast that sent a film of powder spiralling from the ceiling. She lay flat, waiting for the noise to stop, straining for the quick breath of the others just across the room. The carpet under her hands was white with dust and the cannonfire rolled on and on. She wondered if it might be possible to sleep like this, to drift away on a great roll of sound, and then, just as she felt unable to bear it any longer, the machine-guns stopped.

'Dolfi, would you make us all some coffee?' Marianna rose gracefully from the floor, but Eva, a hollow in her ears, found she could not get up.

'Manu,' she wailed, 'Manu,' and with a deep sensation that things could never be put right she began to cry so loudly and so hard that she didn't hear the shouting in the street below and the violent knocking on the door.

Marianna looked down at the body of her husband, lying where the men had left him, stretched out on her bed. He had not been shot, riddled with machine-gun pellets as she'd first feared, but had simply had the life squeezed from him by the pressure of the crowd. His eyes were closed, his glasses lost, and the deep frown jutting in a fork along his brow had loosened, giving him a look of calm. Two revolutionaries, apologetic and polite, had found him in the square, lying limp against a wall. They removed their soldier's caps in the presence of Frau Belgard, and looked down sadly at their toes. 'Caught up in the crush, poor old fellow,' one said, blushing and looking round to check that he hadn't spoken out of turn. There were footprints stumbling across the thin wool of Wolf's suit, and his mouth was open, as if to catch a last thin gasp of air. Bina and Martha watched their mother, their hands over their mouths, while with a gracious nod she showed the soldiers out. 'How can I thank you?' She pressed their hands, and a tiny tremor passed over the pale set of her face.

*

The revolution lasted for three more days, but Marianna hardly noticed. She heard the guns below her window only faintly and the sound of fighting rising from the Reichstag. Her old aunt Cornelia arrived, the black umbrella flapping by her side, full of outrage over the armistice. 'Dear Wolfgang may be better off,' she lowered her voice, 'wherever he is now,' and the corners of her mouth turned down. 'Another long winter of root vegetables, without fat or salt or sauce.' She sat down opposite Marianna and loudly blew her nose, telling her how a young woman in her street had turned the gas on herself and her small child rather than face another winter with the blockade still in place. 'There will be revenge, that's the worst part of it, there will be some terrible revenge.'

Marianna longed for her to leave. She offered her a cup of coffee, made from carrot, and nodded and sighed as the old woman cheered herself with talk. Aunt Cornelia remembered Marianna as a child, the beauty of her handmade dresses, brown velvet over cream, and the day of her magnificent marriage. 'Oysters and caviar,' she sucked her lips, 'and before the ices, roast goose with new potatoes.'

Marianna gave a small smile.

'Cucumber salad in February! What a sensation!' And old Aunt Cornelia raised her eyes to the ceiling.

Marianna and Wolf had been married at the rooms of the Society of Friends along the street at Potsdamer Strasse 9. Almost a hundred people had been invited and many came from out of town. Marianna saw herself, dressed for her wedding and running down to where the local children were gathered in admiration round her bridal coach. She was wreathed and veiled and bursting with excitement, and then, on the seat of the coach, she saw a letter. A stark white envelope addressed to her. She gasped, looking round for anyone who might have left it, a blackmailer, a cast-off mistress, and in her panic she pushed it unopened into her purse. But all through the ceremony the thought of it hummed in her ears. As soon as it was over she rushed away to tear open the letter. 'It was the congratulations of our house porter,' she told Aunt Cornelia, and even now the relief of it made her want to cry.

'It's all right, my dear girl.' Aunt Cornelia stroked her head, and Marianna, finally giving in, sobbed on to the damp cloth of her old shoulder.

Marianna woke one morning to the watery sound of talk. She could hear a flow of chatter like a stream, and slowly rising up out of her dreams she recognized the rambling, unanswered tones of Eva. She turned towards the window, guessing that it must be shortly after dawn. A dull, cold light was rising and there was silence in the street. In a sudden panic she sprang up, flung on a coat and hurried out into the hall. 'Eva?' The chattering voice had stopped and, doubting herself suddenly, she ran back to check that her daughter's bed was empty. 'Eva,' she called, more sternly now, unsure where to look next, and she moved through the apartment, squinting for her silhouette behind the coloured glass of the front door. Then she heard a splutter of short laughs and from behind the panelling came the unmistakable deep gasp of Eva as she realized that she'd been overheard.

Marianna pulled open the airing-cupboard door and, to her surprise, she saw two faces looking up at her, the startled faces of young children, dark eyes and open guilty mouths. There, sitting beside Eva, his hands twisting in his lap, she found her son.

Emanuel sat surrounded on the sofa. He sank back into the cushions, dazed and shrinking fast under the hard, passionate scrutiny of his family. Dolfi poured out coffee, splashing little drops on to the tray as she looked up at him in disbelief.

'How did you get here?' Bina asked.

'Why didn't you let us know?' Marianna leant over her shoulder.

'Will you eat something?' Martha urged.

Emanuel tried to puff back into his old smooth self. 'Where's Papa?' He smiled round at them. And Bina and Martha, taking his hands in theirs, stared up at their mother as she stumbled to explain how they had lost him on the last day of the war.

Emanuel retired to his bed. He thought of his gold medal, stolen with his socks, the raised letters of his father's name in a curve across the back. Belgard and Son, he mouthed into his pillow, and he forced himself away into the long dark tunnel of his sleep.

When he woke he found his sisters hovering. They stayed with him, singing soft songs, pushing at his pillow and tucking his toes under the quilt, until he was forced to consider getting up simply to be rid of them. Marianna had to fight her way into his room, past Bina with her tray of scavenged medicine, bowls of cold water and old linen shredded into strips, over Martha who sat reading to him from ancient myths – dark stories of the underworld and the miracle of Zarathustra's birth – while Eva perched sideways on his high-backed chair and dripped small words of code into the blotter on his desk.

Marianna resorted to visiting him at night. She pulled her sleeve into her palm to smooth the opening of his door, and trod carefully over the squeaking floor. Emanuel lay, just like in childhood, with one hand curled above his head, and she had to stop herself from lying down beside him as he slept. His eyelids, once an arc of milky blue, were run with purple veins, and she saw the flicker of his thoughts rolling back and forth under the skin. A line was forming in a fork between his brows, knitted even in his sleep, and it made her want to call for Wolf, to glance from one to the other and gloat over the resemblance. As she stooped closer, listening to his breath, her foot caught against a sheet of paper. She bent instinctively to examine it, when Emanuel twisted, threatening to wake. In a sudden panic she scooped the pile of scattered pages up from the floor, and backed with them out of the room.

Emanuel didn't venture out until after the New Year. He wrapped himself in Wolf's old overcoat and with one dragging leg, he limped off towards the Tiergarten. Eva followed. She'd volunteered her company, but Emanuel seemed not to have heard and so, at a safe distance, she slipped along behind. Occasionally he stopped and exchanged greetings with some acquaintance passing in the street, and then for a moment the old charm, the curve of his shoulders and his smile turned him back into himself. Eva watched him tilt his head and saw the glitter in his eye, but as soon as he passed on, the smile fell from his face and his shoulders hunched higher and more hopeless than before. Eva dragged her own feet so as not to overtake him and tried to think of new and untried ways to cheer him up.

Since Christmas Bina had been promoted to staff nurse at the hospital. She no longer boiled the implements, washed the patients down, or spoon-fed the most injured, but with firm fingers she pressed gauzes onto wounds and artfully arranged new bandages. Abscesses were drained and old wounds quickly dressed. She answered questions and scribbled notes onto the files of men who, now that the war was over, weren't necessarily going home.

Martha was studying classics at the university. In her first week she befriended another girl, who was reading Sanskrit in a course all of her own. The two girls, happy to have found each other, wandered in their ancient worlds, arm in arm around the city.

Eva had no plans except the ones she'd made with Emanuel. Dear Manu, she thought, as she followed him along, what are we waiting for? But she was distracted by her brother who had stopped to talk to someone. He had straightened his limp leg and was leaning forward, listening, while the woman, her shoulders covered by a dark brown shawl, appealed to him for something. Eva could see only the dark shape of her coat, patched and splashed with mud and decided she must be one of the many widows who came to him for details of their missing men, poor scraps of news that they'd already heard. Eva watched as, with a sudden tender move, he took both her gloved hands in his. Then she turned and, very slowly, walked back the way she'd come.

Marianna shuffled Emanuel's pages into order. I am simply trying to help him, she told herself, thinking of the stack of schoolboy poems she had stored for years under her bed, and she noticed that his reminiscences were written on the backs of letters. They were letters from Eva, full of day-dreams and mysterious plans, and it made her unsure which she should read first.

'My dearest Manu,' Eva's words were fine with care. 'Of course you must rest, let's not even think about going anywhere until after the winter. I won't even mention it again, except I had wondered if, on all your travels, you'd seen anywhere that was without doubt more beautiful than Gaglow?'

Marianna turned the pages back and forth, noticing how Emanuel had lost his languid lines, his sloping, boyish curves. The pages, although recognizably in his hand, were cramped and small, running up and catching in one corner. Marianna picked out words here and there, and then, at random, she began to read.

The strong, hot winds that rolled across the steppe made it unbearable to stay outside for long, and after endless pleading and negotiations we finally succeeded in getting permission to go swimming. Fifty prisoners were led along a dusty path towards the river. The sight of the still green water, floating into view after a steep twist in the path, was so exhilarating that even men who couldn't swim were ready to fling themselves in fully clothed. But dangerous currents swelled under the surface of this river, threatening to drag us down, and even the strongest swimmers were forced to clamber back on to the bank to catch their breath. The water was so deep, sloping steeply from the shore, that we went in packs, calling out warnings to each other and sending men to help the ones in trouble. Despite this, on the third trip, as we were all about to leave, a pile of clothes lay unclaimed on the ground. A German lieutenant had gone missing. Our guards, rather than show sympathy, became greatly excited, convinced that an attempt had been made to escape, and even when after two weeks the corpse of the lieutenant was washed up, so eaten away by worms that it was only possible to identify him by his gold teeth, they still refused to let us ever swim again.

Marianna lay awake wondering about the slow green bend of river, like smooth glass on a beach, and tried to push away the sight of the lieutenant with his ears nibbled into rags. Had his gold teeth been removed and sent back to his mother? She twisted and turned until morning in her bed.

The following night she read a little more.

The unbearably long days, the monotony and claustrophobia, the dreadful disquiet in the rooms, the bad air in the barracks and the long nights, where one hears men coming and going, the snoring, and quite often the fearful shrill cries of a comrade twisting out of a dream, have a slowly disturbing effect. In time all these accumulated things rob one of strength and health and good spirits until the degree of depression becomes so great that some people quite often in irrepressible rage clench their fists and ask themselves whether there is any point in living such a life. Even if the external conditions were any better, each day would still be a new punishment and each month a new torment. It is difficult for a man who has not lived for any length of time amongst prisoners to realize how unhappy he can be when he comes out of the stifling barracks and sees all around him the high and hated fence.

Marianna began to make herself a copy, taking each page as he completed it, so that when she had to slip the story back under his bed she would still have something of her own. She sat up late into the night accumulating her own neat pile on thick grey sheets of paper. She copied the story of his capture, his long slow journey east, and the descriptions of hospitals and camps, of doctors and soldiers and guards he'd known over the years. She saw how he had occasionally received the money she'd sent him, using it in tiny plots and plans, and she kissed each page that stood for his survival.

There were about a hundred of us crammed into the hot-room, and although at first the heat was pleasant, soon it forced us out on to the deck where the joy of staring up at a night sky full of stars made up for the cold and the hardness of the ground. We formed a choir, which sang as we travelled down the Volga, sailing through the changing countryside which was sometimes wild with high rocks and then a moment later laid out prettily with fruit trees, cereal fields and woods of birch. The Russians, many of whom were refugees, listened to us peacefully and even I was surprised at how strangely beautiful the German songs sounded so far away from home. The steamer stopped on most days by a bridge, which teemed with traders, where we all took the opportunity to stock up on necessary provisions as the prices on board were high. Unfortunately, after a week, we arrived at the train junction at Samara where thirty of us were packed with six Russian prisoners into a filthy cattle wagon. The further east we travelled, the more run down and disorganized things became: our train actually collided with another, and at one point we even lost a carriage and had to go back to find it. Soon, from the open doors of the train, we saw the Urals rising up around us. At that moment I was convinced we were destined to spend the remainder of the war working in its mines, but we crossed over the Urals and passed from European Russia into Asia, which I actually saw marked in white letters on a border stone. The people here seemed more friendly and the food for sale at the stations was, to our indescribable joy, at least half-price.

We managed to pass our days quite tolerably, crouching round a tiny stove, playing cards and singing while we watched the countryside go by. And after weeks of travelling on various ramshackle trains we finally reached our destination. If I had arrived in Nova Nikolaiesk any sooner than I did, I would very likely have been wiped out by the typhoid epidemic, which had been raging there since the previous winter. Thousands and thousands of prisoners, housed in squalid, lice-ridden camps, died within a few weeks, and once dead they were thrown into a makeshift mortuary. In their greed the local people crept out at night and robbed them of their clothes, and so, of course, the typhoid spread into the town and became even more impossible to control. There was a story circulating that a prisoner, assumed dead, was thrown into the mortuary only to appear again to lodge an official complaint that his trousers had been stolen. But by the next day he was also dead. There were no lists kept, and out of ten thousand prisoners, eight thousand are said to have died within a few weeks. And I don't suppose their families will ever know what happened to them.

Eva had a plan to celebrate her sixteenth birthday. A circus was reopening near the Bourse Exchange and she hoped that all the family might go. When it was mentioned, Bina frowned, insisting that it would be undignified, so close to Papa's death. Martha agreed. 'Apparently,' she said, 'only three out of the herd of elephants survived the food restrictions of the war.' But Eva would not be put off. On the opening night she went to look at the huge tent. Band music was swelling up inside, and people were arriving in a steady stream, sailors, girls, old women and young men, all pushing their way forward. The air was full of children, chattering like birds, some smart and scrubbed and tightly held while others, barefoot and in rags, scrambled to get in for nothing under the canvas walls. Through the open curtain of the door, Eva caught sight of the arena. A golden round of sand lit up from above with arcs of light. She stood and watched the audience push in and swore she'd find the money somehow. If no one else wanted to go, she'd take Emanuel as his birthday treat. And then the cymbals of the orchestra began to ring, splashing in the beginning of the show, and a rumble rose up as the crowd, intent on having fun, forced themselves forward in their seats. Eva caught sight of a clown, jumping through mid-air, his mop of orange hair standing on end, before the cloth door of the tent was pulled tight behind him.

Eva walked slowly towards home. She crossed the Friedrichs Bridge and headed for the Linden. Then laughing and rushing out of a side street, two people arm in arm knocked her down. The woman was large and loud and, without giving her companion a moment even to catch his breath, she whisked him on, shouting that they'd miss the best part of the show.

'Emanuel?' Eva scrambled up. She was convinced that she recognized her brother's dragging leg, but they were off over the bridge, laughing and grabbing at their open, flapping coats. Eva, her nose stinging with the shock, stood stranded in the road. She'd hesitated too long, and she took off after them towards the high dome of the tent. 'Wait! Wait for me!' But they had a good start on her, and although her brother stumbled as he ran, the strong arm of his companion swept him up and carried him along.

She arrived in time to see them disappear, the last of the latecomers, into the circus tent. She saw a slice of darkness and felt a low hush of suspense as the audience waited, breathless, on a wave. Manu must have already bought the tickets, she thought, and a surge of resentment rose up for his hideous laughing friend, as wide as a house in her old clothes, and her feet in great black boots. She considered waiting for them to come out, catching them as they recrossed the bridge, but it was already dark and growing cold and for all she knew the show might last and last.

I owe my life [Marianna read] and the use of my legs to a Hungarian doctor, who worked tirelessly in the camp to make life bearable. I was lucky to end up there and not at the hospital where I was first sent, where there was a Tartar doctor who had a great lust for operations. He would roam the wards looking for a likely victim, and

223

every few weeks indulged in an orgy of amputations, cutting off the arms and legs, quite unnecessarily, of up to forty people in a night. I was in a hospital in Tarkov, another in Saratov, and finally with thousands of others in a camp in Astrakas, a town famous for its caviar. Unfortunately nothing so delicious reached us there, and we existed on watery tea, fish soup and a scrap of bread. The real reason there was so little to eat was because the camp commander used only a fraction of the money set aside for food. It is common knowledge that, since the start of the war, he had saved enough to buy himself a house, a cart and a horse. Many of the men were so weak they gave up hope, and if you talked to them they answered only with a monosyllabic grunt. On the day that I arrived there, a thin and filthy man, wearing only his underwear, made a protest, by cutting open an artery with his shaving knife on the steps of the barracks.

But then something quite extraordinary happened. Two officers escaped, and in an attempt to conceal the error, the camp commander decided to transfer two ordinary men to make up the numbers. And I, an ordinary man, was chosen, and was moved from the barracks where three hundred men are packed in so tightly it is impossible to sleep in any other position than on your side, to a house on the edge of the Volga where the officers live in relative comfort, with beds and a view of the river.

Marianna slipped across the hall with Emanuel's rough pages in her hand. She twisted the handle of his door and, knowing which floorboards to avoid, tiptoed into the room. It was after midnight and she'd copied the final instalment of his story, surprised to find that it ended so abruptly with Emanuel slipping like a thief across the line. It should have finished with a trumpet call of honour for his safe return and she'd been tempted to add one more page in which he received a medal for his bravery. Marianna bent to push the pages under his bed when she noticed that it was empty. She stared at the smooth outline of the quilt, the undented pillow and, frightened suddenly that she might meet him coming in, she hurried from his room.

*

Eva watched her brother balefully over breakfast. It was true that he looked less grey, the whites of his eyes less yellow. He caught her and smiled their own conspiratorial smile, his hands trembling as he raised toast to his lips.

When he went out she followed him and walked at a safe distance towards the newly opened cafés around Kurfürsten-damm. She wandered up and down while he drank a cup of coffee, followed by long glasses of water. He must be waiting for someone, but eventually he stood up to leave, and after a long and meandering walk he led her back to Potsdamer Strasse 12.

As they reached the door she called out to him in mock surprise, 'Well, Manu, hello,' and finding she had nothing else to say, she told him to expect a birthday treat.

Emanuel leant against the door as if the thought of it exhausted him. 'Have our birthdays come around again so soon?' he asked, and Eva remembered the length of the last year, the endless months and empty hanging weeks, and wondered if this was meant to be a joke.

'Not quite yet,' she said, 'but when they do, will you be my guest at the circus?'

Emanuel raised his eyebrows. 'The circus? Is that right?'

'Next week,' she assured him. 'We'll go together and sit high up at the back.'

'The circus,' he repeated, as if the thought of it was quite extraordinary. And, thanking her, he turned to go inside.

Eva began to doubt that it had been her brother whom she'd seen in such high spirits flapping along over the Friedrichs Bridge. She'd have to watch him closely to see if his reactions to the clowns were new and if the sight of the three elephants surprised him. She crept into her room and opened up her treasure box. It was a long time since she'd added anything and small webs of dust had collected in the hinges of green felt. The wood looked scratched and dull and she spat against the inlaid flower, rubbing at the mother-of-pearl until it broke back into life. Inside, her photograph had curled in on itself. She had to turn the edges back to get a good look at Fräulein Schulze's eyes, staring straight ahead and ringed with light. Dried flowers hung together on their fragile threads and her thimble, once overlaid with silver, had turned into a little pewter cup. She tipped the contents out on to the floor, cupping small beads as they threatened to roll off and picking out the severed stalks of roses. Eva stared down in dismay. She had been convinced, if she could bring herself to part with anything, that she'd have no trouble raising money for two circus seats, but now as she rolled the missing marble from the solitaire around her palm, she realized that there was nothing here of any value. With her fingertips she brushed the green felt of the lid and closed it again. Then it occurred to her that she had another box. Her birth box, locked up in the safe. 'We'll keep it for you here,' Papa had said, 'until you need it.' And the gold to celebrate her seventh birthday, brought from Hamburg by her uncle Dagebert, had been dropped in with the rest. Eva rushed through to find her mother.

Marianna opened up the airing-cupboard door and, standing on a stool to get a better view, unlocked the safe. In Eva's box there was one single gold coin. It had been placed there by Wolf's father the week before his death and she hesitated to remove it. Bina's box was empty, but in Martha's there was still a small assortment of coins. She took one of these and quickly closed the door.

Eva turned it over in her hand. It was dense and heavy, warming so quickly that she had to stop herself from placing it like chocolate on her tongue.

'Thank you, Mama,' she said, and for a moment she felt tempted to invite her to the circus too.

Marianna bundled up her stack of neatly written pages and tied it tight with string. The sight of those last coins had given her an idea and as she walked across the square she wondered what it would cost to have Emanuel's memoir printed into a book. She could make a limited edition of fifty private copies, bound up in leather with a thread of gold, and inside the front page a portrait of the author. She might have to use the last of her daughters' gold but she would present it to Emanuel on his birthday as a present from them all.

The printer laughed at her mention of leather and suggested instead a cover made from cardboard, offering her a choice of grey or blue. Marianna chose pale blue and asked to see the paper. She touched the loose sheets, nodding over the light tint and the tiny horizontal lines. 'I'll need the copies soon,' she told him, and the printer put his head to one side and said that that might cost a little more.

Marianna had to make do with a photograph. She found one, taken on the first leave of the war, Emanuel, clean-shaven, his sweet smile just hovering, his head a little to one side as he leant against the perfectly smooth fingers of one hand.

Marianna helped Eva to get ready. It gave her pleasure to shake out her yellow Chinese shawl, the silk downy with age. It was dotted through with tiny perfect darns, but the fringe was still intact, long and thick, and reached down below her daughter's waist. Marianna brushed her hair. 'One hundred times,' Eva demanded, remembering Omi Lise's strict regime, but Marianna stopped before she got to twenty and, with a mouthful of long pins, piled it on top of Eva's head.

'What a shame,' she mumbled, through the pins, 'that we can't have a ball for you.' But Eva only laughed, open-mouthed, into the mirror and said she'd much prefer a circus.

Emanuel had rubbed black on to his shoes and his hair was flattened back against his head. He took Eva's hand and kissed it, tucking it away under his arm, and together they walked out into the summer street. It was true, Emanuel had changed. His face was fuller, and his waistcoat did not hang so loosely on his

227

chest. Eva adjusted her quick walk to his, hardly noticing his limp, and adding up admiring glances on the fingers of one hand. He let her choose their seats. She wanted to be high, high up, and they climbed, stumbling over benches until they were nearly at the back. They had only just sat down when the first clash of the cymbals cut through the round of tunes and, with one great, thrilling flourish, the clowns were ushered in. Eva gripped her brother's hand and stared down at a troupe of dwarfs, their white faces painted into smiles, their huge shoes spraying sand into the air. They chased after each other on short legs, grappling and butting, pinning down and tripping up, their tricks growing more violent with each lap of the tent until the laughter of the crowd began to mingle with shouts and shrill wild cries. The ring-master in his shiny suit put up his hands and shooed them like children from the stage. Martha had been right about the elephants. Their skin looked sad and old as they loped, heads down, one close behind the other, the round grey circles of their feet falling into step, their knees like knitted underwear creasing obediently in time. Even when they dipped their trunks and showered the strong man with spray, they might have been in mourning for their friends, the water sliding down the flat sides of their heads like tears. Eva glanced across at Manu, anxious that he might want to leave, but he was bent forward in his seat, his eyes fixed on the circle of gold sand, waiting with the others for the next act to come on.

The orchestra were whispering among themselves, plucking strings and tightening their bows, while the crowd, restless, shuffled their feet and let out small impatient grunts. A rumour rippled through the tent that the trapeze artist had been injured in a fall, and Eva wondered what, after the horses, there was left to come. A trickle of despair seeped into her heart and she clenched her fist, holding tight onto her hopes and trying not to cry with disappointment. Then the tent began to hum. All along her row feet drummed against wood and Emanuel, his face burning, knocked his knuckles on the bench.

The arc lights twisted up to brilliant white and a man in a

top hat and tail-coat sauntered into the ring. He pushed back his shoulders, tilting his chin, and there, far above him, a rope was being strung. It was a silver wire, as sharp and tight as gut, and with a low rolling of the drums the man began to climb. He climbed slowly, pausing half-way as the violins rattled after him, urging him on. Eva thought she saw his shoulders swell as he took a last great gulp of air and then, with a hissing of the lightest drums, he slithered to the top.

He pointed a toe and stepped out on to the line. There was a silence, thick with swallowed breath, and then the orchestra began to play. They played quietly, gaining strength as he stepped out, until with a flourish he began to dance back and forth across the wire to the tune of a Hungarian march. His coat-tails flapped, his top hat spun, and his feet, invisible, picked up speed until he was whirling, shimmering in a gloss of black. Then, with both hands, he picked up a small table and holding it above his head he skipped with it along the rope. He placed it, swaying, in the centre of the wire, returning a moment later with a matching chair, and then a stove. The drums hissed and burst and a frying pan was tossed up to him. The frying pan began to sizzle on the stove and from his pocket the man took an egg and broke it high into the pan, scattering the shell on to the sand below. He broke another and another until the drums were beating in a frenzy of delight, and Eva gasped to see the pan of eggs sending up a trail of steam. He tucked a cloth into his collar and then, stirring his omelette with one hand, he caught a bottle of champagne. The drumbeat eased into a waltz and the man sat down to enjoy his meal.

Eva felt her smile stretched wide across her face, her heart skipping in and out of love as she watched the magician on the wire polish off his food. He took one last leisurely mouthful of champagne, and then, holding up his glass, he raised a toast, and the whole tent exploded in a cheer as the stove, the table and the chair were all tossed down to the ground.

Eva joined in the thunderous applause. Her mouth was aching with delight and she stood up to continue clapping. 'The diner on the wire,' Emanuel shouted to her, 'I knew you'd like him.' And he began to cheer as the man swung down to earth.

'I love him,' Eva said, while, with a quick bow to the left and right, the diner skipped out of the tent. Eva felt her heart heavy and hot with longing, and in a daze she let herself be led out into the night, the crowd humming all around her.

'It's better than before the war when Houdini appeared at the Wintergarten,' someone shouted over her head.

'He freed himself from a closed water tank,' an indignant voice yelled back. 'Nothing could be much better than that!'

And Eva whispered to herself that it was better than anything ever in the world.

'Manu?' She looked around for him. He had let go of her hand, and she'd been so caught up in her reverie that she hadn't seen him disappear. People everywhere were shoving and hurrying, swirled up with excitement for the new sensation of Berlin. Breathing hard, she pushed her way out of the crowd, keeping her head tilted up to catch sight of her brother. She'd almost given up when she saw him standing at the edge of a group. He was staring down at his feet, his head a little to one side, and she was surprised to find he wasn't looking round for her. 'Manu.' She began to run towards him, and then a woman in a pale green coat stepped out from the group and took his arm. She turned him towards her and let her arms circle his back. Eva saw her face over his shoulder, eyes closed, wide cheeks bunched up in a smile, and in a strange cold flash she recognized her.

'Schu-Schu?' she gasped, and Fräulein Schulze's eyes opened and stared right into hers. Eva came a few steps nearer, shivering suddenly with cold and wondering why, after all this time, she wasn't happier to see her. Schu-Schu's red hair had darkened. It was brushed upside down under a straw hat, and her hands, out of their gloves, were large and blotched.

'Emanuel?' Fräulein Schulze turned him round to face her. He blushed and smiled weakly, nodding at them both, but she was ordering him with her eyes to speak.

'Eva,' he said, 'Evschen, let me explain,' and he gulped and stumbled round for air. Schu-Schu took hold of his hand. 'I'd like you to meet my future wife,' he said, and the governess's face opened up with triumph.

Eva walked slowly towards them, extending her hand, and then at the last minute, dangling and out of place, she saw her mother's ruby earrings. They hung snug against her freckled neck, the red dull below her hair, and, without intending it, she pulled her hand away. Her sandals clattered on the cobbled street as she turned round and ran, and with Schu-Schu's blind smile in her eyes she kept on till she reached home.

CHAPTER 20

After a week my passport came back with Sonny's name and birth-date printed in the back. 'My last excuse,' I wailed to Pam, but she was off to a hotel near Macclesfield to watch Alan play a business game of golf.

'Shall I drop in on my way?' I could hear her guilt at finding a new man with such indecent speed, and I remembered just in time that I was going to baby-massage. 'Actually,' I told her, 'the man who runs it's quite attractive.'

'It's run by a man?'

'He's a sort of gentle, brawny type with a tattoo.'

Pam was unconvinced. 'Listen, in case I don't speak to you before you go, have a great time.'

'Thanks, I will.

'I will,' I said again, because I still didn't know where I was going. I sat down and wrote John Godber a card. 'I'm so sorry to have called at an inconvenient time and I hope your wife is . . .' I crossed out the last line. 'I hope Elisabeth.' No. 'I hope everything –'

It was impossible. I was too frightened of her death to send a get-well card.

'Dear Mr', I began once more without much faith, but just then the telephone rang.

'There's a letter for you here.' It was my father. 'Shall I open it?'

I could hear him ripping at it before I'd had a chance to

speak. 'How very peculiar,' he was talking away from the phone, 'it's from my cousin,' and he read out the address of Gaglow, the directions from the train and the news that I was expected there in three days' time. 'Has he roped you in to do his dirty work?' He was bristling for a fight, and I had to calm him with assurances that it had been all my own idea.

'I just wanted to see the house before it's sold.' I had been going to tell him. 'And I happened to bump into your cousin . . .'

'You'll be able to tell me what it's like.' His voice was almost inaudible and then, slowly, carefully, he warned, 'I hope you realize that some of what I told you may not actually be true.'

I pressed my ear against the phone, 'That's all right,' and I smiled at the shiver that had run right through me at the story of the curse.

'So,' he went back to the details of the letter, 'you can either hire a car or take the train. Of course, I only remember driving down in my grandmother's carriage. Four horses, or possibly six . . .'

'With a coachman in gold cuffs.' And we both began to laugh. 'Dad.' It was true, suddenly, that I was going. 'Why don't you come too? Just think how fascinating it would be, and if it's not,' I grasped wildly around, 'you can do charcoal sketches of Sonny while he's asleep.'

There was a silence at the other end and my heart slowed down.

'I think not,' he said kindly. 'But if there's anything you need?'

I assured him that I was fine. 'Just one thing.' I caught him as he was about to go. 'What happened to Emanuel, after the war?'

My father sighed. 'Well, after the war he wrote a book, or some kind of thesis, predicting how inflation would get out of control. His mother tried to get it published. She took it all over Berlin but no one showed any interest, said it was rubbish, but Emanuel had the foresight to collect all the family assets and exchange them for gold. And so, of course, while everyone else was desperate with piles of useless banknotes the family still had their supply of gold, which proved to be the one thing of lasting value.'

'So was she accepted eventually, his wife?'

'Absolutely not.' I could tell that this was the part he most enjoyed. 'She was blamed for everything, and mostly for taking my uncle away. They went to live in Palestine. He was offered a job as the manager of Barclays Bank. The bank was on the Mount of Olives. The Olive Branch, I called it,' and he laughed in silent gasps into the phone.

'The Olive Branch.' I grinned, imagining him as a small boy, revelling in the joke.

'My mother would never discuss him, but I know my grandmother did go to Jerusalem for his funeral.' He stopped and then, under his breath, he muttered in a singsong voice, '"We are going to Jerusalem." It's just a song, a game my mother used to play with me when I was small. "We are going to Jerusalem . . ."' and he drifted off, so that I could hear him, opening the lids of empty paper boxes, looking half-heartedly for food.

'I suppose his health was all broken down from being in those Russian camps. Is that why he died so young?' I tried to draw him back.

'Yes,' he agreed, 'it must have been,' and he promised to call me the second I got back.

There was a pile of green mats in one corner and I took one and laid Sonny out. 'How's he been?' It was Martin, the massage teacher, standing over us, remembering that my baby was a boy. I blushed and struggled with his dungarees. 'Fine, really good.' I took him in with one quick close-up glance. His hair was short and dark, his face wide open, and as he leant in I noticed the nails on his fingers, round as moons. Martin laid a hand on the sweet white of Sonny's tummy, 'He's a lovely boy,' and he turned to me with an approving look. 'Very relaxed.' It was the ultimate in compliments and I filled up inside with warmth, basking in smiles, as he moved off around the room.

'OK, let's start with those legs, hand over hand, plenty of oil.' The class had started, and all my concentration was taken up with looking into Sonny's surprised eyes while I stretched and soothed and greased his rollmop legs. 'Loosen those hips, tap the ankles, one two three.' We moved on to the arms, letting their elbows glisten through our grip, easing out fat fingers.

Sonny lay on his stomach and stretched his shoulders up into an arc. 'Strong boy.' Martin nodded as he passed, and I swelled under the rosy glow of praise. But none of the babies would tolerate much more on their fronts, and soon they were slipped and flipped into soft towels while the women turned to each other with stories of vaccines, sore nipples and the endless broken saga of each night.

I bundled Sonny up into my arms and took him to where Martin was standing in the centre of the room. 'Would you hold him for a moment?' I nodded in the direction of the loo.

My face was flushed as I caught it in the mirror, washing the oil off my hands, 'Ssh,' and I tried to shake the wild, unlikely thoughts out of my head.

When I came back Sonny was lying along Martin's folded arm, his chin cushioned against muscle, his body lounging lion-like along a branch. He raised his eyes lazily to mine and smiled. Martin hadn't seen me and he kept on around the room, rocking Sonny gently as he went, answering questions and stooping down to give advice. 'This is a great way to hold your baby.' He saw me and smiled. 'It's very soothing and it balances out the weight.'

I held out my arms for Sonny. 'I'll try, but he's too heavy for me like that,' and I showed Martin how I liked to hold him, up against my shoulder, nuzzled into my neck.

'Well, get your partner to come along.' He raised his eyebrows, and I smiled without answering in a way I hoped made everything quite clear.

Once I'd packed away my towels I lingered by the door. 'I won't be here next week, but I'll be back.' And with Sonny already drooping into sleep I sparked my eyes in his direction.

The next morning there was a card from Mike. It had a picture of the sea, rough green against a jagged beach, and when I scooped it up I saw it was addressed to me. 'Sarah, I've got a week off suddenly and it coincides with the ferry. I've got to see you both. I'll ring as soon as I arrive. Please please don't be busy.'

I took the card upstairs and set it with the others. I wanted to spit at it, blot the writing out with bile, but instead I stood and read it over until the words had turned into a song inside my head and I had to turn it round to face the wall.

I went and got the tickets, smoothing them over with my hands. 'Please please don't be busy.' And I thought how we'd always been just out of step. We lacked timing, and our dreams were made of fragile, separate things. Our last fight had been over a car. Our last before we knew about the baby. There was a Citroën parked out on the street, a beautiful pale blue with cushioned seats, its long back drooping out on to the road like soup. I'd often watched it, rising off the ground with steam, and now it had a little cardboard sign, For Sale. I swung myself against him. 'We could set off across America, have an adventure. Take it in turns to drive.'

But he only pulled away and said he didn't want an adventure. 'Anyway, you know that I can't drive.'

'You could learn? Don't you want to learn?' I was too excited to let him alone.

'All I want to do,' he said, 'is work.' And suddenly it occurred to me, standing out there by the velvet car, that this might be the truth.

'It doesn't appeal to you at all, to drive across America with me, not ever?' Little cracks of glass were splintered across my chest and it was difficult to hear what he was saying.

'No,' he said. 'It doesn't.'

'So what do you want?' I was pushing things too far. His eyes contracted, each iris spinning with alarm, but instead of 'Nothing,' he put out his hand, just in time, and suggested lunch.

We spent an ice-cold afternoon, hand in hand, wandering through Camden Lock. His fingers felt all floury, the palms half drained of blood, but I wasn't going to be the one to lose my hold. We walked round and round, using the objects on each stall to give us time, pushing our way through people, united warmly for a moment against the pushing crowd. It only needed one more word from either of us, but as soon as we got home Mike leant into the television, pulling it as close to him as it would go, so I took a book and climbed straight into bed. My chest was aching, hardened with suspense, and the half year's doom was like a wrap around my throat. The light was out when he came in and we lay sleepless, side by side, our knees bent up like ice picks in the sheet.

When I woke Mike was lying with his arms around me. 'Sarah,' he said, half laughing, and we made love with our eyes wide open for the first time in months. It's over, I thought, it's over. It seemed pointless to be careful, to abide by any normal laws, and I argued hotly in the tangle of the bed that, if we were too distant for America, there was no point in stooping into intimacy while I scrabbled in the bathroom for my cap.

I turned the postcard round again. 'Please please don't be busy', and I had to conjure up the dark look on his face when I'd told him that my period was late.

I took courage from John's letter and called to thank him for arranging Gaglow. 'How is your wife?' I asked, and he told me that she was remarkably recovered. 'Mr Godber?' There was one more thing I wanted to know. 'Could you tell me what happened to your aunt . . . the woman that Emanuel Belgard married?'

He paused, and I wondered suddenly just how much my father had made up. 'Of course, of course.' I could tell that he was smiling. 'Schu-Schu? She went to live with my grandmother after Emanuel died. Surely Michael remembers. She lived out at Gaglow as Omi Marianna's companion, Schu-Schu, an enormous woman with red hair and great feet like a man.'

'Of course,' I said, as if I'd simply forgotten. 'I see.'

'It's why they hated going there, the sisters. It's why we never went.'

'Of course,' I said again. 'Thank you so much.'

'But, sadly, there were no children.'

'No, no children, I knew that.' And we said goodbye.

That night, while Sonny slept, I calmed myself with packing. How many different outfits could a baby get through in four days? But all the same I laid out jumpers, sun-suits, hats and vests, and a tiny pair of stripy swimming trunks.

I weeded through my wardrobe taking down the clothes I never wore. I tried them on, admired them and then, unable to see a reason why I'd want to wear them simply because I was abroad, I hung them up again. Eventually I packed my favourite jeans, some shorts and sandals, and for travelling, my tulip summer dress.

That night I dreamt about the ice-house. It was flooded with a golden light, its pillars rising, the fluted tops floating off into the clouds. Underneath the floor my feet were freezing cold. I woke up and pulled a blanket over me, and as soon as I went back to sleep my dream picked up where it had drifted off.

I saw my great-grandmother drinking beer, just like my mother with a thin cigar, and then there she was, an old frail lady, holding Emanuel's uniform up to her throat, pleading with the new Nazi soldiers, not to take away her house, 'He gave up his strength for the Fatherland,' but her voice trailed off, the words turning into tiny smoky rings so that the men pushed past her to smear their painted signs over the ice-house walls.

I left Sonny bouncing in his chair and heaved the bags down to the front door. They bulged with nappies, sun-cream, books and clothes, and I hoped the driver of my mini-cab would be prepared to help. I propped the door open with the pushchair and, racing up again to collect the boy, I pushed the bags out on to the step. I could feel the sharp corners of Mike's letter, stiff against my hip, and relishing the postmark I thought I'd wait to post it at Heathrow. I'd written first thing that morning, before getting out of bed. Nothing personal, I'd insisted, just bad luck, and I saw even in the sharp ink strokes of his name how much I'd changed towards him. Then my cab drew up against the kerb. I could hear its engine running noisily, and the door swung open before I'd had a chance to turn round. But it wasn't for me. It was a gleaming London taxi, not my cab at all, and Mike, with one small bag, was stepping out. 'Sarah, for Christ's sake.' He·glared at me, surrounded by luggage, and then flying round he reached over to the driver for his change.

I sat with Sonny on the basement wall and watched him. I could see the fluster of his hands as they dipped into his wallet, and then the taxi flashed on its orange light. 'Do you want to take this on, love?' the man called out, and I told him I had a mini-cab coming.

Mike surveyed us both, his face creased up with travel, his eyes confused. 'How long have I got?' I reminded him, in case he'd forgotten, that the local taxi firm was always late. There was a silence and I felt my heart slip sideways. 'I'm only going for four days. It wasn't planned – I mean . . .' Furious to be caught up again so fast, I fingered the white corner of his letter.

Just then my car pulled up and I began to drag one bag towards it. Mike picked up the pushchair and it unfolded in his arms. 'Where to?' the driver asked, and lowering my voice, I said to drive fast to the airport.

Mike held open the door for us, and then, instead of closing it, he slung in his own bag, and walked round to the other side. 'All right, son?' He leant over to the baby, and Sonny blazed a gummy smile into his eyes.

The car swerved round a bend. 'I would have brought his seat,' I started, 'but I couldn't carry anything else.' But Mike wasn't listening. He was crooning and whistling, singing and smiling, while Sonny reached up to catch his chin.

'Where are you going, then? Which terminal?' the driver asked, and I leant over the seat and told him we were flying to Berlin. There was a sudden silence, and when I glanced round to explain, I saw that Mike had produced a tube of bubbles and was blowing pink and purple volleys into the car. 'Mind yourself.' The driver batted them away and Mike opened a window, turning Sonny round so he could watch the bubbles drift out into the day.

'How did you think you were going to manage?' Mike rammed our luggage with an unwieldy trolley.

'I'm fine,' and I tried to demonstrate by keeping both sets of wheels running in the same direction. 'You'd be surprised how helpful people are when you're on your own.'

'So you're going all the way to Germany to escape me?'

We were wandering through the lanes of checking-in, looking for our queue. I waved my ticket at him. 'I bought these last week, long before I got your card.'

Mike shook his head at me. 'Let's see,' he said, easing them out of my hand. 'Are these refundable, do you think?' Before I had a chance to stop him he had backed away.

'You bastard!' I hoicked Sonny up out of his pushchair and gathered up the bags. 'Mike!' But he had disappeared.

The people in my queue were watching me so I shrugged my shoulders and settled back into line. I'd simply explain that my tickets had been stolen, robbed right out of my hand, and, after all, I had any amount of witnesses.

The queue shuffled slowly forward and I hardened my resolve. It was as if, until now, I hadn't wanted to go, hadn't been quite sure. But, now, nothing was going to stop me. I heaved my bags back onto their trolley and moved forward in the line.

We were one stop from the desk when Mike struggled through to us. He had a shiny British Airways folder and from inside he took our tickets. 'No problem, the plane's only half full.' He handed them in to the desk. 'We'd like to sit together,' he said, and I hugged Sonny against me as if nothing unusual was taking place.

'So, you're prepared to follow us across the world?' I looked sideways at him as we stepped out across the shiny floor.

'I don't seem to have much choice.' He smiled.

'As long as we stay away from America?'

'Don't push your luck.' Awkward, suddenly, and shy, we walked through into the lounge.

We had to take a taxi from the station. 'Will there be room for me?' Mike asked, doubtful now as we drove fast along newly patched roads.

'The house is huge.' I laughed him down. 'It has fourteen bedrooms at least, or maybe forty, and the teachers will all be off on holiday.'

The taxi driver was a large, red man with over-knuckled hands, who talked loudly at us while we strained out of the window to see. There were wheatfields and rye, and cows in clusters flipping their tails for flies, and then we were rattling up the drive towards the gritted oval of the porch.

'It's beautiful,' I gasped, 'beautiful,' although what struck me most was that really it was hideous. The house was newly painted in apricot and cream, and roses, bred to flower right through the summer, grew from the gravel in tubs. I climbed out of the car. A man was clanking open the glossed double doors, but already I was edging towards the garden.

'Good evening, welcome.' The man strode towards us, and I introduced him to Sonny and then Mike. 'Come, come inside,' he called. 'You'll see we have some of your family's original furniture. The grand piano, for instance, and some interesting tapestries.' As he talked I found myself slipping off, clanking open the new wrought-iron gate, and skimming off alone across the lawn. The garden was mostly grass, with wide beds of roses, short bushes in pink and gold and red. They were set out squatly, divided up with fat, ferocious stems and without a weed between them. I turned to look up at the house. There were long french windows, closed against the heat, and under the shade of a veranda was stacked a large consignment of plastic chairs. The teachers, I imagined, breaking off to sit out in the sun, and I walked towards the edges of the garden where the lawn had been left to grow tall, running wild against a fringe of trees. From here I could see the high windows of the attic, and the orchard, gnarled and green, spreading out to one side of the house. There was a path of longer, rougher grass that led into the hill, and as I followed it under leaves of lilac I came upon the ice-house. It was dilapidated, its pillars peeling paint, and the leaves from last winter lay curled and dried across its floor. A stone bench curved into the wall and there was the square outline of a door. There was no handle and no catch, and as I traced it with my fingers I found that it had been sealed shut. I lay down on the bench and looked out through the avenue of leaves from where I could just see the shadows on the evening lawn. 'Sarah,' I heard Mike call, and then the little whimpering of Sonny, hungry for a feed.

I tried to imagine my great-grandmother living here, alone with her companion, Emanuel's wife, while Germany boiled up towards another war. Schu-Schu, I thought, Gabrielle Belgard, and I wondered if they had minded much when Bina, Martha and Eva refused to come. They would walk the paths together, not always in their widow's black, and in the early evening, drink coffee with cream out on the porch. I should tell my father how the curse must have been lifted, when Marianna went to Jerusalem and brought Schu-Schu home and I thought I caught their shadows, playing cards into the night.

'Sarah,' Mike called again. 'We need you,' and after a moment I jumped up and ran through the long grass towards the house.

I'd like to thank the following people who helped me with information, translations, photographs, memories, encouragement and notes: Gerta Calmann, Marianne Calmann, Dick Mosse, Lucy Mosse, Katharina Bielenberg, Josh Lacey, Kitty Aldridge, David Morrissey and the late Jo Kaufman.

Also for source material: *Memories of My Youth* by Elise Brash, *The Letters of Carl Heinrich Hertz*, *Life in Russia, 1915–1917* by Richard Samson (with special thanks to the Institut für die Geschichte der deutschen Juden), and *An English Wife in Berlin* by Evelyn Blucher.